The Vampire's Masquerade

Paranormal Literary Society Book 1

Nellie Peters

Contents

For Mom
Thank you for believing in me—I finally did it!

I miss you...

1

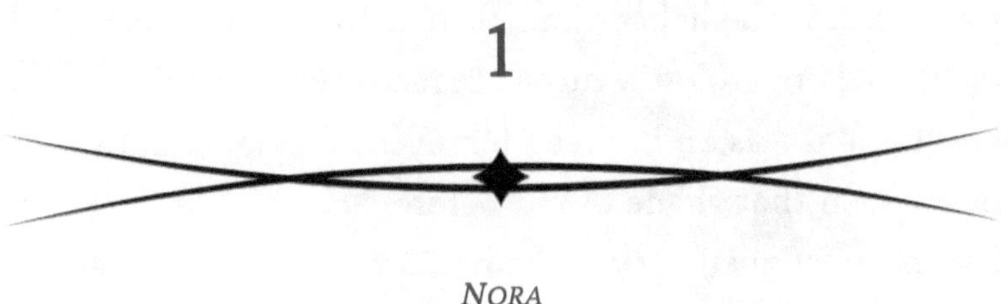

NORA

"Your performance is utterly unacceptable. If not for your late father's influence, I would have had you banned from the premises years ago."

My father's influence? He built *this company!*

I ground my teeth to keep the outrage from spilling out. "I apologize, Mistress Loralai." Her required honorific coated my tongue like poison. "I promise it won't happen again."

"I sincerely doubt that," the woman sneered, her flawless complexion twisting.

I forced myself not to clench my fists. She would notice. She always noticed.

"I assure you, I am completely in earnest," I said, giving her a blinding—and totally fake—smile.

She narrowed her eyes. "Unfortunately, I do not doubt *that*. It is your competence that is in question... Very well— return to your mindless tasks." She dismissed me with a wave of her hand as she turned to her computer.

"Thank you, Mistress," I ground out, giving the shallowest bow I could manage. I turned on my heel to escape the suffocating space.

Miserable old cow.

Some of my internal growl must have leaked out. As I reached for the doorknob, the air in the office seemed to drop ten degrees. The lights dimmed. The hair on the back of my neck prickling, I slowly turned to face my doom.

Loralai was on her feet, her eyes blazing. Literally—I'd never seen that shade of red before. She rounded the desk, her pace clipped. My fight-or-flight response flew into overdrive. I felt like one of those gazelles in the documentaries that's stuck in a mudhole and surrounded by a pack of hungry lions.

She stopped barely a hand's width away. I was already plastered against the door in terror. There was no sense pretending—my time had come.

"Ms. Jensen, do you know why I am here?" Loralai examined her nails. Her wicked, *pointed* nails.

I swallowed thickly. "No, Mistress."

She fixed me with her stare. The veining in her red irises swirled like lava flow. My neck strained as I fought against her compulsion, but I couldn't force myself to look away.

"I am here because no one is better suited to continue your father's work." Her voice seemed to come from inside my head. "Do you know why *you* are here?"

No, Mistress. I wasn't sure if I spoke out loud or not. Loralai's molten eyes appeared to grow until they were all I could see. My vision swam. I couldn't tell which way was up.

"You are here...because I have not yet disposed of you." Her response was whispered right beside my ear. I jumped in surprise, and the world lurched.

Everything went black.

I woke up at my desk. Or sprawled across it, rather. Loralai must have had someone dump me back there. I cradled my head in my arms for a moment, my temples pounding. I *hated* when she used that vampire crap. Pulling some ibuprofen out of a desk drawer, I gulped down a couple of tablets, grimacing when I realized I needed to replenish my supply soon.

The clock chimed, and my mood lifted. There was one bonus to my boss knocking me unconscious: my shift passed a lot quicker.

I stuffed my laptop into my bag and peeked in the compact mirror I kept in my desk for times such as this. There was a keyboard imprint on my cheek. Better than a black eye or claw marks. I shouldered my bag and joined the crowd in front of the elevator banks.

I squeezed into a car with my coworkers but kept my head down. No one bothered talking to me—they all learned long ago it was hazardous to their health to befriend me. Someone pushed the call button as the doors closed, but one look at the cramped interior kept them from joining us. We only made it down one floor before stopping again. The doors opened, revealing a single person.

Or *thing*, rather.

The vampire looked young, but that didn't mean anything. He was tall and wore a fine, tailored suit and carried a briefcase. The elevator car held its collective breath.

The vamp appeared unconcerned as he stepped forward. We all moved back. Toes were crushed, boundaries were crossed, but space was made. He nonchalantly faced the doors and pressed the button for the ground floor.

No one made a sound. I was plastered against Richard from Accounting's back like we were re-enacting the cover of a trashy romance novel. I was all for it, as long as he stayed between me and *it*.

I clenched Richard's shoulder. He awkwardly patted my thigh.

The car stopped, and the bell chimed. You could have cut the tension with a knife. Thankfully, this vamp wasn't as vindictive as Loralai. Or he was just in a hurry to be vindictive elsewhere. Either way, he stepped out as soon as the doors opened. We all waited a beat before rushing to exit ourselves.

Richard and I avoided eye contact.

I hurried across the lobby, only pausing when I spotted Alistair, the kindly old guard my father hired, at the information desk. He was speaking to someone but looked up when I stopped. His smile grew, and he waved.

"Have a great weekend, Miss Nora!" he called across the room.

I blushed at the looks I received, but waved back. "Thanks! You too, Alistair!"

I faced the doors and noticed the vamp from the elevator watching me. Feeling courageous, I glared at him. He gave me an odd look—almost amused. Before my feathers had time to get really ruffled, he dug a cellphone from his pocket and walked out.

"Whatever," I mumbled. It was the weekend. I was done pandering to vamps—or any other paranormals, for that matter. Unless I got fast-food...but at least I could use the drive-thru for that.

A cheery *ding* sounded, alerting me to a text message. I pulled my phone out of my bag.

Lina: Are we still on for PMS?

I snickered, knowing what was coming next. Sure enough, another message popped up.

Lina: Ugh! I meant PLS! Stupid autocorrect..

I smiled at my friend's familiar annoyance. She had a brilliant literary mind but wasn't a fan of modern technology. I typed a reply.

Nora: Yeah, I'm just leaving work. Be there soon.

I tossed the phone back in my bag and headed out the door. After retrieving my old, dented Toyota from the employee lot across the street, I set off toward the city library, reflecting on my week during the drive.

Loralai used her brain-bending on me twice. A new personal low. And my job duties had been cut back again, leaving me as basically a glorified gopher. My boss's fury this afternoon was incited over my forgetting the whipped cream on her latte.

Angry tears pricked my eyes. If my father hadn't passed... No, if *they* hadn't shown up, I wouldn't be stuck in this hell. I'd be well on my way to becoming a junior editor. I wouldn't be publicly browbeaten for the printer running out of paper or the pens having the wrong color ink.

The paranormals first stepped onto the world stage eight years ago, in what was later coined the "Grave

Awakening." Funny, considering it supposedly coincided with a bunch of vamps being woken up from hypersleep or whatever it is they do. I was a sophomore in high school at the time. The initial human reaction was a mixed bag of fear, I-told-you-so's, and excitement. Everyone was curious. We all wanted to know which pop culture version got it right. The Team Edward and Team Jacob flags were flying high.

Turns out, we'd all mostly gotten it wrong.

The vampires drink blood, but prefer it chilled, and from a blood bag. They are supernaturally strong and fast, plus, you know, the mind control thing. They have no aversion to sunlight. Near as anyone can tell, they only prefer night because there are fewer dumb humans around to trip over. They are suave, intelligent, and ridiculously organized. Like, *The Godfather*-level, but on a global scale.

When they first came out, the world governments nervously welcomed them, but immediately started enacting paranormal-focused laws and restrictions. It lasted about two seconds. No one's sure if our leaders saw the futility of laws in the face of the overwhelming power—physically and politically—of the vamps, or if they just got brain-bent until they fell in line. Either way, the vamps are pretty much running the show nowadays, even if nobody admits to it.

The werewolves really change into huge, wolf-like creatures. They tend to be more bipedal than straight-up wolf, but it seems family heritage plays a role in which of the two they lean toward. They maintain strong family units, but their "families" aren't necessarily blood-related; I think everyone is just too embarrassed or afraid to refer to them as packs in open conversation.

Call them what you will, the groups mostly keep to themselves. I don't know a single human who can say for sure they've met a werewolf, and certainly none who've seen one transform. Most of us learned what little we know about them from mandatory social studies classes that were introduced shortly after the paranormals' appearance.

Oh, and the age-old feud between werewolves and vampires is apparently completely fictional. The two basically ignore each other's existence.

Ghosts and zombies were the final two players in the big reveal. According to the scant information we were given, it seems when a person dies, they sometimes can choose to return to life. I guess they don't ever remember that they're not going to *want* to come back, because everyone who does gets split in two: a nearly mindless shell of their former self, and a completely intelligent but amnesiac carbon copy.

The zombies have just enough wit left to learn basic tasks, and so are relegated to the routine, no-creativity-needed type jobs of the world. Really, the news that most telemarketers are actually zombies didn't come as much of a surprise to anyone. On the plus side, whatever makes them come back reverses what happened in death, so they have normal, non-revolting bodies. They also don't try to eat anyone's brain.

The ghosts are a little trickier. Officially dubbed "Apparitions," they maintain all the intelligence of their former selves, but the amnesia apparently leaves them permanently stripped of everything but speech and the most basic of life skills. They're the ones that wander into shops in a daze, get a free cookie, and wander back out with a gentle but insistent pat on the back. Scientists have decided most homeless people are probably apparitions. The sad thing is they're perfectly capable of learning to live normal lives, but they feel so lost they wind up disappearing from whatever job or program they start before they make any real progress.

The vampires hinted once or twice at "lesser beings" beyond the Big Four but never explained further, and none of us humans could figure out what they meant. We knew they weren't talking about us—they made no effort to hide their disdain for puny, weak-minded humans. Scientists immediately got to work trying to pin down exactly what the other beings might be, but haven't had much luck. Most people just quietly congratulated themselves on being right all these years about the chupacabra and Bigfoot.

As far as I'm concerned, four of them are a great plenty. In fact, just *one* has been enough to completely derail my life.

Prior to vampires, my dad and I had it pretty good. Jensen Publishing was already a successful company by the time I was old enough for a job, and since my goal in life was to become an editor, what better place to get started? My dad was happy to take me on, but he definitely believed in the value of hard work. He had built the company from the ground up, after all. I think it helped him cope after my mom died.

My first job was in the mailroom. It was boring, but easy, and it introduced me to everyone in the company. I didn't really understand the importance of networking at the time, but it was an invaluable experience. I moved up to an office assistant role within a year.

The Grave Awakening happened a month later.

Everything changed from then on. My father was one of the first to welcome the whole new field of potential clients. As such, Jensen Publishing was awarded a lucrative contract to edit and distribute the plethora of new learning materials the world suddenly needed. Our fortunes quite literally changed that day.

My dad had always been a conservative type, saving rather than spending, but he sat me down after he signed the contract with the vamps and filled me in on all the nitty-gritty details. (We were always very open with each other—we'd had to be, after losing Mom.) The payout for the contract was staggering, and spaced over the lifetime of the agreement, which was basically indefinite. As long as Jensen Publishing stayed afloat, and the vamps had propaganda to distribute, we'd all be very comfortable.

Unfortunately, there was a stipulation to the deal. For our company to properly edit their materials, we'd obviously need a subject matter expert on staff.

Enter Loralai.

I hated her from the moment she stepped off the elevator. She was a perfect fit for all the worst vampire stereotypes. Beautiful and possessing of an otherworldly grace, yes, but also vain, haughty, and cruel. She preyed on the staff mercilessly—doing everything short of physical assault to keep us all afraid and compliant—and ensured her claws were deep in everything that went on at the company, paranormal-related or otherwise.

But the worst part was her relationship with my father. She must have brain-bent him constantly, because no one could possibly buy her syrupy sweet, batting-eyelash act.

Especially since all it took was one look around the office to see the truth. Nevertheless, he bought it hook, line, and sinker. He praised her work constantly, gushing nauseatingly over "that remarkable woman." It wasn't long before she was running the day-to-day operations and Dad was just a figurehead. Thankfully, his continued presence in the office kept her mostly away from me, aside from nasty looks and the occasional veiled threat.

I gave up on trying to convince him of her true nature pretty early on. It was like everything I said just bounced off him. His responses were always along the lines of, "Oh, I'm sure there was just a misunderstanding," or "Loralai is a good person, and she only wants the best for our company."

We eventually fell into an unspoken agreement to avoid the subject.

Then, three years ago, Dad started getting headaches. At first, he said it was just eye strain from staring at a computer all day. But when they turned into full-blown migraines, we met with the doctor. Dr. Engle suggested a regimen of pain relievers, but the migraines continued and increased in frequency as time went on. The doctor completed all sorts of tests and imaging but couldn't find a root cause. I began to suspect it was a side-effect of Loralai's manipulation, but the one time I blurted that out, Dad got really upset and his condition worsened. I didn't bring it up again, but as he continued to decline, I became more and more convinced I was right.

The day came when he couldn't leave the house anymore. I arranged for a home health worker through the hospital but didn't know what else to do, so I went on acting as though everything was normal. I went to work every day and faced Loralai's nastiness. I continued attending part-time classes at the community college. And I went home every evening and sat at Dad's bedside and told him about my day. We kept his room dark and quiet and encouraged him to rest as much as possible, but he insisted on listening to all my meaningless stories. Whenever he asked about the company, I'd tell him everything was fine, Loralai was handling things.

When he deteriorated further, the doctors decided it would be best to move him to the hospital. Sitting in his dim room had been bad enough, but visiting the hospital every day and seeing all the tubes and wires hooked up to him was heartbreaking. When had my funny and irrepressible father turned into this unrecognizable shell? I teetered on the edge of a crippling depression but held on for Dad's sake. I had to be there for him—he'd need me to help him through his recovery, after all.

The call came during my Literary Theory class. I recognized the hospital's number and walked out of the lecture hall. I never went back.

After all the funeral arrangements and legal matters were taken care of, and I spent a considerable amount of time sitting alone in my empty house, I switched to online classes. I returned to work—to my normal desk and insignificant tasks. My coworkers were compassionate, and everyone offered their help in anything I might need, but it wasn't long before they stopped approaching me.

In my fog, I didn't really notice at first, but the day I saw Loralai looming over Mary from HR after the sympathetic woman had delivered a foil-covered casserole to my desk, I put the pieces together. The vamp was causing my isolation, making me easier to manage.

It was probably for the best, I thought. I didn't want the others to suffer unnecessarily. And without the contract with the vampires that had taken over our entire operation by that point, we'd all be out of work.

So, I kept my head down, avoided everyone, and watched my future gradually slip away.

2

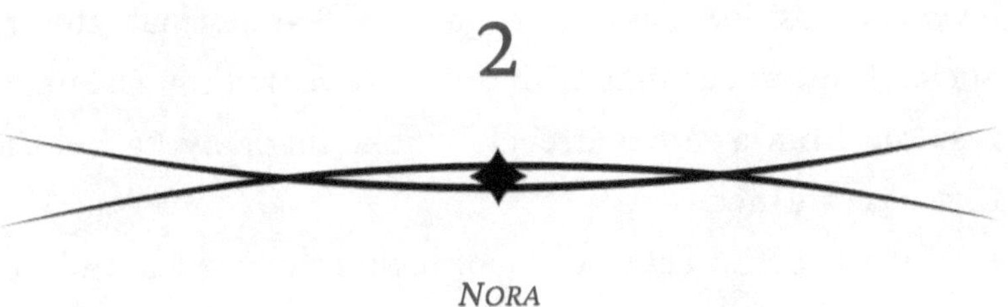

I PARKED BEHIND the library and sat for a few minutes. I looked forward to seeing my friends, but sometimes it was just hard. These were some of the last connections I had from before my dad's death. There was everyone at work, of course, but that situation was such a mess, I mostly tried not to think about it.

My friends in PLS were different. They were all around my age, for one thing. They had been like sisters to me during Dad's sickness, but as a result, they were sometimes far too observant for comfort. As much as I wanted to pretend my life was fine, and paranormal creatures didn't exist, my friends could always tell when Loralai had been especially vindictive. It made hiding from my problems a lot harder.

I heard my phone chime and sighed. No sense putting it off any longer. Grabbing my bag, I hurried up the stone steps and entered the red brick building through the back entrance. It put me in the green-and-brown jungle scenes of the children's section. I smiled at the stifled giggles coming from a tree-shaped reading alcove and continued on to the series of small meeting rooms next to the non-fiction section. The girls and I had basically laid claim to the one with the floral motif painted on the wall years before when our little group started.

After being assigned a group paper in our freshman-level composition class, we began the "Paranormal Literary Society" due to our shared love of creative writing. The name resulted from a rather irreverent joke made by Rachel the first time we met.

It was definitely a stroke of luck for our teacher to put the four of us together. Even though none of us had previously spoken, the arrangement led to amazing friendships. I couldn't have handled everything that happened—and continued to happen—without the support of these three incredible ladies.

I pushed through the door and found I was the last to arrive. As usual.

"Sorry. Work ran a little long," I lied. They all knew it was a lie. I don't know why I kept up the charade.

"That's alright," said Lina, the kindly, soft-spoken member of the group who also happened to be an in-house librarian. She gestured at the laptop screen displaying our sole remote attendee. "Rachel was just filling us in on her mom's latest pickling attempts."

I snorted. Rachel's mom was eccentric, to say the least. She had been an extreme end-times prepper before the Grave Awakening. The event tipped her over the edge. She packed up Rachel and their cat and hustled them all into the underground bunker they owned and didn't seem to have plans to leave. None of us were brave enough to ask, but the general consensus was that Rachel probably hadn't been above ground in the past eight years. She mentioned her dad sometimes, but only in reference to speaking to him on the phone. It seemed he hadn't gotten on board with the bunker plan.

Despite the strange situation, Rachel had a sweet and bubbly personality, and often kept us in stitches with tales of her mom's efforts to keep life interesting. I admired her courage and optimism. I couldn't imagine the number of times she had to explain why she attended all her classes via webcam. That alone would have driven me nuts.

"Asparagus," came Rachel's tinny voice over the speaker, rehashing the pickling story for me. *"Which is bad enough, except she used the curry seasoning mix. It. Was. Awful!"*

Everyone laughed. "Did the cat at least eat it?" asked Izzy. Rachel's poor cat had become the designated taste-tester/garbage disposal in their bunker.

"No, Tam has pretty much taken to running for the hills whenever she hears jar lids opening. I think she's living behind the toilet paper tower now."

"Smart," said Izzy. The dark-haired, black-clad girl wasn't much for wasted words.

"So..." Lina turned to me. "How was work today? Did anything *interesting* happen?" she asked tactfully.

"Did that witch accost you?" was Izzy's plain-spoken version.

"Oh, I hate her!" Rachel's contribution summed up everyone's opinion. I couldn't imagine anyone on the face of the Earth actually liked that vindictive woman.

"No," I replied brightly. "I didn't even see her today. Everything was fine. So, who wants to read first?"

"Nora." Lina's tone was gentle.

I cringed inwardly. She was too empathetic for her own good.

"You don't have to tell us, but you know you don't have to pretend, either. We're always here for you." She leaned over and squeezed my hand.

I gave her a sad smile. "Thank you. It's just easier to ignore it." I returned the squeeze before pulling away.

Rachel broke the brief pause in the room. *"Can I read first? I wrote an entire new chapter this week!"* The blonde bounced at her desk in excitement.

I shared a smirk with Lina and Izzy before nodding at Rachel.

Izzy heaved an exaggerated sigh. "If you must."

Rachel let out a small squeal before clearing her throat and flipping open the technicolor Lisa Frank notebook before her. Her mom must have been stashing stuff in that bunker since before Rachel was born.

"'Ambassador Ravia felt heat climb her neck and spread across her cheeks, despite the chill in the strange planet's air. The towering man before her, if he could be called that, with his pale blue skin and unearthly purple eyes, was the most gorgeous creature she had ever laid eyes on. His gaze swept over her, leaving a trail of goosebumps in its wake.

"'Human,' his deep voice set the butterflies in her stomach fluttering. 'You are not what I expected.'

"The glint in his eye and slight curve of his sensuous lips betrayed his pleasure at the fact...'"

I heard a faint choking sound from Izzy's side of the room and stifled a snicker.

Oh, Ravia.

In the comically deep, theatrical voice reserved for her readings, Rachel continued the space epic of spunky—and concerningly promiscuous—Ambassador Ravia.

It was impossible to miss the correlation between Rachel's steamy, escapist fiction and her isolated lifestyle. The first time she read to us, I think everyone was a bit shocked. Her characters were all fantastically capable, in every conceivable way, and found themselves in a suspicious number of compromising situations, despite the impending doom they were always supposed to be averting. Even though I'm fairly sure none of the rest of us would have ever picked up a book like that, it soon became something of a guilty pleasure. Rachel's dramatic delivery made it all the better.

Lina read next. Another surprise at the start, the sweeping landscapes, valiant knights, and evil sorcerers of Lina's high fantasy writing belied her quiet demeanor. Her stories were exciting, the prose vibrant and beautiful, and her soft, lilting voice had the added bonus of being extremely relaxing. Listening to Lina read was probably my favorite way to decompress.

Izzy's turn introduced us to her latest psychological thriller. She usually wrote mysteries in short story form, often featuring a grim and deeply flawed male protagonist. The current work seemed to be shaping up to be lengthier, though. When she closed with a gory description of a murder scene, delivered in her typical bleak reading voice, I doubted I was the only one with a case of the creeps.

"Your word choice was so vivid, Izzy! I could picture exactly what you were describing," said Lina, grimacing. "It seems like a pretty complicated plot, though. Are you planning for this to be a novel?"

Izzy shrugged. "We'll see what happens."

Lina shot me a knowing look—Izzy's ability to brush off any form of compliment was nearly as remarkable as her writing skill.

"Yeah, Izzy, that was great. I'm excited to hear more," I said.

"It needs work," Izzy deflected smoothly, straightening her already-straight stack of papers.

I returned Lina's look with a small grin as I pulled a folder out of my bag. "I didn't write anything new this week, but I *did* get some proofs back from that illustrator!" After passing around the sketches featuring a cute, compassionate-looking mouse in various poses, I held one up for Rachel to see.

"*Oh, that's so perfect!*" she gushed.

"It is," agreed Lina. "It's exactly how I imagined June."

Izzy nodded thoughtfully as she studied a picture of June with her paws on her furry hips.

With the help of my friends' critiques, I had recently finished writing a children's book about a mouse who befriends a lonely little girl and teaches her important lessons about kindness and loyalty. I'd contacted several illustrators about the project, but this was the most promising. His drawings perfectly captured the sweet mouse without being too *Looney Tunes*-ish.

"I emailed him back this morning and said I want to work with him. I had to explain the situation a bit, so hopefully he'll still be willing to take on the project," I said.

Lina looked sympathetic. "He obviously put a lot of care into these mockups," she said, holding one up. "Maybe he'll take it on for the enjoyment rather than publicity. He's getting paid either way, after all."

"I still don't understand why you don't just take it to a different publisher. I know you want your family name on it and all, but you could rub that vamp's face in it—you got published even without her permission," said Izzy.

"Yeah! You could give her a signed copy for Boss's Day!" squealed Rachel.

The idea was tempting, but I knew the fallout wouldn't be worth it. Publishing the book wasn't the problem—it was the public reminder that my mind wasn't under her thumb as my father's had been that would send Loralai flying off the handle. Besides, I'd once promised him I'd be a famous author someday and would have all my books printed by him. Even though I'd said it when I was six, and now wanted to be an editor more than an author, his passing made it seem imperative that I keep this one promise at least. I was already failing at the other, mostly unspoken, ones—live a full life, marry a nice boy, be happy, etc. The least I could do was ensure any printed book with my name on the cover carried the Jensen Publishing stamp.

Unfortunately, with Loralai now acting as the final voice on submissions, that dream was unlikely to come true. I was determined to be content with an author copy and a dedication page to my dad. This seemed infinitely more doable now that I'd seen my sweet June come to life, thanks to "C" of C-Sketch Illustrations (according to his email signature).

The group of us chatted for another half-hour about everything from the early season heat wave we were experiencing to the uptick in vampire political activity the news had been quietly reporting on lately.

When the conversation reached a lull, Izzy closed her bag and stood abruptly. "Well, I'll see you all next week," she said. She certainly made goodbyes easy.

Lina reached for her laptop, waving goodbye to Rachel.

"*Bye everyone! I'll text you, Alina!*" the bubbly girl called.

I saw Lina's hesitation. "Couldn't you email me, instead? You know how finicky my phone can be..."

"*Oh, of course! Sorry, I forgot. I hope you can get that fixed soon. See you next week!*"

Lina closed the computer and tucked it into her bag. She turned to me with a lopsided smile. "You know how she is over texting," she said sheepishly. "I can't ever keep up."

Rachel's rapid-fire messaging and penchant for acronyms *was* rather overwhelming.

"Don't worry," I replied with a smirk. "Your secret is safe with me."

3

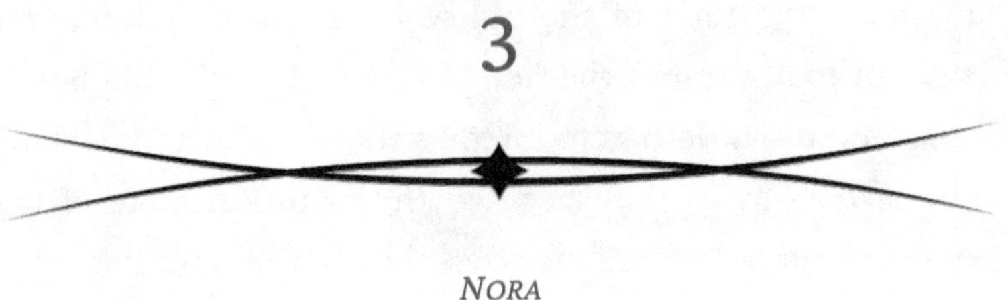

NORA

STANDING IN MY silent kitchen, I let out a sigh. I'd always appreciated peaceful stillness, but the complete void of sound in my house was oppressive. I was considering getting an apartment, if only to have some version of a fresh start, but the idea of putting further distance between Dad and myself was frightening. He was gone—I knew that—but at least here at the house there were knickknacks that triggered memories, and clothes that still carried his scent.

But if I compromised and took those treasured possessions to a new home, wouldn't that defeat the purpose of a fresh start?

The girls from PLS and I often went to dinner after our meetings, but with Izzy's quick exit and Lina needing to get home to her uncle, I was left to my own devices. I smiled as I recalled the single attempt we made at taking Rachel out with us. We tried to pick the least busy restaurant we could, but the ambient noise still flooded the laptop mic and resulted in everyone loudly repeating themselves all evening, much to the annoyance of the other customers. The rest of us were willing to try again, but Rachel always refused, saying it was easier to chat with us during the meetings, anyway. I think she felt worse about us getting shushed by strangers than she let on.

Settling on leftover Chinese takeout for dinner, I escaped the deafening quiet of the house for the back porch. Our neighborhood climbed the side of a small hill, with our house being one of those perched along the ridgeline. When my parents bought it, they decided the beautiful view of the expansive park behind us was worth the sacrifice of a backyard. Besides, there was still enough grass in the front for toddler me to have plenty of outdoor fun.

I finished my sweet and sour pork and sat back to admire the shifting colors of the sunset as growing shadows crept across the park. A beautiful, but bittersweet, sight. My dad and I watched the sunset together from the porch as often as we could. It had been one of my mom's mandatory family activities—one which we were more than happy to continue in her absence.

A chime from my phone provided a welcome distraction from my increasingly morose thoughts. I swiped at a few stray tears and pulled the device from my pocket. My notifications announced an email reply from C-Sketch Illustrations.

Dear Ms. Jensen,

I'm so pleased you are happy with the samples I provided. Thank you for taking the time to explain your unique situation. Despite your stated concerns, I am

happy to accept your offer to collaborate on this project. I greatly enjoyed your charming tale and am very much looking forward to meeting and working with you. I would like to schedule an in-person introduction in the coming week, if your schedule will allow it.

Yours sincerely,

C

My mood lifted as I read, leaving me with a wide grin pasted on my face by the end. I had hoped "C" would be willing to work with me, but told myself to expect a rejection. Someone as talented as him (her?) likely wasn't starving for work, and accepting a project with zero publicity wasn't an overly smart move for someone who relied on referrals for their next paycheck.

I immediately hit the reply button.

Dear C,

Thank you so much for getting back to me! I'm thrilled you've accepted and am also excited to meet and get started on this. My schedule is—my grin turned to a grimace—**basically wide open. Let me know what works best for you and I'm sure it will be fine for me as well.**

Thanks!

Nora Jensen

I plopped my phone on the patio table and drummed on my thighs in excitement. Finally, something was going right!

Dad would be thrilled!

For the first time in nearly a year, the thought of my dad wasn't solely one of sorrow and regret. Before I could examine the realization further, my phone announced the arrival of another email. The guy/gal must have been working at their computer that evening. Or was as glued to their phone as us young folk. I was leaning more toward the computer scenario. Given the abundantly polite and formal tone of all the emails I'd received so far, I was pretty sure "C" was an older person. Maybe a retiree doing illustrations just for the enjoyment of it, as Lina had suggested?

I pulled up the message.

Dear Ms. Jensen,

Not to worry, my agenda is also rather bare at the moment. Are you averse to conducting business on the weekend? I know of a pleasant coffee shop downtown, if you would be willing to meet with me tomorrow morning.

Best regards,

C

Surprised and delighted at being offered something to fill my empty weekend hours, I quickly typed out an affirmative and soon had a scheduled time and place to meet my new partner the following day.

That night, I organized and packed up my manuscript and my jumble of notes for the illustrations before going to bed. According to the map on my phone, the coffee shop wasn't far, and our nine am meeting wasn't exactly the crack of dawn, but traffic into the city usually swelled on Saturday mornings as all the suburbanites raced to be first in line at the fancy shopping mall downtown. I wanted to give myself plenty of time to get there and ensure I didn't forget anything important. I was already nervous that this person would be less than impressed when they saw how young I was—I didn't need to add to it by showing up late and forgetting half my stuff.

My phone chimed as I was climbing into bed, alerting me to a message of congratulations from Izzy. I'd shared the news with my friends as soon as I had the final meeting details and was promptly flooded with all-caps excitement from Rachel and kindly worded I-told-you-so's from Lina. Rachel was especially delighted by the name of the meeting spot, Bean Me Up. I was given strict instructions to make detailed notes of any and all *Star Trek* references and memorabilia the coffee shop might have on display.

As expected, Izzy waited until the hysteria died down before adding her two cents. I smiled at the thought of my somewhat standoffish friend. I imagined she probably turned her phone off as soon as the group message notifications started.

I jumped out of bed the next morning, eager to start the day, without even a single push of the Snooze button. *Another first...*

Dressed in a simple blouse and knee-length skirt, I pinned my hair into a neat bun and headed to the kitchen to wolf down a quick breakfast. I preferred to avoid embarrassing myself with a noisy stomach during the meeting.

As I gathered my bag and headed out the door, my phone alerted me to a new email from "C." I opened it with a considerable amount of apprehension, leaving the front door standing open in my distraction. *Has he already reconsidered?*

Dear Ms. Jensen,

I apologize for my foolish lack of foresight; I realized this morning I never provided you with a description of myself, so you would know who to look for at the coffee shop.

My anxiety left in a whoosh, and I had to shake my head at myself. The last few years were rough, but when had I become such a determined pessimist?

I am of average height and build, with brown hair. I will be wearing a blue button-down.
See you shortly!
C

Well, he sounded pleasant enough. And apparently not old enough for gray or white hair, unless he was one of those elusive male hair dyers you hear about. Wait, he never actually said he was a *he*... Nerves forgotten, I locked the front door, cutting off the escaping flow of "bought air," as my mom used to call it, and soon joined the stream of suburban women in their polished SUVs headed toward the city center.

Traffic hadn't reached an unreasonable level yet, and I arrived at the coffee shop sooner than expected—much earlier than our agreed-upon time. The rising temperature, intensified by the downtown sea of glass, steel, and pavement, sent me scurrying inside the shop to wait. I ordered an iced tea and claimed a quiet corner table.

The place was busy, but most of the customers got their orders to go with only a few lingering patrons. The nearby university skewed the customer demographic toward the younger side, but several sharply dressed business professionals dotted the line as well, apparently punching the overtime clock for their offices. Rachel would be proud to know I did spot a collection of signed headshots of various *Star Trek* actors. None of the big names, though—the place wasn't *that* trendy, apparently. But still trendier than I expected of the staunchly proper "C."

A sudden chill slithered down the back of my neck, setting the hairs on end. I rubbed a hand over my skin and covertly glanced around for the source of the prickly sensation. It wasn't hard to find. A few tables away, in the darkest corner of the shop, sat a pale, bald man wearing a dark suit. His eyes were a creepy shade of ice blue and were fixed on me. I looked away quickly and took a sip of tea, trying to resume my former calm. A reflective napkin holder told me he was still staring. I fought the urge to shudder.

As my unease grew, my temper rose to match it. I turned back and was preparing to tell him off when someone approached the table in my peripheral view. My quick glance and split attention only revealed that it was a young, attractive man—exactly the type I'd been dutifully avoiding for years.

"Not now," I said, waving a hand vaguely at the stranger, my eyes back on Creepy Guy, whose expression hadn't changed in the slightest at the interruption to our standoff.

The newcomer didn't leave. "Ms. Jensen?" His warm voice sounded mildly amused.

My reason for being there rushed back like a smack in the face. I whirled around, Creepy Guy forgotten, heat flooding my cheeks. Sure enough, my brain now registered the stranger's brown hair, average height, and blue button-down. It also registered that "C" had entirely failed to mention he was drop-dead gorgeous. And at least twenty years younger than I expected.

I shot out of my chair, dumping my bag off my lap and its contents all over the floor.

Real nice, Nora. I'd never wanted to kick myself so badly.

Mr. Dreamy stepped back in surprise as a container of lip balm bounced toward him. I dropped to my knees to gather my belongings, ducking my head to hide my burning face. Dreamy made matters worse by crouching to help me.

I was certain my cheeks would spontaneously combust when he plucked the flower pouch containing my feminine products out from under the table. I snatched it from his hand, along with the lip balm, bottle of lotion, and two pens that he offered, and stuffed the whole mess back in my bag, immensely grateful I had previously taken my paperwork out and arranged it neatly on the table.

Dreamy stood and offered a hand to help me up. I hesitated a moment before accepting, briefly tempted to just live the rest of my life under that table and not have to face him. He pulled me gently to my feet and then had the nerve to look apologetic.

"I'm terribly sorry for startling you. You are Ms. Jensen, are you not?"

I nervously touched my hair, ensuring it hadn't collapsed along with the rest of my presentation. "I am. How did you know?"

His look of apology turned to bashfulness. "I've actually seen you before," he said. "At the university."

That was a surprise; I didn't recognize him at all. *I'd remember a face like that...* "Did we have classes together?" I asked dumbly.

"Just one. And you were only there for part of the semester..." he trailed off.

Oh. *That* year. No wonder I didn't remember him.

"Um, yeah... I had a lot going on at the time." I picked at a loose thread on my bag.

"I saw the announcement in the paper. I know it's rather late, but I offer my deepest condolences on your loss."

I peeked up at him and was surprised at his kind expression. Most people's condolences had blurred together into nothing but noise long ago. Something about the sincerity on his face set me more at ease. I gave him a small smile. His returning grin revealed perfectly straight white teeth. He seemed relieved. I guess I wasn't the only one feeling concerned over this debacle of a meeting.

Suddenly, his eyes widened, and he slapped a hand to his forehead. "I haven't introduced myself!" he exclaimed. "My goodness, please excuse my rudeness!"

Our definitions of rude must be very different...

"My name's Cal," he continued, offering me his hand again. I took it and began to shake at the same time he bent over to kiss the back of mine, resulting in me nearly punching him in the mouth. I half-expected my hair to turn red with the force of my blush.

Cal gave my hand a quick peck and released it, his mouth twisting into a lopsided smile. "I apologize," he said. "My mother raised me to be rather...old-fashioned."

I self-consciously rubbed my hand and glanced around. A brunette girl across the room smirked at me and whispered to her friend. I narrowed my eyes at them and turned back to Cal, indignation bolstering my nerves.

"That's okay," I said. "The world would be much better off if more people taught their kids manners these days. Besides, I'm the one who should be apologizing for the disaster I've made of things so far."

"I haven't found it to be disastrous at all," he replied with another gorgeous smile. "And thank you. My mother would be gratified to hear you say that." He gestured to my seat. "Shall we sit?"

I plopped into my chair, grateful for something to do besides gawk at him. He settled into his seat with infinitely more poise. I noticed the pristine leather folio sitting in front of him and wondered when he'd set it down.

Probably right before he went fishing for my tampons. Ugh.

"So, Ms. Jensen—"

"Nora," I interrupted. "Sorry... Just Nora is fine."

He smiled. "As you wish. *Just* Nora."

Did he even realize he was quoting the dashing Wesley from *The Princess Bride*?

I mentally rolled my eyes. *Turns out, he's the real-life Wesley.*

He opened his folio and took out a stack of papers. "I know you'll have your own vision for the illustrations, but I hope you won't mind that I took the liberty of coming up with a few ideas of my own."

Cal began handing the sketches over, one at a time. I took them slowly, pausing to appreciate each one. He was right—I did have my own ideas for the illustrations—but it was hard to remember what they were as I marveled at his work. He was extremely skilled, to be sure, but more than that, he'd perfectly captured the nuances of the characters and situations. It wasn't long before I was grinning like an idiot. Cal didn't seem to mind.

Then he held out the final drawing.

It was me.

4

I STARED AT the little blonde girl on the page. Her sad blue eyes gazed back. She sat alone under a red maple tree. Memories flooded my mind: another sad little blonde girl, sitting alone on her tricycle, wondering where her mom was. Suddenly she was grown up, sitting alone on the back porch, wishing her dad would come home.

A tear splashed onto the paper, smearing the colors.

I gasped and snatched a napkin off the table, but the damage was already done. "I'm so sorry," I said miserably, handing the paper back. An ugly splotch marred the center of what had been the most detailed of Cal's sketches.

He took the paper silently and set it aside without a glance. Wrapping his hands around my own, napkin and all, he looked at me earnestly. "Never apologize for being human, Nora. Our humanity is a gift. And one not everyone gets to experience."

I smiled weakly. *He's right. I could be a vampire or zombie instead. Blech.*

He returned the smile and gave my hands a reassuring squeeze before letting go. "Now," he continued in a brighter voice. "Why don't you tell me what you envision for the illustrations, and I'll see what I can come up with for our next meeting?"

———

"*Your* next *meeting?! Meeeoow!*" Rachel's shrill catcall proved too much for my laptop speakers. The audio went static-y and cut off most of whatever else she said. The parts that came through sounded an awful lot like the sort of morally questionable advice Ambassador Ravia would give.

I laughed as I readjusted the settings. The audio came back just as Rachel finished with "*—to jump on that!*"

I shook my head in amusement. "It wasn't like that. He's just working with me on this project."

Lina, Izzy and I were sprawled around my living room, with Rachel's screen perched on the coffee table. In a rare fit of normalcy, I'd decided to play host to this week's PLS meeting. It had mostly devolved into a big social hour so far; it was nice. I began to wonder why I worked so hard to avoid people.

"*Pfft. He's 'just working' with me,*" Rachel mimicked, pairing her air quotes with a dramatic eye roll. "*He's also* just *young and cute, according to you! What's holding you back?*"

I flopped back into my armchair and stared at the ceiling. "Well, for starters, he's not interested in me."

Another screech blasted out of the laptop, Izzy scoffed, and even Lina snickered.

"Uninterested guys don't kiss your hand, Nora! They don't pick up all your purse junk! And they especially don't console you after you just ruined their stuff!" Rachel's logic made me cringe.

"She's right, you know," said Lina. "He sounds like a perfect gentleman, but even gentlemen have their limits."

"He's into you," Izzy said matter-of-factly. "Why else would he mention having seen you at college before? He probably liked you then, but you dropped out before he worked up the nerve to say anything."

"Oooo, good point, Izzy!" trumpeted Rachel. *"See, Nora? It's settled. You need to date him."*

"It might be easier to believe all that if it actually came from him," I laughed.

Izzy shrugged. "So, ask him."

I blanched. "I can't just *ask* him if he's interested in me! What if he said no? I'd die of embarrassment *and* would have to find another illustrator!"

"And what if he said yes?" replied Lina.

"Well... I don't know." I picked at a seam on my chair. "I guess I'd probably still be embarrassed."

Silence descended, and I peeked around at the others. Lina gave me a sympathetic look. Rachel was tapping on her keyboard. Izzy stared at a bookshelf in the corner.

I sat up. *"Anyway.* If we're done dissecting my nonexistent love life, should we get to the actual meeting?"

Izzy continued her perusal of the bookshelf. "That's easy. We didn't bring anything to read."

"What, really?"

Lina nodded. "We actually texted each other after you invited us over. We all wanted to come, of course, but we thought you could use just a casual get-together. And it happened to work out nicely. Izzy didn't have anything ready, and I was too busy with...home stuff, to write at all."

"*I wrote a ton!*" Rachel chimed in. "*But I want to rework it before everyone hears it.*"

I smiled. "Thanks, guys. That means a lot."

"You're welcome," said Izzy. "Let's order dinner."

An hour later, we were still sprawled around the living room, but now with empty takeout containers scattered between us.

"*What I really miss is going to the movies,*" Rachel sighed. We were in various stages of after-dinner sleepiness and Rachel was recounting her list of everyday things she missed the most. "Plain old store-bought pickles" was one of the first entries.

"Movie theaters are overrated," replied Izzy. "People talk through the whole thing, the candy costs too much, and somebody huge always sits in front of you."

Rachel looked slightly embarrassed. "*I did get hushed a few times when Mom took me.*"

I chuckled. *No surprise there.* Another thought jumped to mind. "Hey! Dad set up a movie projector in the family room downstairs just before..." I trailed off awkwardly. "Anyway, I've never used it, but I'm pretty sure it works. We could have a movie night sometime."

An excited *whoop* provided Rachel's answer.

"I have my next weekend off in two weeks," said Lina.

"Weekends work fine for me," replied Izzy.

"Well, alright. I guess I'll plan on two weeks from now, then."

"And that'll give you two whole weeks to seal the deal with Cal so you can bring him to meet all of us!" Rachel exclaimed.

Two whole weeks, indeed.

I stood in the driveway later that evening, bidding my friends goodnight. Lina hugged me tightly and murmured a quiet reassurance.

"You're not alone."

It was the first time her words weren't met with an immediate internal denial. Something was changing. Strangely, I welcomed it, rather than running or pushing it away. I felt genuine hope for the first time in ages.

"Don't worry about Cal," called Lina from her car. "If he's not Prince Charming, he doesn't deserve you, anyway!"

I laughed and waved goodbye, my heart the lightest it had been since Dad's passing.

––––––––––

Monday morning brought me crashing back to reality.

Loralai had been gone the previous week on vacation or a business trip or an extended haunting of some poor, innocent soul. Whatever it was, the week without her was pure bliss. Coworkers spoke to one another instead of staring at the floor and scurrying around like a bunch of kicked puppies. By Tuesday, there was actual laughter heard.

Any thoughts about continuing such behavior were quickly—and thoroughly—quashed at Loralai's return. Perhaps her haunting didn't go so well, because the moment she stepped off the elevator, it was as though a black cloud descended over the office. She swept up the aisle, leaving a noticeable chill in her wake. The sound of her door slamming was probably heard on the next street over.

No one said anything, but it was obvious everyone was doing their utmost to avoid approaching her. It wasn't until that afternoon that someone finally broke. When poor Richard from Accounting passed by on the way back to his office, he looked as though he might be sick. Or already had been, in her office.

On second thought, if that'd happened, I doubt he would have escaped her with his head still attached.

Mercifully, I made it through without any summons.

The following day was worse.

A new vamp arrived. Charna was tall and curvaceous with caramel skin that still managed to come across as weirdly pale. Loralai presented her to the rest of us as her new assistant, but it only took a glance to see Charna obviously didn't regard Loralai as her superior in any way. As my desk was closest, I had the pleasure of listening to them hiss at each other all day—sometimes literally.

Although I frequently suspected the hands on the clock were actually going backward, the day finally came to an end. I quickly gathered my things, eager to escape the palpable tension hanging over the office. I stepped into the aisle and nearly collided with Charna. Hustling backward, I mumbled an apology and stared at the floor. She didn't reciprocate. Her maroon eyes entered my field of vision.

"Watch it, *mortal*," she snarled. Startled, I scurried farther back into my cubicle. Aside from Loralai, a vamp had never gone out of their way to address me before. They mostly seemed to ignore the existence of any human they didn't need something from, much as we disregard ants.

Now holding my gaze, she straightened back to her full, imposing height, fairly towering over me. Her stilettos didn't help the matter. We stared at each other a moment longer, anger radiating off her, apprehension swelling in me, when the sound of a closing door caught her attention. She sliced her eyes over her shoulder and an inhuman growl crawled out of her throat. Whipping around, she stalked toward the elevator.

Assuming Charna's reaction meant Loralai was on the move, I stepped behind the edge of my felt-covered office wall and waited for her to pass. I didn't care to run into her on the best of days, and with how the week was going, I wasn't sure I'd survive the encounter. Her footsteps passed and faded in the direction of the elevator banks. I waited until I heard the *ding* announcing the arriving car before leaving my cubicle. The doors hadn't closed yet as I approached, but thanks to the angle, I couldn't see the occupants.

Loralai's perpetually condescending voice drifted out, halting me. "This is my company, and I will not stand for a repeat of your behavior today. *I* am in charge here and *you* will do well to remember that—unless you prefer I bring the matter up with the Elders."

"Your childish posturing is pathetic." Charna's reply dripped venom. "The Elders will soon realize you've served your purpose. When that time comes, I can only hope our Lord Miroslav allows *me* the joy of ripping your disgusting throat out."

The doors closed on whatever response Loralai might have given.

I stayed frozen in place. I knew the vampires were ruthless and followed their own set of rules governing their society, but geez! Had I just stumbled into some horror movie? Something else about the conversation tickled at the back of my mind, but I couldn't place it.

After finally working up the nerve to call for my own elevator, I continued puzzling over the conversation as I descended to the lobby. The bell sounded, and I stepped off, colliding with the solid chest of the same well-dressed vamp who had ridden the packed elevator with all of us a couple of weeks before. I recoiled violently, crashing into the back wall of the car. He stepped in and gave me a mildly amused look. I stared back, my mouth hanging open in horror.

"Did you need to get off here?" he asked.

"Uhh," was my eloquent response. I chanced a quick glance at the screen on the wall and realized I'd only gone down one floor. *Stupid!*

He waited.

The ground floor! You need to go to the ground floor! Hurry up before he decides your *throat needs ripping out!*

"Are you—" he began.

"Ground!" I choked out.

He stopped and just looked at me again.

I cleared my throat. "Sorry. The ground floor. I got distracted and thought I was already there—"

My rambling explanation cut off when he smiled, showing his fangs and sending my fear through the roof.

"Not a problem," he said, and pushed the button for the ground floor. He turned to face the front, a healthy distance away from me.

I peeled myself slightly off the wall, but kept my eyes on him, determined not to be caught unawares. Not that I could possibly do anything to defend myself, but I guess it's the thought that counts. A reflection caught my eye, and I realized I could see his face in the shiny metal paneling on the wall. He wasn't looking at me, despite my staring, but I noticed his eyes were so dark red they nearly appeared black. *Interesting.*

"Did you say something?"

My eyes widened. "Did I?" I whispered.

He smiled again, this time without teeth. "You may ask me something, if you like. I know humans have many questions about us."

"No, that's okay," I answered in a rush.

The elevator chimed, and the doors opened. I double-checked that it was the ground floor while waiting for the vamp to exit first. He didn't move.

"Don't worry," he said. "I won't bite."

My head whipped toward him. He wore a serious expression, but his eyes crinkled in amusement. The elevator doors stood open, and the lobby was empty. I could see Alistair at his desk over the vampire's shoulder, so at least there might be a witness if anything happened. I turned my gaze back to the vamp and saw the corner of his mouth creeping upward. Indignation overruled my fear.

"Fine. Why are your eyes darker than other vampires'? Does it mean something, or is it just the equivalent of blue versus green?"

His mouth quirked higher. "An excellent question. You're a very observant human."

I nearly scoffed, and prepared to sidle around him, expecting this patronizing non-answer to be all I would get, as per their usual tendencies.

"A vampire's eye color is actually an indication of age, although generally in the reverse of what you would see in a human. A darker color signifies an older vampire. As one enters what might be deemed 'old age,' the whites of the eyes become red as well."

I could only stare in shock at his candor.

He stepped closer and pointed at his eyes. "Look, you can see the way the red is deepening and spreading through my irises."

That snapped me out of it. No way was I going to willingly stare into a vampire's eyes. I jerked back, banging my elbow painfully on the wall. Before I could try to push past him, he held up his hands in a placating gesture.

"It's alright," he said. "I understand why you wouldn't want to. But it really is a fascinating process. If you'll allow it, I'll look into the corner there, so you can see my eyes without fear of manipulation."

True to his word—amazingly—he stood still and turned his gaze slightly to the side, giving me an excellent view of his blood-red eyes. Curiosity overtook me, and I stepped closer. The dark color wasn't uniform, as I first thought, but actually contained a number of lighter striations. I peered even closer. The darker areas seemed to be *bleeding* into the lighter in narrow, curling rivulets, almost as though they were two bodies of water intermixing.

With a start, I realized the vampire was looking directly at me. "Fascinating," he murmured. "The blues of your eyes twist and pool as mine do."

My mind still felt clear. Emboldened by his openness, I pressed my luck. "How old are you?"

His eyes crinkled once more. "Alas, I am approaching the dreaded middle age, just shy of two hundred and forty."

Middle age, indeed. Give or take a couple of centuries.

His answer reminded me exactly *what* I was in such close quarters with, prompting me to step back and drop my gaze.

He sighed. "Forgive me if I've upset you, Ms. Jensen. As you well know, humans don't usually appreciate scrutiny from vampires. I couldn't resist the opportunity."

"How do you know my name?"

"Most everyone in this building knows your name, do they not? Your father was a fixture here for many years. I was sorry to learn of his passing." He stepped out of the elevator. "Have a pleasant evening, Ms. Jensen."

———————

I finally made it home, pondering the strange encounter the entire way, and was unlocking the front door when it hit me like a bolt of lightning.

Our Lord Miroslav.

According to the social studies classes we were all required to take back in high school, Miroslav was the name of the very first vampire—*fifteen hundred years ago.*

5

MIROSLAV

"WILL YOU NOT *tell me what it is?" The mock pout did nothing to diminish Iva's beauty.*

"If you knew, I fear I would lose your interest, and then what would I do with myself?" I teased, holding the cloth-wrapped trinket just out of her reach.

Her brilliant smile never ceased to cause flutters in my stomach.

"Oh Mir, you know you shall always have my interest and affection."

A delicious warmth spread through me at her words, though I knew she did not mean them the way in which I yearned to hear. Our childhood friendship had long since established me as nothing more than a dear brother in Iva's eyes.

"My lady, you always know how to disarm me," I said, offering her the item.

She snatched it and eagerly unwrapped the plain cloth, revealing the brilliant blue gemstone hidden within. Her lovely brown eyes widened, and her heart-shaped lips parted in surprise.

I had never wanted to taste those lips more. Unable to help myself, I moved closer. Iva looked up at me, awe still written on her features. I could see the light of the gemstone reflected in her eyes. Rational thought fled my mind. I ducked my head toward her.

Iva held the gemstone up between us, taking care to touch only its cloth wrappings. "Where did you find such a thing?" she whispered.

I squeezed my eyes shut a moment, trying to banish the haze of desire clouding my mind. Upon reopening, I found Iva still peering up at me expectantly. She had not moved away, instead leaning even closer, as though we were sharing a secret. As usual, she was completely ignorant of my regard. I smiled fondly at her. Her innocence and sense of wonder were two things I cherished.

"The soldiers who passed through the village yesterday, their leader used it to pay for a shoe for his horse."

"A shoe? But that is not even worth a sack of grain! This stone must be worth a fortune!"

"Would not the soldier have known that, though? He did not appear destitute and would surely have known the value of the stone," I replied, feeling rather unsure myself.

"Perhaps...or perhaps it does have some value, but he knew a person from our tribe would have no way of using it as currency?"

Iva's logic made sense.

"That seems likely. He thought he was getting the shoe for nothing but a shiny rock."

Iva squeezed my hand. "Oh, Mir, I am sorry. I know how hard you work to provide for your poor mama."

I threaded my fingers through Iva's. "You mistake my meaning. Whether he realizes it or not, he gave me a priceless treasure for nothing but a single horseshoe," I pressed her hand gently, desperate for her to understand.

Her gaze met mine, scant inches away, the stone still casting an ethereal glow across her face. Her eyes widened minutely, and a lovely blush warmed her cheeks. Her lips parted once more and hope like I had never felt before bloomed in my chest.

The scene suddenly swam before my eyes, the colors running until they morphed into a flickering orange glow. The sound of screams tore at me. Blurred images slowly resolved themselves. It was night. The village was burning. Our people ran to and fro, interspersed with sword-wielding invaders. Heat pressed against my legs. I looked down and everything else faded away.

Iva. My precious Iva. Her stunning eyes stared up at me lifelessly. Her thick, beautiful hair I had longed to run my fingers through a thousand times was unbound, spilling across my lap. I reached to touch her, and blood dripped from my fingers. I froze as the metallic scent flooded my senses, threatening to overwhelm me.

It was everywhere. My legs were drenched. The entire front of Iva's dress was soaked, down to the swell of her belly. I carefully touched her, but felt no signs of the fragile life she carried within. Tears poured down my face, and I shifted, gathering her in my arms. I pressed my face to hers and willed her to return to me.

"Please," I whispered. "Please do not leave me."

My tongue felt coated and heavy. I pulled back to wipe my tears from Iva's creamy skin and was instead greeted with the sight of a gruesome red smear across her cheek. Shocked, I touched my face, but found no sign of injury. My mouth was full of the taste of blood, but I felt no pain. A sudden prick on my lip startled me. Probing carefully, I discovered my two canines had elongated into sharp points. A moment later, I saw two ugly, damning holes in Iva's neck, just above her shoulder.

An entirely new sense of horror dawned on me. I tried to jerk away but Iva's hands were wrapped in the front of my shirt, as though she had been trying to pull me near. Numbness spread through me as I carefully disentangled her fingers. Distantly, a steady humming grew louder. The sound reached a dull roar, and I realized it was the ringing in my ears at the same moment Iva's hand opened to reveal the blue gemstone.

"My Lord Miroslav," a voice called.

My eyelids fluttered in response.

"My Lord, the Elders have come to a decision on the Ritual. They believe the heir is ready to take his rightful place as our new Lord."

Iva's smile drifted before me, the memories fading.

I twitched a finger in acknowledgement of the unstated message: the Elders intended to revive me soon. I had slept for many centuries before existing in my current state of semi-consciousness. Though lucid enough to understand and respond in minute physical ways, it had been so long, I wasn't sure I even remembered what it was like to be fully awake.

My vivid dreams were always of when I was mortal, or of my Turning. They never served to remind me of what it was like to have my senses heightened and emotions deadened, to have time become nothing but a word oft used by humans. Was I still Lord Miroslav, the father of the entire vampiric race? Or had my torturous dreams warped my mind back into that of simple Miroslav, the feeble peasant? The man who couldn't protect those most precious to him. The man whose memory filled me with disgust.

I returned my senses to my surroundings. The messenger was murmuring to someone near the door to my tomb, for that was what this room had become. I'd learned the humans had coined the phrase "the living dead" for creatures such as me, but in truth, I had drifted much closer to death than life in the past five hundred years.

That would soon change.

"Tell Elder Kael our Lord approves of their decision and awaits the presentation of the heir," the messenger whispered.

At last.

I would awaken. And the vengeance I had dreamed of for millennia would be poured out upon the world.

6

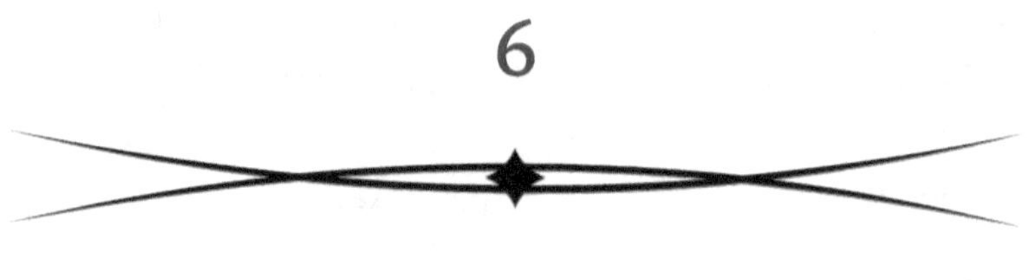

"**MY FRIENDS AND** I are getting together this weekend and I wondered if you'd like to come?" I asked my reflection.

Too friend-zone.

"Do you want to come watch movies at my house on Saturday?"

No! That sounds like some frat-boy hookup invitation!

I scrubbed my hands over my face. "This is a disaster."

My fourth meeting with Cal was in half an hour, and I still hadn't figured out how to invite him over. Rachel had pestered me about it endlessly, with Lina and even Izzy joining the group text onslaught. They finally let up when I promised to invite him to our movie night, but this was my last chance to ask him in person. There's no way I could ask over the phone or in an email—with my luck, he'd assume it was a booty call and never speak to me again.

Maybe he doesn't know what that is; he is very proper...

I shook my head at myself. I had to do it in person.

"And here's the last one."

"Oh, it's perfect!" I exclaimed. Cal captured the bright future I described in my writing by portraying June the mouse and her little human friend, Anna, standing on a small hilltop overlooking a picturesque meadow full of wildflowers. June perched on Anna's shoulder and they both pointed into the distance, ready to embrace their next adventure.

Cal smiled modestly at my praise. "Thank you, Nora. I'm so glad you approve of my work."

This latest collection of sketches marked a turning point in our project. Cal had created all the illustrations the book required, and I had now signed off on them. Technically, we wouldn't be required to meet in person again, as I needed his final drafts to be in digital format, anyway. This really was my last chance. Our meetings had fallen into a predictable pattern of polite chit-chat at the beginning, followed by project discussion and review, before going our separate ways. Since I hadn't worked up the nerve during the social portion, I'd lost all chance of a smooth segue. Directly to the point with maximum embarrassment was my only option.

Cal tucked his sketches neatly back into his folio. "I'll get started on the final drafts right away. If you have any more ideas, or decide you'd like to revise something, please—"

"Doyouwanttocometomyhouse?"

Turns out, there's a level of embarrassment beyond "maximum." I couldn't say which of us looked more shocked. If I'd had a mirror, I'm sure I would have voted for myself.

"Um..." The most inelegant phrase I'd ever heard cross Cal's lips hung in the air, shocking me further.

Fix this, you idiot!

"Sorry, that didn't come out right," I stammered. "I meant tomorrow. I'm having a movie night with some friends, and I hoped you might like to come..." My courage failed me, and I trailed off, picking at a scratch on the table's edge.

Cal was silent. My collar chafed my flushed skin.

"Nora."

I met his eyes reluctantly. He wore a soft smile. "If you're certain your friends won't object, I would be honored."

Relief flooded me. Thinking of Rachel's enthusiasm, I smirked. "I'm sure they won't mind."

By the time we packed up to leave—my address saved with Cal, along with several reassurances that *no*, he did not need to bring anything—I felt giddy with excitement. Even Creepy Guy in the corner, who had turned out to be a regular fixture at the coffee shop, couldn't dampen my mood. I flashed the weirdo a brilliant smile and a jaunty wink before sailing out the door, which Cal gallantly held open for me.

My enthusiasm lasted all night and into the next day. Lina came over early to help me figure out the projector and rearrange furniture in the basement, as my dad had never gotten around to completing his planned theater space. Seating options established, we brought snacks from the kitchen and selected a variety of movies for us all to choose from.

At that point, my nerves returned. What sort of movies did Cal like? What if he thought the movies I liked were awful? What if the movies *he* liked were awful?

Lina laughed at my voiced fears. "Don't worry, Nora. He's not some great cinema critic coming to crush all your hopes and dreams. He agreed to this because he obviously likes spending time with you. That means he'll enjoy watching a movie with you, whether it's one of his favorites or not."

Although Lina's reassurance helped, my palms were still sweating by the time the doorbell rang ten minutes before six. Leaving Lina to set up Rachel's video feed, I nervously smoothed my shirt and headed upstairs. Rachel had insisted this be a pajama party, but I couldn't bring myself to dress down below jeans and a casual tee after Cal agreed to come. Thankfully, Lina also forewent the pajamas, although I doubt she could ever bring herself to leave the house in something so frumpy. If it was girls only, she probably would have brought pajamas to change into once she arrived.

I quickly checked my reflection in the hall mirror and took a deep breath before swinging open the door, a smile plastered on my face. Cal and Izzy stood together on the porch. Cal looked the most casual I'd ever seen him, in a soft plaid flannel with the sleeves rolled to the elbow, jeans, and black sneakers. Izzy wore a character-appropriate black tunic-length shirt with spider web-printed leggings. Her red hair band and purple combat boots provided a splash of color. She held a few DVDs, while Cal cradled a two-liter bottle of orange soda with...a ribbon on it?

"Hi guys," I said. "I'm glad you came! I assume you've met...now?"

Izzy quirked an eyebrow at my awkwardness while Cal flashed her a charming smile.

"Yes," he said. "Miss Izzy and I have just become acquainted."

Izzy turned her eyebrow in his direction before stepping through the door. "Indeed. He's very polite." She kicked her boots off next to Lina's sandals and headed toward the basement stairs.

Cal followed her inside, but lingered while I closed the door. When I turned to face him, he held out the soda. "A bottle of wine is a customary hostess gift, but I felt something more casual might better fit the occasion."

"Oh," I said, taking the bottle. "Well, thank you. That was very thoughtful."

"You're very welcome," Cal replied with another blinding smile.

"Um…" I wanted to shake myself. "I'll get the rest of the drinks and cups from the kitchen, and then I'll introduce you to the others."

"I'll help you! Just let me remove my shoes."

I padded down the hall to the kitchen while Cal took off his sneakers. He arrived in time to collect the orange soda and three other bottles I took out of the fridge, leaving me to stagger under the weight of four plastic cups. When I attempted to take a bottle from him, he gave me a warm smile and stepped out of reach. I led him downstairs, smirking to myself at the sight of his blue- and green-striped socks. The small display of goofiness seemed simultaneously completely out of character and perfectly apt.

Upon our arrival in the basement, all conversation suspiciously ended. Rachel's feed was set up and stationed on the coffee table. I could see her peering at her screen, trying to get a better look at Cal.

"Guys, this is Cal. Cal, this is Lina," I said, gesturing, "and Rachel."

Lina gave him a warm smile. "It's very nice to meet you, Cal."

"Hi, Cal!" Rachel waved.

"I'm very pleased to meet you, Lina, Rachel." Cal, his arms still full, nodded his head politely at each of them.

"We've heard soo much about you," purred Rachel.

I wished I could reach through the screen and strangle her.

Izzy rolled her eyes and flipped the computer around, holding movies in front of it. "Which one do you want to watch?"

With Rachel distracted, I directed Cal to unload the bottles onto the console table behind the sofa.

"I went ahead and ordered the pizza," said Lina as she poured herself a cup.

"Great, thank you! I hope pizza is okay," I said, turning to Cal.

"Absolutely," he replied. "Although I insist you allow me to pay for it."

"What? No! You're my guest. I'm paying."

"I can't possibly allow a lady to pay for dinner, especially after you've so graciously welcomed me into your home and introduced me to your friends."

I glanced at Lina and knew from her smirk that she'd be no help. Izzy's face was blank and Rachel, who was now conveniently turned to see us again, looked like she might pop from excitement.

I recalled Cal's earlier words. "But as the hostess, isn't it my job to provide dinner?"

"Only if you intend to cook."

I sighed. "I'm not going to win this, am I?"

Cal grinned. "If it helps, you may recall you're paying me for my illustrations, so, in a way, you *are* paying for dinner."

Rachel squealed in delight, and I admitted defeat.

When Cal offered to pour Izzy a drink, Lina took the opportunity to whisper smugly in my ear, "The jury's still out on that Prince Charming thing." She chuckled at my glare and claimed a seat at the end of the couch.

A lighthearted rom-com was chosen as the first movie of the night, with Cal abstaining from the vote. Once it was ready to go, we chit-chatted until the pizza arrived. The time was mostly spent with Rachel explaining her bizarre living arrangements to Cal and preening over his generous sympathies. When the doorbell rang, Cal insisted the rest of us relax while he took care of it.

Rachel, whose computer had been moved again so she could see everyone, waited a few moments after he left before letting out a shrill squeal. *"Nora!"* she exclaimed. *"You never told us he was so* hot!*"*

The room fell into a dead silence. The rest of us had a perfect view of Cal, perched on the bottom stair, his mouth open as he prepared to say something. He met my eyes, and I wanted to die.

"Well?" pressed Rachel.

Izzy, bless her, leaned forward and flipped the screen around to face Cal.

"*Oh...*" By her tone, Rachel's neck likely disappeared into her shoulders.

The doorbell rang again.

The corner of Cal's mouth quirked. "Forgive me. I was going to ask if anyone needed anything from upstairs."

Lina glanced at me. My eyes felt like they were the size of saucers. "No," she answered. "I don't think so. Thank you, Cal."

He nodded politely and continued up the stairs.

Once he was safely out of the room, and with several extra moments to be sure, Rachel groaned. *"Nora, I'm so sorry! I had no idea he was still there."*

"That's why you shouldn't say dumb stuff," scoffed Izzy as she turned the screen back toward us.

Rachel nodded miserably. *"I know! Mom tells me so all the time."*

Lina patted my shoulder. "Cheer up. There are worse things than to hear that someone thinks you're good-looking."

"I know, but—we're working together!" I covered my face. "I don't want him to think I'm just some silly girl."

"Considering how hard he worked to pitch himself to *you*, I highly doubt you're in danger of being seen that way."

Izzy nodded her agreement.

"Lina's right!" said Rachel. *"If anything, he'll just think* I'm *silly, and that hardly matters."*

I smiled weakly at my friends. "Thanks, guys. Sorry I'm a mess."

Lina, sitting next to me, patted my hand. "We're all messes. And we're all here for each other, no matter what."

At the sound of footsteps on the stairs, Izzy proclaimed in a loud and utterly flat tone, "Oh look, everyone—Cal is back."

I couldn't help the giggle that leaked out and was relieved to see he wore an amused grin as well. Soon, the pizza was divvied out, the movie started, Rachel was turned around to see the tv—and Izzy plopped into the sole armchair with a smirk, leaving Cal and I to sit awkwardly next to each other on the couch. Lina tucked her legs underneath her on my other side and settled in with a comfortable sigh, forcing me closer to Cal.

Traitors.

7

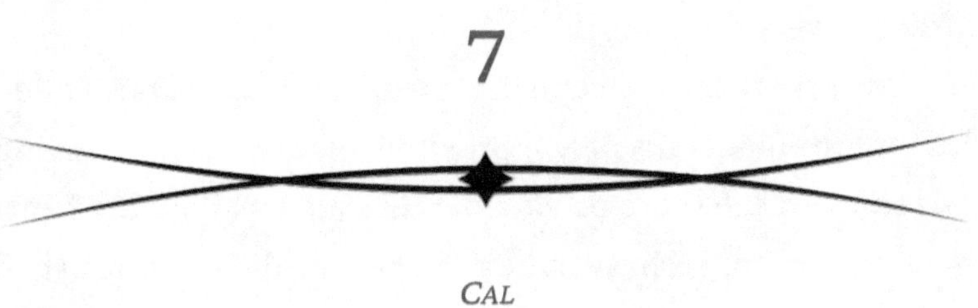

CAL

"PERHAPS I SHOULD get you a bracing mug of chilled blood?"

"Huh?" My attention snapped to Alden standing before me with his arms crossed and an annoyed look on his face.

He rolled his eyes. "That's only the third time I've asked if you want a refill on your coffee."

"Oh. Sorry." I hefted my Styrofoam cup self-consciously, gauging the contents. "No, thank you. I still have quite a bit left."

My friend strolled away to order a drink for himself from the petite barista behind the counter, who stared at him in awe. Her reaction was nothing new. My thoughts returned to another petite young lady, and I fought the dopey grin trying to spread across my face.

Alden claimed the chair across from me, expertly ignoring the gawking collection of coeds at the table next to us. "So, I gather from your distracted state that it went well last night?"

I tried to hide my smile by taking a sip of coffee, which had cooled during my daydreaming. "It was...very pleasant."

"Very pleasant?" Alden's flat look spoke volumes.

"What?"

"You called me Friday, practically gushing over this woman inviting you to her home, and now all you have to say is it was 'very pleasant'?"

My grin turned sheepish. He was right, of course. I filled him in on the details of the previous night's events, leaving out some of the more private details, such as how my heart galloped in my chest when Nora accidentally brushed against me when she reached for her drink, or how I had to talk myself out of taking her in my arms when she bid me goodnight, rather than simply clasping her hand.

Alden chuckled. "It sounds like she really likes you."

I buried my hope under nonchalance. "She was just being friendly. We didn't even make plans to meet again."

"After your prior disastrous encounters with the opposite sex, I would expect you to be a little more attuned to people's intentions. Does she know who you are?"

"No!" I cleared my throat and lowered my tone. "No. I'm just a plain old illustrator to her."

"A *plain old* illustrator, huh?" He looked skeptical.

I smirked, remembering Nora's adorably stricken expression after her digital friend's rather embarrassing outburst. "Well, maybe not *too* plain and old."

Alden gave me a knowing look. "I imagine not. However, if you plan to further this acquaintance, you'll have to tell her the truth. And sooner, rather than later."

I sighed. *If only it could be much, much later. Or never.*

"Hello, Mother. You needed to see me?"

My mother was a stately woman, usually clad in fashionable business attire. Today was no different—her tailored dress accessorized with simple jewelry and her dark hair swept up in a complicated-looking style. Everyone said my features came from her, although I wouldn't know any different as I'd never met my father.

"Caliban, my dear!" Mother rounded her desk to embrace me. I internally cringed at her insistent use of my full name. "Yes, we have important matters to discuss. Sit down." She gestured to a sitting area at the other end of her private office. "Would you like something to drink?"

I declined and chose a cushy armchair. She perched on the edge of the opposite chair. "Caliban," she began.

"Please, Mother, call me Cal."

She gave me a stern look. "*Caliban*, we've been over this many times. You have a perfectly respectable name that honors our family's heritage."

"I know these things don't mean much to you, but the Shakespeare reference is bad enough without adding in the fact it sounds entirely too similar to the name of the terrorist group. I would very much prefer it if you called me Cal, like everyone else."

She was quiet for a moment. "If I call you Cal, will you stop shirking your duties to this family?"

Ouch. I slumped in my seat. "I don't mean to shirk my duties. I just... I wish I could follow my own path and not be tied to the family business."

"I know, dear." Mother gave me a sympathetic look. "But that isn't the life we've been given—you *or* me. So, we must do our part and make the best of it."

I sighed and nodded before straightening. "Alright. So, what is it you wanted to talk about today?"

"The board has decided it's time for you to take on more responsibility, to start really learning the ins and outs of the company. They want you to officially step in as CEO soon."

Soon? What about C-Sketch? And Nora?

Although I'd known it was coming, I had no idea it would be this early in my life. I had always pictured it happening when I was at least middle-aged, if not older. "Already? Doesn't the board think it a bit reckless to hand the reins over to a glorified youth, especially when you've been running things so well?"

Mother waved a hand dismissively. "Nonsense. This was their plan from the start, and you'll have all that collective knowledge to draw on as you go."

It seemed Hollywood had artificially raised my hopes for a greedy chairman who refused to relinquish control.

———

Monday morning saw me dressed in a new suit, riding the executive elevator to the top floor of our company's headquarters. Mother's parting advice rang in my ears: *"Just be yourself and don't be afraid to ask for help if you need it. No one there wants you to fail."*

The doors opened and my escort, a burly, older man wearing an earpiece, gestured for me to exit first. A woman around my age met us at the reception desk. "Mr. Vasile! I'm so glad to see you again! I was excited to hear you'll be here full-time from now on," she gushed.

Instead of saying "Don't remind me," like I wanted to, I smiled politely and responded that I was glad to see her, too. Except I wasn't. Besides the fact I didn't want to be there at all, the way Leanne's eyes followed me almost hungrily always made me uncomfortable. Maybe once I was CEO, I could assign her to another office.

My silent companion led me past the desk and down the hall to a frosted glass door etched with my name. There really wasn't any getting out of this. Behind the door was an anteroom, gleaming and pristine, with a wall of glass overlooking the city. The room featured a potted tree in the corner, a bank of white filing cabinets, and a tidy desk manned by an unbelievably gorgeous woman.

"Ah, I see you've met Sandra." Neal Lind, head of the company's board of directors, bustled into the room behind us. "She's your new executive assistant and will handle anything you need."

Sandra's red eyes flashed as she smiled coyly and extended a hand tipped in scarlet, pointed nails.

Unbelievable, indeed.

My upbringing demanded I show courtesy and shake her hand, but that was all I would do. "No," I said, turning back to Lind, who gave me a confused look.

"I beg your pardon?"

"My assistant. The position must be filled by a human. I'm sure you understand why."

The man wore a startled look. "Mr. Vasile, I assure you, no one would dare—"

"But how would anyone know?" I interrupted. "I'm aware there are theoretically methods to protect oneself from compulsion, but there's enough responsibility weighing on me as it is without adding unnecessary difficulties or potentially questionable circumstances to it."

Turning back to the vampire, I dipped my head. "My apologies, Sandra. I'm sure you're a perfectly lovely person,"—*maybe*—"but I'm afraid I must insist you be reassigned elsewhere."

Sandra looked disappointed, but gathered up her belongings and left the office without a fuss. Maybe she was a decent person after all.

Lind grimaced at the door the vampire had retreated through. "I'm terribly sorry for the inconvenience. I'll have Human Resources assign you a new assistant immediately."

"Thank you," I said. "And please ensure Sandra is given a comparable position. It truly wasn't personal."

"Of course," replied Lind with a smile. "She'll be relieved to hear that." He gestured to the door across from us. "Please, look around your office; make yourself comfortable. I'll make arrangements with HR and then be back to take you to the ten o'clock meeting. I'll leave Andros here in case you need anything in the meantime."

The burly man didn't say anything but crossed to open the inner door for me, revealing a much larger, and just as brightly lit, interior. I wandered around the corner office, admired the view from the glass walls, peeked in all the drawers and cupboards, wondered if I'd be able to request a less ostentatious desk chair, and was just beginning to figure out the remote that controlled the level of tint on the windows when Lind returned. It was the first time I'd ever been relieved to attend a meeting—Andros' stony silence was beginning to chafe.

My relief was short-lived. The ten o'clock meeting lasted until lunch and didn't seem to accomplish anything of note, beyond re-introducing me to the board members. I hadn't been in the building in nearly six years and didn't remember most of those present. Topics of discussion included various political matters, whether the executive bathroom should be renovated this year or next, Thompson's satisfaction with his new tailor, and the itinerary for select members to visit the company's various subsidiary holdings.

Frustratingly, lunch was catered. Lind's explanation that it was "in honor of your first day, Mr. Vasile!" didn't soothe my aggravation. I had been counting the seconds until I could escape the conference room. The extravagant spread seemed utterly impractical for the middle of a weekday: lobster, filet mignon, fine wine and expensive liquor. I wondered if the leftovers would wind up in the staff refrigerator or the dumpster.

After engaging in as little small talk as could be deemed polite, I finally retreated to my office, where I occupied myself with the all-important task of contemplating the white paneled ceiling. Lind said he would send over files for me to review as a way to become better acquainted with the business, but I had no idea when to expect them, or if they'd even make it into my office now that my assistant was dismissed.

A firm knock at the door returned my mind from its wandering. At my call, a middle-aged woman clad in an ill-fitting pantsuit bustled into the room. "Good afternoon, Mr. Vasile. My name is Marge Newman. Mr. Campbell in the HR office said that you requested me as your new executive assistant."

As I took in the thick glasses hanging from the bauble-clad chain around Ms. Newman's neck, her lopsided salt-and-pepper curls, and her sturdy brown pumps, I realized Mr. Campbell in the HR office thought he was teaching me a lesson. Little did he know, I'd take an army of dowdy grandmothers over a svelte, Prada-clad vampire any day.

"Good afternoon, Ms. Newman. I voiced some concerns about your predecessor's qualifications to Mr. Lind this morning. I'm sure you're aware I am new to this position and will need a fair amount of help to navigate office operations at this early stage. It's also important that my assistant be someone with whom I can build a strong working relationship as I take on more responsibility in the months to come. I trust Mr. Campbell selected you with these requirements in mind."

Ms. Newman studied me for a moment, a shrewd look upon her face. "Mr. Vasile, I have never been a part of the upper echelons of this company, but I hear enough to have some inkling of the circumstances surrounding yourself and your family. I am also self-aware enough to recognize that Mr. Campbell did not take me from my fifteen-year tenure in the archives department because he's been secretly grooming me for greatness all this time." She paused for a moment to straighten her brown jacket. "Although he *was* kind enough to give me a bit of insight into my new position by way of a pass-along from Ms. Ortiz."

At my questioning look, she clarified, "Sandra."

"Ah," I replied. "I'm afraid I don't see much value in such insight, as Sandra was in this office for less than an hour."

Ms. Newman's placid smile turned slightly lopsided. "She said as much herself."

I smiled in return. *Another point in Sandra's favor.* "May we speak bluntly, Ms. Newman?"

"Of course, sir."

"Do you feel you are capable of fulfilling the requirements of this role?"

Ms. Newman lifted her chin slightly. "I do, Mr. Vasile. It may be my first time as an executive assistant, but I've been leading the archives department for many years now. I'm confident in my abilities."

Rather than reassure me, I cringed at the admission. "I have no desire to take you from a position you've worked so long to attain, especially to replace it with a mere assistant's role. I'll speak to Mr. Campbell and get this straightened out."

"A *mere* assistant?" Ms. Newman outright scoffed. "Mr. Vasile, I don't think you quite appreciate your own position in this company. I've just been given the biggest promotion of my life. It may be new and a bit uncomfortable, and I'm sure I'll forget to press the up button on the elevator instead of down, but I welcome the challenge. I'm not too old to appreciate a new adventure in life and, after this conversation, I feel certain that working for you is exactly the place I want to be."

I was touched. People were constantly reminding me of my importance to my family and the business—as they had been my entire life—describing the greatness I'd achieve, and the loftiness my name carried with it. But no one beyond my loved ones had ever made me feel as though I, personally, could be exceptional. No, Mr. Campbell truly had no idea what a favor he'd bestowed. "Very well, Ms. Newman. I don't believe there is anything else on my agenda for the day beyond some paperwork being sent over for review. Please don't hesitate to request anything that will make your new office more comfortable."

Ms. Newman nodded briskly. "Thank you, Mr. Vasile. I'll watch for those documents to arrive."

As she left the office, I thought I heard her mumble something about "an industrial-sized bottle of Windex." I chuckled and turned my chair to appreciate the view out the windows. I wasn't far into my daydreaming when Ms. Newman returned.

"Here are your reports, sir, and there is a Mr. Lancaster here to see you."

"Perfect!" I grinned at her. "Please send him in."

Ms. Newman left the papers in a tidy stack on the corner of my desk and returned to hold the door open for my visitor.

Alden strolled in wearing his usual crisp business wear. He thanked Ms. Newman, giving her a stunning smile. She responded politely and marched back out to her desk. Alden stared at the closed door for a moment. "Huh."

I smirked. "Surprised a woman didn't notice you, Al?"

My friend gave a mock shudder. "You know I detest that nickname. And yes, I suppose that was a bit of a surprise. But I was more shocked at the, um, *caliber*, shall we say, of your assistant."

"Oh, she seems very capable," I assured him. "Her appearance was apparently meant to be a dig at myself, though."

I proceeded to relay the day's events.

Alden lounged in an expensive leather chair in front of my desk, sipping an Artesian water pilfered from my sideboard. "Sounds like Mr. Campbell is a real character. Lind doesn't seem to have anything to do with it, though."

"I agree. Although I imagine he had some input into my *first* assistant's choosing. There had to have been some measure of public appearance taken into account for it."

"No doubt. You're a young, attractive guy set to take over a global company. They wanted a young, attractive gal standing behind you during the tv spots."

I grimaced at my friend's teasing and the reminder of my future. "I'm not sure I can do this, Alden."

His expression turned serious. "Of course you can. Not only have you been groomed for this your whole life, you're a smart, capable person. I know you wish you had other options, but I also know you're going to give this your all and make it something you can be proud of, like you do everything else."

My frown twisted into a wry smile. "Thanks, *Al*. I appreciate your confidence in me."

Alden laughed, then deposited his glass on the desk and rubbed his hands together. "Now, let's talk about something infinitely more enjoyable. When do you see Nora again?"

I chuckled in return. "I'm not sure. I plan to call her this evening and hopefully arrange something." My frown threatened to return. "I still don't know what to tell her about all this."

"You'll figure it out. And she'll understand. So, what do you have on the agenda for tomorrow?"

"I'm accompanying Lind and some others on a trip around town to visit the subsidiaries." I answered distractedly, still thinking of what I might say to Nora.

Alden's face twisted like he was fighting a smile. "Subsidiaries...like Jensen Publishing?"

8

NORA

I WAS SPRAWLED on the couch, fantasizing about a tropical vacation, when my phone began to buzz, alerting me to an incoming call. I lazily felt about the floor, searching for where it had fallen during my initial collapse. I finally found it and tapped the answer button without really looking at the screen. "Hello?" I droned, staring at the ceiling.

"Nora? Is that you?" Cal sounded worried.

I bolted upright, nearly falling on the floor in the process. "Cal! *Ahem.* Sorry, I didn't see who was calling." I squeezed my eyes shut and thumped my forehead on the arm of the couch.

He chuckled. *"That's alright. I wanted to thank you for hosting me the other night, and also apologize for not calling sooner. I had some...unexpected family issues arise over the weekend."*

"Oh, that's no problem. I figured you were just busy." I hadn't been worried at all. I definitely hadn't checked my phone every other second for the previous two days.

"I was, unfortunately, but it's no excuse for not taking the time to thank you properly. I won't be so rude again in the future, I assure you. I had a lovely evening with you, and very much enjoyed meeting your friends. They're a fun group of ladies; I can see why you're close with them."

"They are. And I'm glad you came," I stammered, struggling to focus beyond "in the future." "I hope everything is okay with your family...?"

Cal didn't seem to mind the awkward pseudo-question. *"They are. We just have a few long-standing disagreements that come up every now and then."*

"Oh. Well, that's good, at least." I liked Cal, but I wasn't sure I was quite ready to deal with a lot of family drama. I already had enough drama of my own.

"Indeed. I confess, I have an ulterior motive for calling. Would you, perhaps, be interested in having dinner with me tomorrow evening?"

I flushed with pleasure and was enormously grateful he wasn't present to see it. *Settle your nerves. Don't be too eager.* "Sure!" I chirped. *Or be super eager—that's fine, too.* "I usually leave work at five. Where should I meet you?"

"I was thinking The Jade Palace, if you don't mind Chinese food."

"I love that place! I get takeout there sometimes after work. It's right by my office."

"Great! I hoped to save you any additional driving during rush hour."

I could hear the smile in his voice and grinned like an idiot in response. "Oh, well, thank you. And that sounds great. I'll just head over after work, then?"

"That'll be perfect. I'll plan to be there a few minutes after five."

"Awesome. See you tomorrow!"

"Um...yes. Tomorrow. Have a pleasant evening, Nora."

Cal's sudden awkwardness threw me off kilter. "Uh, okay. Bye."

I ended the call and looked at the screen in confusion. Cal was never awkward. Was he only asking me to dinner because he felt obligated after the movie night? *No, that's not right. He was completely normal for the whole call, right up until the end. He must have just gotten distracted by something.*

I shook my head and pocketed the phone.

———

By the next morning, I was back in high spirits. I waved merrily to Alistair as I flounced through the lobby, feeling sassy in my flowered sundress. I whistled a jaunty tune on the elevator, reveling in being the sole passenger. When I stepped onto my floor, I nearly collided with Mary, who was rushing through the entryway, balancing a towering stack of files.

"Nora, where have you been?" Mary hissed, looking nervously over her shoulder. "Loralai's been looking for you all morning!"

My stomach plummeted. "What do you mean, all morning? My shift doesn't start for another ten minutes."

Mary started shaking her head before I even finished speaking, further tightening the knot of dread in my gut. "She sent out a late-night memo telling everyone to come in an hour early! Apparently, her boss and some other bigwigs are checking in on us today. She's cracking down on everyone!"

"I-I didn't check my email," I stammered.

"I'm sorry, dear." Mary gave me a sympathetic look before glancing around again. "If you want to leave, I won't tell anyone I saw you," she whispered.

I gave her a half-hearted smile. "Thanks, but I think I'd better face the music. Do you need help with those files?"

The woman jostled the pile back into line with her shoulder. "No, that's okay. You just worry about yourself. Good luck, sweetie!" She gave me a final, commiserating smile before hustling away.

I took a deep breath, smoothed my hands down my dress, and marched out to meet my doom, who met me at the entrance to my cubicle.

"Where have you been?!" Loralai's growl lifted the hairs on the back of my neck.

"I'm sorry, Mistress Loralai, I didn't see the email. I didn't know—"

"You didn't *know*?" she interrupted. "Or you didn't *care*? You prance around this office, looking down your nose at everyone simply because of who your father was—"

What?!

"—and now, when I need everything to be flawless, you think you're too important to even show up! Do you have any idea who's coming here today?"

I struggled to reign in my fury. "Someone from V-Corp," I ground out through gritted teeth.

Loralai's eyes looked like they could burst into flame at any moment. "Not *someone*. THE one. Caliban Vasile, himself, and the entire board of directors!"

Somewhere beneath my growing fear of Loralai was a spark of surprise. *I thought some woman from the Vasile family was running the company...*

The fuming vamp brought me violently back to the present when she grabbed my collar and shoved me backward into the cubicle wall. "You've disrespected me for the last time, *mortal*," she snarled, her nails pressing into my skin.

My rescue came from an entirely unexpected source.

"Loralaaiii," drawled a bored voice. Charna stepped into view, holding an emery board and languidly inspecting her manicure. "The old man in the lobby says they're on their way up." She briefly ran her gaze over Loralai, her lip curling. "You may want to freshen up."

I was glad I wasn't on the receiving end of the sound that erupted from Loralai. Charna didn't even flinch. She merely strolled away, filing at a wayward nail. Loralai dropped me in a heap and stalked off, growling to herself as she went.

I staggered into the cubicle and flopped into my chair, pressing my hands against my eyes. *What just happened?!* I expected Loralai to be unreasonably angry, as per usual, but figured she'd brain-bend me, or maybe even fire me. *I honestly think she was going to kill me!*

I was dimly aware of some manner of commotion happening by the elevators, presumably caused by the arrival of the higher-ups, but couldn't bring myself to care. I stayed crumpled against my desk and hoped everyone would pass me by, unnoticed.

Sure enough, Loralai soon paraded down the aisle past my cubicle, leading a mass of suits. "...this way to the editorial section. As I'm sure you know, the printer is two floors down from us, allowing our firm to maintain some of the highest output rates..." her smarmy tone trailed out of earshot, much to my relief.

An hour turned into two, and I remained relatively undisturbed. I didn't see much of our visitors beyond an occasional glimpse through the conference room window once they returned from their office tour. Loralai appeared to be ingratiating herself at a nauseating level. Charna, always standing nearby, alternated between looking bored and murderous, apparently depending on Loralai's conduct.

I was deciding between taking my morning break before or after the meeting, when the suits started filing out of the conference room. I huddled over the paperwork I was sorting for the records department and prayed for invisibility.

"Charna." Loralai's imperious tone came from the other side of my fabric-covered wall. "Run to my office and fetch those annual performance reports for Mr. Vasile to take with him." The vamp's voice did a creepy sort of flirtatious thing when she said the man's name. I shuddered.

Charna scoffed. "I'm not a dog. Run and fetch them yourself."

You could have heard a pin drop, even on the carpeting. I held my breath, terrified of rustling a paper. From the silence, everyone on the floor—possibly in the building—

had the same idea. Just how much collateral damage would there be in the imminent bloodbath?

"Fiine..." The vamp's drawn-out response sent goosebumps racing down my arms. "NORA!"

I jumped so high I bashed my knees against the underside of my desk. Wincing, I stood on tiptoe to look over the top of the wall. "Yes, Mistress Loralai?"

Someone in the crowd of well-dressed backs facing me made a hum that sounded like displeasure. Loralai cast a glare in their general direction before returning her attention to me. "Get the performance report files off my desk. Now!"

"Yes, Mistress Loralai!" I skirted around the crowd and hustled for her office. Snatching the stack of folders off her desk, I hurried back, keeping my eyes glued to the floor. When her five-inch heels and leather skirt came into view, I stopped and held out the files. "Here are the reports, Mistress."

"They are for *Mr. Vasile,*" she growled.

"Sorry," I mumbled and turned toward the others, internally shrieking. *Which one is Mr. Vasile?!*

Thankfully, a pair of shiny leather shoes stepped forward, saving me from further disaster. I nearly slumped in relief. I offered the reports and raised my gaze, intending to convey as much silent gratitude as was humanly possible to this stranger. My eyes met a pair of very familiar warm brown ones, and I froze.

Cal at least had the decency to look mildly embarrassed as he gently tugged the folders from my unresponsive fingers. "Thank you, Nora," he murmured.

His voice broke my trance. *"Cal?!"* I blurted without thinking.

I was jerked around so fast it made my head spin. "How *dare* you address *Mister* Vasile so informally!" Loralai nearly spat in my face in her fury. "Leave my sight this instant!"

My mouth was gaping like a fish, but I didn't know how to stop it. Too much was happening at once. I tottered away, risking a glance back at Cal as I went. He met my gaze, but quickly returned his attention to Loralai.

Somehow, I made it to the ladies' restroom, collapsing into the random chair that was kept in there for some reason. Emotional trauma was apparently the reason. After an indefinite amount of time spent staring at nothing, I heaved myself up to splash cold water on my face at the sink.

"Caliban Vasile?" I asked my reflection. It was similarly clueless.

9

NORA

I STOOD OUTSIDE The Jade Palace, staring at the entrance. I had made it through the afternoon of work unscathed. A remarkable feat. Loralai seemed to think Charna's slight was more notable—and therefore required more retribution— than my own slipup, which I definitely wouldn't complain about.

Now, I just needed to work up the nerve to face Cal. Caliban. *Mr. Vasile.*

Ugh.

Whoever he was, he owed me an explanation. I squared my shoulders, lifted my chin, and marched through the door.

"I'm supposed to meet my friend here," I told the hostess. "He's in his twenties, with brown hair, about *this* tall." I held a hand vaguely above my head.

The woman's smile grew. "Are you Nora?"

"Yes," I said, surprised.

She nodded knowingly as she turned toward the seating area, beckoning for me to follow. We wound through the tables, passed the dragon fountain, and crossed a miniature bridge over the koi pond I had never noticed before. The hostess pulled back a heavy velvet curtain hanging across the back wall, revealing a cozy recessed dining area lit by paper lanterns. Cal stood next to the table, twisting a cloth napkin in his hands.

"Enjoy your meal," said the hostess, softly closing the curtain behind me.

I stayed put, unsure what to say or do.

Cal laid the napkin on the table and gestured politely to the seat opposite. "Would you care to sit?"

"I suppose," I said, and slowly made my way to the table. He moved to pull the chair out for me, but I held up a hand to stop him. "I can manage." I settled into the seat and looked at him expectantly.

He cleared his throat and sat down, reaching for the crumpled napkin again.

I eyed him warily. "So...*Cal*. Am I even allowed to call you that?"

"Of course you are!" He reached across the table for my hand, but I pulled away.

"It seems some people would disagree with you."

Cal grimaced and dropped his gaze, clenching his fists convulsively. "I'm sorry for that. I'm sorry I didn't defend you."

"Why didn't you tell me?"

He returned to his torment of the poor napkin. "I wanted to tell you; I just didn't know how."

I opened my mouth, but he shook his head, seemingly at himself, and continued, "No, that's not true. It would have been perfectly simple to tell you. I was just afraid."

I picked at my own napkin. "Afraid?"

"Afraid...of what you would think of me. Afraid you wouldn't want to see me anymore."

I hesitated, remembering how Loralai had fawned over him. "You didn't think I would like who you are?"

He smiled crookedly, still looking down. "I was fairly confident you liked who I am. But I wasn't as sure you would like who the world thinks I am."

"Oh." I blushed at his implication.

We sat in silence for a few moments.

"Would you have ever told me?" I asked softly, tracing a swirl on the tablecloth.

Cal's hand covered mine. I raised my eyes and was taken aback by the intensity in his. *"Yes!"* he stressed. "I'm so sorry I didn't tell you from the start, but I never would have kept you in the dark! I'm growing very fond of you, and it would have been impossible to build a relationship if I didn't tell you the truth about myself."

"Oh," I repeated dumbly, blushing a little more intensely this time. I returned my attention to the tablecloth, unsure of what to say.

Cal curled his fingers under my palm and gently squeezed my hand. When I kept my eyes lowered, he bent his head to recapture my gaze. "Nora, I *want* a relationship with you. You're smart, and clever, and kind. You've been through so much, but you keep facing each new day head-on. You're an incredible, beautiful woman, and I would consider myself the luckiest man in the world if you would give me a chance." It was his turn to wear a slight blush, but he didn't look away.

It was the perfect silver screen moment, but I didn't know what to do. He was right; I *did* like him—very much. But I'd had plenty of time that afternoon to imagine what it might be like to be involved with one of the richest, most powerful men in the city. I knew myself. I hated catching people's attention. I was a loner, whose only friends were a ragtag bunch who wouldn't appreciate any residual limelight cast their way. I was awkward at meeting new people, and I abhorred the idea of being on television or in tabloids. With my family gone and crazy vampires running roughshod over my father's legacy, privacy had become paramount in my life. Continuing to see Cal would mean a quick and permanent end to that.

"I don't know," I said. "I think it's all too much for someone like me. You need a girl who's comfortable with attention and knows how to talk to people without stumbling over herself."

"I have sycophantic employees for that," he replied, waving his free hand dismissively. "What I *need* is someone down-to-earth who won't be blinded by glittering facades. Someone who will help me keep my head above water, and who I can laugh with about all the nonsense we'll have to muddle through. I need someone like *you*, Nora, but I'm asking because I *want* it to be you."

My mouth twisted in indecision. Part of me wanted to let him convince me—to dive in headfirst and never look back. Another part knew if I didn't take the time to really weigh the options and come to a decision freely, I'd always second-guess myself.

Cal smiled. "Please, don't answer now. I can wait. Let's just have dinner and keep getting to know each other." His smile turned to a grin as he picked up his menu. "Besides, you might find you can't help but fall for me before long."

Relieved by his offer, I laughed at the flirtation. "Oh, really?" I looked him over with an air of mock disinterest. "Or I might find there are much greener pastures to be found elsewhere."

"I'm certain there are." The twitch in the corner of his mouth belied his solemnity. "But I shall do my best to appease your wandering eye."

Huffing a laugh, I turned to my menu. He knew perfectly well the only "wandering" my eyes did was to the nearest exit in an uncomfortable situation. *No, I don't think he's wrong about falling for him...*

A waiter appeared moments later to take our order and deliver a plate of spring rolls. Suspect timing, but I had to admit it was convenient. Clearly, there were more perks to being rich and famous than I realized.

Our order submitted, I selected a roll and began peeling off bites of papery skin. "So, Cal," I casually repeated my previous opener.

He smiled. "Yes, Nora?"

I ignored the way the sound of my name in his smooth baritone made my stomach flip-flop. "What's your favorite color?"

His eyes crinkled pleasantly. "Blue. What's yours?"

"Also blue. But specifically royal blue."

"A wise choice," he nodded sagely. "I'm partial to navy, myself."

"That seems fitting." *I'm sure all the office girls would swoon if you showed up in a navy suit.* "Your turn." At his questioning look, I clarified, "To ask a question. Everyone knows the best way to get to know someone is to play Twenty Questions."

"I'm afraid I missed that tidbit in my psychology class," he said.

I *tsk*ed. "Your professor ought to be ashamed."

Cal chuckled. "Indeed. Well, since you are clearly the expert here... Hmm... When you were little, what did you want to be when you grew up?"

"A famous author. I told my dad I was going to write dozens of books, and he would print them, and everyone would buy them." I smiled fondly at the memory, my eyes misting a bit.

"Is that why you wrote *Anna & June*?" Cal's tone was gentle.

"Partially. I got the idea after an assignment to write a short story portraying some moral lesson during one of my composition classes in school. That's actually the class where I met Lina, Rachel, and Izzy. We had a group project together and found out we all really enjoyed creative writing, so after the class ended, we just kept meeting and helping each other with our writing."

"That's wonderful! They seem like a delightful bunch."

Rachel will swoon when she hears Caliban Vasile thinks she's delightful.

I nodded. "They're great. They really kept me together when my dad passed."

"I'm glad you didn't go through that alone." Cal reached over to give my hand another squeeze.

"Me too." I gave him a weak smile in return.

"I believe it's now your turn?"

"You're right. Wait! You didn't say what *you* wanted to be when you grew up. I'm guessing..." I screwed my face up in concentration. "A rodeo clown?"

"Close," Cal laughed. "I had a whole list of things I wanted to be. The most enduring ones were a fighter pilot or an underwater treasure seeker. I used to run around the house carrying strips of cardboard, pretending they were my airplane wings. Then, after we camped at a lake one summer and I found an old necklace while swimming, I became obsessed with finding treasures in every body of water we went near. Mother fished me out of the wishing fountain in Monument Park dozens of times."

I laughed, imagining a miniature Cal bobbing for slimy coins in the park. "Your poor mom. You sound like you were a handful."

"She likes to remind me of it," he agreed.

"I have to admit, I can't really picture your family camping. Is it something your dad enjoyed?"

"No." Cal's mouth twisted. "That is, I don't know. My father has never been a part of my life. I'm not even sure he's alive."

Nice, Nora. Maybe you should have read some of those tabloids.

"Oh. I'm sorry," I said lamely.

He smiled. "Don't be. I made peace with it a long time ago. And to better answer your question, I went camping with my friend, Alden. He's always liked that sort of thing. I enjoy it, too, but I haven't had many opportunities for it in my life."

"I imagine not, what with your family running V-Corp. Besides, camping wouldn't be very fun with a bunch of paparazzi hiding out in all the bushes."

"Thankfully, the paparazzi have only recently become interested in me," Cal chuckled. "Although, you make a compelling point. Alden may not want me accompanying him on his next trip."

"You mean he *doesn't* like reveling in your limelight? What an oddball," I said dryly.

"Don't worry, he gets plenty of his own attention. He has a rather...*noticeable* appearance."

Coming from Mr. Gorgeous himself, that's saying something. Maybe I can introduce Alden to the girls, so they'll have someone new to fixate on.

Cal gave me a bemused look as I snickered over my inner musings, but didn't ask.

"I guess it's still my turn, isn't it?" I thought for a moment. "What do you do at V-Corp? For that matter, what does V-Corp do, other than own things?"

"So far, I mostly sit at my desk and twiddle my thumbs. The board is expecting me to assume the position of CEO before long and wants me to get better acquainted with the company in the meantime, but I haven't received much insight so far. As far as what the company actually does, you've essentially summed it up. V-Corp owns, or has holdings in, a variety of smaller businesses."

"But if that's its main function, won't you mostly just be hanging around collecting dividends?"

"That's often how it works, but V-Corp has always preferred to take a more active approach in the running of its subsidiaries. The businesses all have their own management hierarchy, of course, but we're there to provide some measure of overall direction."

"Like the captain of a ship," I offered.

"More like the owner of a ship." He smiled at my raised eyebrows and amended, "Not to be boastful. The captain directly controls the crew and operations of the ship, but even though he makes all the day-to-day decisions, he is still acting in the interests of the person who owns the ship."

I nodded, but confusion set in a moment later. "Wait, when did you start overseeing Jensen Publishing, then? Dad never told me about someone buying majority holdings in the company. And if V-Corp is in charge, why is *Loralai* running the place? She came to us straight from the vampires. I assumed they sort of unofficially took over once we started printing basically only their stuff."

Cal's mouth twisted unhappily. "Well, that's the other part of things... We also maintain the primary business partnership with the Vampire Elite. All of their professional dealings are funneled through V-Corp and nearly all our subsidiaries have contracts with them."

The Vampire Elite. The ruling class of the entire race. "I guess the company name is even more apt than I realized," I said, a touch sarcastically.

"It would seem so," he agreed. He hesitated a moment before continuing, "It's easy to see why you're not fond of the vampires you work with, but how do you feel about the rest of them? Or the other paranormals?"

"I wish they didn't exist," I replied bluntly. I figured it was pointless to mince words since he'd already witnessed Loralai's behavior. "Vampires make my life a living hell more often than not, and the rest don't seem much better. We all would have been better off if they'd never revealed themselves."

"Surely, they're not all bad. You must have had *some* positive interactions with paranormals."

I immediately thought of the vamp on the elevator, but decided not to volunteer that information since I still didn't know quite what to make of him. "The crew at Taco Town occasionally get my order right," I conceded.

Cal nearly sprayed the water he was sipping all over the table, prompting me to join him in laughter. "I'm not sure I've ever heard such a positive recommendation," he gasped, wiping his chin with the wrinkled napkin.

I grinned. "Yeah, they probably wouldn't appreciate my Yelp review."

Our food arrived and the rest of the meal was thankfully spent on much lighter topics. I left the restaurant feeling simultaneously better and worse. Better, since I now felt confident that Cal had been in earnest in his dealings—and flirtations—with me. Worse, because knowing that only made me like him more.

Now I had to decide if I could handle the awkwardness of dating not only a celebrity, but my *boss*.

10

"I'm confused." Izzy didn't look confused. She looked exactly the same as ever. "How does Cal own your company? I thought *you* own your company."

"*I* don't," I picked at the same loose thread on the blue lounger. The chair was receiving a lot more abuse now that PLS had begun unofficially meeting at my house instead of the library.

"Why not?"

"*Yeah, didn't your dad leave it to you?*" Rachel chimed in through a mouthful of preserved apricots. It seemed her mom had finally achieved some manner of canning success.

"He was supposed to, but the vamps started running the place before he died. I think any kind of earlier succession plan just fell to the wayside." I shrugged. It had been a while since this topic was last brought up, but that didn't make it any easier of a conversation.

Unsurprisingly, my friends had freaked over the news about Cal. Rachel actually ran off, knocking her webcam askew in the process. When she came back a few minutes later and made us all seasick with how much she jerked the camera around trying to recenter it, she was waving a worn copy of *Entertainment Today* and screeching, "I knew he looked familiar!"

We were then subjected to the presentation of a vapid quiz entitled "Which Rich Hottie Will You Marry?" with a late-teens Caliban Vasile being Option #3. Thankfully, Rachel distracted herself with a lengthy discussion on the pros and cons of the actor whom she was allegedly to marry.

"Plans may have fallen to the wayside for *them*, but have you actually seen your father's will? Have you spoken to his lawyers?" Izzy pressed.

"Well...sort of. The only documents I received were for the house and Dad's bank account. A lawyer called me not long after Dad died and had me come in to sign some stuff so I could take ownership of the house and accounts, but that was all. I just assumed there wasn't anything about leaving the company to me since the lawyer didn't mention it."

"Izzy's right," said Lina. "I think you ought to make an appointment and go through his will again. If something was overlooked or mishandled, you need to set it right."

I didn't relish the idea of diving back into Dad's personal affairs, especially now that I'd finally started feeling like my life was getting off to a bit of a fresh start. But my friends had a point. Dad talked about leaving Jensen Publishing to me from the beginning. It made no sense for him to list all his personal accounts and major possessions in the will, but then not say anything at all about the company he owned.

"Alright," I agreed. "I'll call them in the morning."

"Good." Izzy nodded sagely. "And then you won't have any excuse not to date the guy."

I stared at her in shock. That was...unexpectedly romantic, coming from Izzy.

"*Exactly! And you can tell all his single friends about your awesome, gorgeous besties!*" Rachel's enthusiastic addition earned a laugh from all of us—even a chuckle and an eye roll from Izzy.

"Actually," I replied with a smirk, unable to resist the opportunity. "Cal *did* tell me about his super good-looking friend, Alden..."

"*WHAT?!*" Rachel shrieked. "*Tell us everything!*"

————

By Friday morning, I was starting to feel good about things again. Cal and I had talked on the phone the previous night for nearly two hours. He never once made me feel pressured to make a decision about us, instead filling the time with silly stories about his childhood and wild adventures with Alden. At one point, he confessed to only remaining in the Literary Theory class we shared in college because of his interest in me.

"*My advisor gave me a list of options to fill an elective slot, and that one seemed interesting. The only other class offered at the same time of day was fencing,*" he said.

"*Fencing?* I must not have received the same course catalog as you. I didn't know that was offered at *any* school. Well, maybe whichever one the British royals attend," I laughed.

Cal joined my mirth. *"I got the feeling my advisor would have offered to let me chew gum for credit, as long as she could keep me on her roster."*

"Ooh. Another adoring fan, then," I teased.

"Hey, sometimes those fans really come in handy! I could have used one in place of the Literary Theory professor. I never managed to get an A in that class."

"I guess all that fame and fortune doesn't equate to intelligence," I said, my voice filled with mock disappointment.

"Or perhaps I was just too distracted by the lovely blonde across the classroom to pay attention."

I scoffed. "That excuse hardly works—I was only in class for a month."

"Believe me, your absence was just as distracting as your presence," he murmured.

Recalling his words made my cheeks heat all over again as I sat in my cubicle, mindlessly sorting documents. Beyond making me blush, Cal was becoming someone I could—and *wanted* to—open up to alarmingly quickly. At this rate, when the time came, would I even be able to say no to him? And if not, could I be happy with him, or would a part of me always resent the loss of privacy and independence?

Like a hound on the scent of perceived disloyalty, Loralai suddenly appeared in the doorway. "Nora. I have not forgotten your *indiscretion* on Tuesday. What do you have to say for yourself?"

It was an obvious trap, but I could see no way out but straight through. "I'm very sorry, Mistress Loralai. It won't happen again," I muttered toward her feet.

A red-tipped nail forced my chin up. "No, it will not," she purred. A demented smile spread across her face, sending chills racing down my spine. "When Lord Miroslav awakens, we will never have to suffer you mortal fools again." She clutched my jaw and leaned closer.

I craned my eyes toward the gray, felt wall, desperate to avoid her manipulation.

Rather than trying to meet my gaze, she bent her head to whisper in my ear like a lover, making me squirm uselessly in her iron grip. "And I will be free to peel the tender, delicious flesh from your bones."

She gave my chin a final, malicious squeeze, causing a sharp pain to bloom in my cheek. Straightening, she ran a nail across her tongue, a dark red line trailing in its wake. She winked salaciously and strolled out of my cubicle, leaving me a sweating, trembling wreck.

I made my shaking way to the ladies' room, passing Mary just outside the door. She gasped and followed me inside.

"Oh, Nora, what happened?!" she cried as she rushed to the sink. She yanked a handful of paper towels from the dispenser and doused them in cold water. I got a brief glimpse in the mirror of the bloody streaks on my jawline before Mary pressed the towels to my face. She grimaced apologetically at my hiss. Glancing around the empty restroom, she leaned closer to whisper, "Did *she* do this to you?"

I met her gaze but didn't respond, taking hold of the paper towels myself.

Anger rose in her eyes and she made a quick circuit of the tile floor, brandishing her plump fist as she paced. "That—that—*thing* is despicable! She makes me sick! If your poor father were still here, she'd never dare come within a mile of you!"

I smiled sadly. "But she *did*, Mary. She might not have done anything physical, but she threatened and manipulated me plenty of times, and he never believed it." I dropped my eyes to the floor and choked on a sob. "I think she killed him."

Mary gathered me into a hug and rubbed my back soothingly, whispering words of comfort. I expected her to refute my words, to tell me my father died from a terrible illness, and I shouldn't torment myself by thinking otherwise.

I expected her to be like everyone else.

Instead, she stepped back and held me at arm's length, a deadly serious expression on her face. "I won't try to tell you you're wrong, because I don't believe you are." Shock must have been evident on my face, for she continued, "And I'm not the only one. We all saw the way she treated your father; the constant manipulation—and plenty of it not even supernatural." She gave a disgusted huff before gently pressing my shoulders, her expression turning earnest. "But you can't go around saying things like that, not as long as you're within her reach. The others and I stayed after your father's death because we loved him, and shared his dreams for this company, but we won't sit by and watch that creature destroy you the way she did him. You need to leave, Nora. Stop coming back here."

"But this company is Dad's legacy," I protested weakly. "I can't just *leave*."

"*You* are your father's legacy! *You* are what he cared about; the reason he came to work every day!" Mary shook my shoulders lightly to emphasize her words.

I crossed my arms and stepped out of her grasp. "Dad loved Jensen Publishing. I won't abandon it."

"Your father would have gladly built a treehouse instead of a publishing company, except that his whole family loved books. He only wanted you to be happy, and he knew you would be here. But that was before the vampires—before *her*. He'd be devastated to see you now. Please, at least consider leaving the company."

"Alright," I said at last. I didn't bother to hide my reluctance.

Mary sighed and gave me a grim smile. She took the soggy paper towels from my hand and gently dabbed at my jaw. "Promise me you'll do something fun this weekend?"

I snorted. "More fun than this?"

The quirk at the corner of her mouth belied her stern *tsk*. It seemed sweet, old Mary from HR was something of a kindred spirit.

My face cleaned up as well as possible, I crept back to my cubicle to wait out the day, thankful there was only another hour until quitting time. Staring at the clock on the far wall, I found my fear and anger being replaced by puzzlement. What had Loralai meant about Miroslav awakening? She made it sound like something big was about to happen; was she talking about things locally, or something more...widespread? And who else knew about it?

Glancing over my shoulder, I pulled out my phone and tapped out a quick message to Lina.

Nora: Hey, are you free tonight? Something happened at work. Need to talk.

I held my phone and watched the clock hand edge toward five. The elevator dinged, and I suddenly realized exactly who I needed to find. Slipping the phone back into my bag, I quickly straightened the papers on my desk and gathered my things. A peek out of my cubicle revealed a clear path to the elevator bank. I hustled down the aisle and was reaching for the call button when a sudden bout of nerves had me turning the corner and entering the stairwell instead.

Common sense caught up with me at the door to the next floor down. I'd only seen that vampire in the elevator twice. He could very well have just been meeting someone, and not actually working here. Even if he did work here, I had no idea what his name was, or which office he might be in. If I recalled correctly, this floor housed two different law firms.

I snorted to myself. *Just what the world needs*—literal *bloodsucking lawyers.*

A buzz from my phone momentarily distracted me.

Lina: Are you okay? I need to check on my uncle but will be free after that. It should be about 630.

Nora: I'm ok, but I think there's something major going on with the vamps.

I hesitated over the Send button. A memory floated back to me of Rachel talking about how none of our communications are truly private. She said it was something her mom worried about all the time, but Rachel, herself, didn't seem to care much either way.

Still... I backspaced and started over.

Nora: I'm ok. Would you mind coming to my house?

Lina must really have been worried. She responded immediately.

Lina: I'll be there as soon as I can.

Relief and gratitude toward my friend bolstered my nerves. Re-stowing my phone, I threw my shoulders back, lifted my chin, and—

Nearly jumped out of my skin when the door opened suddenly, revealing a familiar set of red eyes.

"Hello Ms. Jensen," the vampire said with a friendly smile. "I was wondering how long you planned to stand out here."

"Don't do that!" I yelped. I pressed a hand to my chest in a feeble attempt to calm my galloping heart. If I knew him better, I would have smacked him for scaring me so badly. *And also if he wasn't capable of ripping my head off...*

His smile turned to a smirk. "I apologize for frightening you. I forgot humans possess the same adorable skittishness as rabbits."

I glared and spun on my heel, intending to leave his smug, pasty face behind. He caught my elbow gently. Much more gently than I would have expected even of a human, much less a vamp.

"I'm sorry, Ms. Jensen. Truly. I only meant to tease, not to insult," he said, releasing my arm.

I narrowed my eyes at him, but his contrite expression never wavered. What did it matter, anyway? I needed answers, and he was the only vampire I could ask. Pride and hurt feelings had no place here.

"I need to talk to you. About…vampire things," I said.

"How illuminating," he replied, his amused smile back in place. "May we move to my office, or is the drafty stairwell a necessary component to this discussion?"

I ignored the sarcasm. "Anywhere private. I can't have anyone else finding out about this."

His smile grew, his expression turning mischievous. "Intriguing! I find myself most curious, Ms. Jensen." He opened the door and gestured for me to go first. "My office is just around the corner to the right."

I stepped inside and waited for him to lead. He brushed past, and I suppressed a shiver. Maybe sequestering myself in an unfamiliar space with a stranger who also happened to be a monster wasn't such a great idea… We reached his office before I had time to rethink my decision.

It was a large, comfortable space with plush, upholstered chairs set before an elegant desk. His window faced the nearby green space. He motioned me toward one armchair and then took the other rather than sitting behind his desk. I perched on the edge of the cushion awkwardly, suddenly very unsure of myself.

"Now, Ms. Jensen. What do you need to discuss with me?" He lounged comfortably in his chair, giving me his full attention.

"Um…" *What am I doing here?!*

"It's alright," he said. "As I told you before, you can ask me anything."

"How did you know I was in the stairwell?" I blurted. *Oh well, at least it's a start.*

The vamp's lip curled slightly. "Your scent is rather...*stronger* than usual, at present."

"I *stink?*"

His eyes dropped pointedly toward my jawline before returning to meet my own. "In a manner of speaking."

"Oh." I touched the scabbed cuts self-consciously. Did I imagine the sympathetic look on his face?

"Would you like a drink?" he asked.

I scoffed before catching myself. "No, thank you."

He smiled again. "I have water. Or brandy, if you prefer."

"Oh, um, water would be nice. Thanks."

I studied his office decor as he retrieved a glass from a cupboard against the wall. There were various framed newspaper articles, presumably related to his work, a photograph of him with an attractive young woman, and a bronze statue of a wolf sitting beside his monitor. He returned, handing me a glass of water, and sat back down, sipping his own drink. I was surprised to see it was also water.

He read me easily. "We don't only consume blood," he chuckled.

"I'm learning all kinds of fun things today," I muttered into my glass.

"Pardon?" Judging by his expression, he heard me perfectly.

"What's with the wolf?" I asked instead, gesturing to his desk ornament. "Seems a little out of character."

He laughed. I was annoyed to find it was a pleasant sound.

"It was a gift from a close friend." He smiled fondly at the statue.

"Her?" I asked, nodding toward the photograph. I'm not sure why I was being so nosy. Maybe I was afraid of what his answers to my real questions might be.

He followed my gaze and brightened. "Oh! No, that's my cousin. She's a sweet girl and has given me plenty of presents over the years. But not that one."

"Oh." I scratched my leg awkwardly. The vamp waited patiently.

Stop screwing around, Nora! At this rate, you're gonna run into Loralai in the elevator!

I took a big gulp of water, wished briefly that I'd taken the brandy, and cleared my throat. "*Ahem.* So, who's Miroslav?"

11

THE VAMP STARED at me for several uncomfortable moments. He took a slow sip of water, his red eyes locked on mine over the rim of the glass.

I regretted my question. I regretted ever meeting the guy. Thing. *Whatever.*

"Miroslav," he repeated flatly.

Well, I'm already this deep in it. Might as well keep digging. "Yup. Miroslav. Is it a popular name among you lot, or is there just the one guy?"

"I only know of 'the one guy,' as you so eloquently put it," he replied with a quirk to his lips.

"Okay... So, he's definitely dead by now, right? 'Cause that was a really long time ago."

He considered for a moment, his eyes narrowed speculatively. "To my knowledge, Miroslav was never slain."

"Uh—good for him, I guess, but that doesn't quite answer my question. Is he dead or not?"

The vamp sighed and looked out the window. "There are some who believe he still lives."

"Seriously?! Do *you* think he's alive?"

He met my gaze again, his eyes suddenly intense. "Why are you asking these questions? What happened?"

"Nothing! I just—I heard the name and was curious, that's all." I brushed my fingers over my jaw again and my eyes wandered toward the door. I needed to get out of there ASAP.

Warm fingers closed over my own, and I nearly leaped off my seat. The vamp gently pulled my hand away from my face and turned my head to the side with a finger under my chin. Leaning uncomfortably close, he inspected the cuts.

"Who did this to you, Nora?" he growled, making the hairs stand up on my neck.

"Nobody!" I choked out. "It was just an accident. And what happened to Ms. Jensen, anyway? I don't know your name at all!"

He didn't fall for my misdirection. "Tell me the truth."

I had no desire to protect Loralai, or try to pretend it really was an accident, but at that moment I had a crippling fear that accusing a vampire to another vampire was a terrible idea.

"I am. It's fine."

He dropped his hand from my chin but remained leaning toward me, wearing a frown. The red of his eyes seemed more liquid than usual, but for some reason I didn't fear manipulation from him.

"Nora—"

I raised an eyebrow at him.

"Ms. Jensen," he amended. "I hope you've realized by now that you have nothing to fear from me." He ignored my quiet scoff and continued, "These marks on your face are unfortunate, but would normally not be my business. However, as they are coupled with your sudden interest in Miroslav, I confess I am rather concerned about the circumstances in which you find yourself."

This wasn't at all where I expected our conversation to lead.

"I don't know why you would be. We're nothing to each other," I replied, my tone harsh.

"Perhaps not." A peculiar twinkle in his eye had me narrowing my eyes in suspicion. "But I do pride myself on maintaining respectable conduct—something I also expect from my peers."

"I see. And what would you do if you found out someone wasn't living up to your standards?"

"Oh, I would have words with them. Nothing for you to worry about, of course." He waved a hand airily.

"Uh-huh. And this individual—where do you think they would put the blame for the interaction?"

The vamp's lips curled into a rakish smile. "My dear Ms. Jensen, I believe you underestimate my powers of persuasion."

Realizing I was sitting forward to mirror his posture, once again placing me firmly within his brain-bending range, I cleared my throat and leaned back into the plush chair, pointedly breaking eye contact. I heard a quiet chuckle and the sigh of fabric as he settled back into his own seat, but maintained my studious inspection of the stitching on my armrest.

"Alright. You don't have to tell me. I'm fairly confident I already know the answer, anyway."

My eyes darted back to him in a panic. Before I could say anything, he held up a hand.

"Relax," he said. "I have no desire to make anything worse for you."

"Frankly, that's a surprise," I deadpanned. "Coming from someone like you."

Maybe don't antagonize the monster, Nora?

Thankfully, the vamp just laughed. "Fair enough. I promise you, though, not all vampires—not all *paranormals*—are evil. Just like humans, we have our bad apples, but we try not to let them spoil the rest."

I nodded, but wasn't sure I really believed him. I'd seen too many examples to the contrary.

"So, getting back on topic," I said. "You never answered my question. Do you think Miroslav is around somewhere?"

The vamp considered for a moment, his mouth twisting like he'd eaten something sour.

Someone sour?

He replied, oblivious to my dark train of thought, "Honestly, I'm not sure. I've heard stories over the years and seen what might be considered evidence of his survival. But I've never seen Miroslav in the flesh or met anyone who has."

"What if—" I hesitated briefly. "What if you heard someone talking about him like he was still alive? Like he was just sleeping?"

"Sleeping?" he asked, his eyes shrewd. "Interesting. I *had* considered the possibility…"

"Possibility? Sleeping for a thousand years seems like a normal thing to you?"

"Not exactly." He smirked. "Vampires are sometimes able to enter a sort of stasis for long periods. However, in all the instances I've heard of, the stasis either wasn't for more than a decade or two, or else the individual withered away and couldn't be revived. And you say someone told you Miroslav was sleeping?"

"Well, no, I didn't say that." Not exactly, anyway.

He gave me a flat look. "Right. So, during your extremely specific speculation, you came to that conclusion?"

"Um. More or less."

I was impressed he managed to refrain from rolling his eyes.

He was quiet for a moment, apparently lost in thought as he studied the ceiling tiles. My eyes wandered the office once more, this time noting a plaque on the wall above the cupboard in which he stored his drink collection. I couldn't make out all the specifics from my seat, but it appeared to be some manner of certificate of achievement and was addressed to an A. J. Hunt.

"Well, Ms. Jensen, you've given me much to think about. I need to follow up on this information with a few of my acquaintances. Might I call on you in the coming days to discuss my findings?"

"Oh, um, okay." I hadn't expected a follow-up on this conversation at all, much less for him to go digging for info.

He accompanied me as I stood and headed for the exit. Memory of the run-in with Loralai rushed back to me when I reached the door. "Wait, I might not be at the office for a while. Can you call me instead?"

He quirked an eyebrow, a grin spreading over his face. "My my, Ms. Jensen. How very forward of you."

I couldn't stop the flush spreading over my cheeks, much to my annoyance. "Forget it," I grumbled, reaching for the doorknob.

He beat me to it with a chuckle. "I apologize for my teasing once again. I would be happy to relay any pertinent information to you as I find it, in whichever manner suits you best."

A sense of foreboding about Loralai's comment overruled my injured pride. "Fine. What *is* your name, anyway? Or should I just use 'Annoying Undead' as your contact title?"

Despite my snark, he gave a winning smile. "I'm sure you can refer to me in any manner you please. However, if you want a real name, you may call me AJ."

"AJ? Seriously? Didn't you say you're two hundred and fifty years old?" There was no way the guy shared a name with a boy band member.

"Close enough."

"So, shouldn't your name be Charles or Thomas or something?"

"My mother was more creative than that, thankfully. Besides, your own name was quite popular in the nineteenth century. Perhaps you're secretly a vampire as well?" He put a hand to his mouth and pretended to study me.

I rolled my eyes and gave the irritating vamp my cellphone number, thankfully avoiding both Loralai and Charna on the way to the lobby.

———

Despite her text, Lina was waiting for me when I got home.

"Sorry!" she said as soon as I reached the front door. "My sister called while I was leaving work. She traded shifts tonight and can stay with Uncle Mark longer than I expected. I sent you a message, but wasn't sure if you saw it."

I pulled out my phone and saw the unopened notification. "Oh, I'm sorry, I didn't hear it go off. I was a bit late leaving work. Well, leaving the building, anyway."

At Lina's questioning look, I huffed a laugh. "It's crazy. I'll tell you all about it."

Forty-five minutes and multiple outraged exclamations later, Lina rubbed a hand over her eyes. "Wow. That's a lot to take in."

"Yeah," I chuckled dryly. "It was a bit surreal."

"I bet," she sighed, and shook her head. "So, what now?"

"I guess just wait and see what AJ finds?"

My phone rang from its place on the coffee table. The screen displayed Cal's name.

Lina smiled and started toward the kitchen. "Go ahead and take it. I'll get myself a glass of water."

"Thank you!" I called after her before answering. "Hello?"

"Hello, Nora. Are you home from work already?"

"Hey, Cal. Yeah, I got home a while ago. Are you done for the day?"

"I am. I was going to call earlier but thought you might still be driving and didn't want to catch you right as you walked in the door, either."

I smiled. "Well, thank you for your thoughtfulness. How was work today? Has your boss given you any more responsibilities yet?"

"It was good. I finished going through the files Lind sent me and feel like I have a firmer grasp on the way things are done around here. And even if I don't, Ms. Newman already seems to be an expert at everything," he laughed. *"How was your day?"*

"I'm sure she'll keep you in line." I chuckled along with him. His previous description of Ms. Newman, as well as the story of her hiring, made me very curious about the woman. As for his question... "My day wasn't that great. I might be taking some time off."

"What happened? Are you alright?"

"I'm alright," I answered a bit too quickly. "Really, it's fine. I just have some things I need to take care of, and then I'll be back at work."

"Alright... I hope you know you can tell me anything. I want to be there for you however I can."

I nodded before remembering he couldn't see me. "I know. And I appreciate it."

Cal being my boss in some capacity made me uncomfortably hesitant to share what happened at work. I didn't think nepotism would do me any favors with Loralai.

Besides, beyond our uncertain working relationship, the few times paranormals had come up in conversation made me suspect Cal didn't share my views on the topic. Not that I needed him to agree with me about everything, but given my uncertainty about the situation with Miroslav and this whatever-it-was with AJ... I didn't know how to explain it yet again without winding up even more anxious about the whole thing. At least with Lina, it was easy—she knew when I needed someone to just listen.

"Of course. I actually called to see if you would like to see a movie with me tomorrow, but it sounds like maybe you have a bit too much on your plate at the moment."

"No! No, that sounds great. I could use the distraction."

"Perfect! I have to attend this meet-and-greet event shortly, so I'm afraid I can't talk for longer today, but perhaps I can send you a link to the movies playing tomorrow and you can decide what you're interested in?"

"That's no problem—Lina is actually here right now, anyway. I'll look at the movies and text you some choices later this evening."

"Great! Say hi to Lina for me. Have a good evening, Nora."

"I will. You, too." I ended the call with a sigh, then noticed Lina leaning against the doorway.

"You didn't seem too eager to tell him what happened," she said.

I groaned and flopped against the back of the couch. "I know. Everything is such a mess. How do I tell him his subordinate is abusive but still convince him I don't want preferential treatment and, oh yeah, the father of all evil might also be prowling around his subsidiaries?"

Lina quietly returned to her seat. "Unfortunately, I have no idea. But I do believe honesty is the best policy."

I sighed again. "You're right. I'll try to talk to him about it tomorrow."

"Have you seen your dad's lawyers?"

"Not yet, but I have a meeting scheduled with them for Monday afternoon. Just one more wrench to throw into all of this."

She gave me a commiserating look. "And what if Miroslav *is* alive, and there really is some kind of major vampire upheaval about to happen?"

I grimaced. "Then I guess we'd all better pray for a miracle."

12

"**Can I freshen** your drink, Mr. Vasile?"

I struggled to maintain a pleasant expression as the woman fluttered her eyelashes and leaned into my arm, her skintight dress straining to support the obscene amount of cleavage on display.

"No, thank you," I replied as politely as I could manage, yanking my eyes upward once more. "Although I wouldn't say no to another of the bruschetta hors d'oeuvres, if you happen to know where the server went."

"Of course! Don't wander off while I'm gone," she said, trailing a manicured nail down my arm.

I shuddered as soon as she turned away. She was easily my mother's age and had the worst wandering hands of anyone I'd ever met. I'd previously overheard a server saying they were nearly out of the bruschetta, so hopefully the errand would keep the woman occupied awhile.

"Having fun?"

I breathed a sigh of relief as Alden sidled up to me, drink in hand. "Hardly. If they're not groping, they're fawning. I don't know how Mother's stayed sane all these years."

"Eh. You get used to them, eventually." He shrugged.

"I sometimes forget you work for this company, too."

His eyes twinkled. "Only when it suits."

I shook my head, smiling into my drink. "I don't think I want to know what that means."

Two women sashayed by, brushing against me unnecessarily and giggling to each other. I couldn't prevent my lip from curling.

Alden smirked. "You know," he began with far too innocent an expression. "They wouldn't be trying nearly so hard if you already had someone on your arm."

I narrowed my eyes. "Is that so?"

"Oh yes," he continued airily. "Someone lovely and witty and intelligent, preferably with blonde hair and blue eyes."

"That's rather specific."

His expression sharpened into something slightly devious. "Someone you'd be too busy mooning over to notice all the vultures."

I couldn't help but smile at the picture Alden painted. "You know I'd love to have Nora here with me, but I can't force her hand. Even though we seem to mesh well, personality-wise, my circumstances make me a less-than-ideal choice for her."

My friend rolled his eyes and groaned in exasperation. "What I know is you clearly aren't doing a good enough job of wooing her. Otherwise, she'd be here, circumstances be damned. After all, as a few wise men once said, all you need is love."

Despite the flat look I gave him for his pop culture reference, Alden's words still caused an uncomfortable twinge in my gut. I knew Nora had serious reservations about being thrust into the spotlight at my side and I couldn't blame her at all, but could it be as simple as Alden claimed?

I wasn't naive enough to believe love just happened spontaneously and if any difficulties arose, then it clearly wasn't meant to be—relationships took effort and dedication from both sides to make them work. But at the end of the day, love itself was the point of all the endeavors, wasn't it?

Could I really sit and wait for Nora to possibly fall in love with me, and just keep my fingers crossed that she would then be willing to put up with everything that came after?

I can't just wait and hope. I have to show her that a life together would be worth the effort.

Armed with this new resolve, I returned my attention to Alden, who had apparently been speaking during my deliberations.

"—said he really shouldn't spend so much time at the gym or his head might not fit between his shoulders before long."

I chuckled blandly at his expectant look.

He sighed. "I take it you've made up your mind about Nora, then?"

"What? No, I wasn't—"

"*Pft.*" His scoff cut off my weak protest. "You haven't gotten any better at pretending to pay attention. Besides, it's obvious when you think about her—you get this ridiculous dreamy look in your eyes." He waved a finger in my face, indicating the offending expression.

"I'm sorry. I didn't mean—"

"Why are you apologizing?" he interrupted again. "I keep telling you to go for it. So, get out there and do it!"

I laughed at his blunt manner. "Don't worry, I intend to."

"It's about time. Now, hurry up with these pleasantries so you can get on with it."

Right on cue, Mother arrived at my side. "Caliban, dear, I want you to meet someone." Turning, she directed my attention to a tall, lean man dressed in what appeared to be some manner of ceremonial robes. "This is Elder Kael, a long-standing member of the Circle."

Elder Kael inclined in a shallow bow, hands tucked into his wide, crimson sleeves. "Master Caliban, I'm honored to meet you at last. Your mother has spoken highly of you." His thick European accent suited his black hair and pale complexion.

"Elder Kael. The honor is mine." I tipped my head respectfully, wondering why a member of the vampire equivalent of Parliament would be honored to meet me.

"I hear you've officially taken over leadership duties of your family's company. A remarkable feat for someone so young." The vampire's mahogany eyes seemed to simmer, showing only slivers of white around the edges. He had to be ancient.

"You flatter me, but my mother is actually still the acting CEO. I'm afraid I'm little more than a figurehead, at present.

I'm still learning the inner-workings of the company and likely won't be truly in charge for quite some time yet."

"Oh, I wouldn't be too sure of that," he replied with a courteous smile. "You seem to be a bright young man; you'll catch on quickly."

"Uh, thank you. I'll certainly do my best."

The vampire gave another gracious dip of his head before removing a long-fingered hand festooned with intricately worked rings from his sleeve to gesture across the room. "Would you care to walk with me? As V-Corp is our primary point of contact with the mortal world, the Circle of Elders feels it is in our best interests to nurture close ties with the leadership of your company."

At my questioning look, I received an encouraging nod from Mother and a barely discernible shrug from Alden. I turned back to Kael, who still had his arm outstretched. "Of course," I replied, stepping up beside him. "I, too, wish to maintain a positive relationship with the vampire community."

Despite his claim, Elder Kael was mostly silent as we circled the room, instead studying the attendees and bestowing occasional respectful nods to various individuals. It struck me as odd. As a member of the highest echelon of vampire society, Kael outranked everyone present. He outranked everyone on the planet, in fact—at least, according to vampire views. The only people he might consider his equals were the other members of the Circle. He certainly had no cause to *bow* to anyone.

"Elder Kael," I began hesitantly.

He immediately turned to me with a pleasant smile. "Yes, Master Caliban?"

I opened my mouth but suddenly realized there was no way I could ask about his behavior without insulting him. That was the last thing V-Corp needed right now. I cast my eyes around the room, searching for another topic. They landed on a familiar face and my brow furrowed. "What is she doing here?" I muttered.

Apparently, my words were louder than intended as Elder Kael followed my gaze to the brunette vampire I'd last had the distinct displeasure of interacting with at Nora's office. She waved a champagne flute around as she pawed at an imposing man in a business suit. I couldn't tell from the distance, but considering her previous manner toward humans, I assumed the object of her affection was also a vampire.

"Are you referring to Loralai?" asked my companion.

Great, she's someone important. Nora will be furious.

"Yes." I tore my gaze away and tried to feign disinterest. "I met her at one of our subsidiary companies the other day. I didn't expect to see her here tonight."

"Ah. You're correct—a vampire of her station would not normally merit an invitation to an event such as this. She is here at the behest of another. There is to be a Council of the Circle later this evening, at which time we must renew our vows to the sovereignty of vampirism. To complete the ceremony, members will partake of a source of pure immortality. Loralai has been chosen to provide that sustenance."

My blood ran cold at the implication. Meanwhile, Kael still wore the same pleasant smile as usual. Somehow, his completely unaffected expression turned my stomach even more than his calm explanation of the coming cannibalism. Some distant, unimportant part of my mind wondered why, exactly, the vampire felt compelled to spell out the intimate—and most definitely illegal—details of a high-level ceremony to a mere mortal.

"I see," I managed. I met Alden's eye across the room and saw my escape. "If you'll please excuse me, Elder Kael, I must speak with my friend before he leaves. It's an honor to have met you. Enjoy the rest of your evening." I bowed and hoped he wouldn't find an excuse to continue speaking to me.

Thankfully, he simply bowed in return. "Of course, Master Caliban. I look forward to speaking with you again soon."

Not if I can help it.

I grimaced as I strode across the room. Alden saw my expression and abandoned the flock of ladies surrounding him.

"What happened?" he asked quietly.

"I wanted to catch you before you leave," I said in a slightly louder than normal voice. "I had a question about that paperwork you sent me." Widening my eyes meaningfully, I tipped my head toward the door.

"Certainly." Alden caught on immediately, to my relief. "Let's step into the hall to discuss it."

I smothered the urge to look back at Elder Kael as I followed my friend out the door. He didn't stop until we were two hallways and a lobby away from the conference hall.

There, he turned to me with an uncharacteristically stern look and crossed his arms over his chest. "So?"

I recounted Kael's words, shuddering at the memory. "Is it wrong to feel relieved Nora will no longer have to suffer under her rule?" I asked.

"No, Cal, it's not wrong to want your loved ones to be free of abuse," Alden replied in a dry tone. "Besides, from what you've told me, it sounds like the woman deserves what's coming to her."

I wasn't sure I agreed. Yes, Loralai was despicable, and I keenly regretted not standing up to her for Nora's sake, but I couldn't bring myself to believe anyone deserved a fate like that.

"Will you tell Nora?" asked Alden.

I considered it for a moment. "I'm not sure. She hates the woman and wants justice for her father, but I don't believe she would agree with this kind of retribution."

Maybe Nora was more right about the vampires than I realized.

13

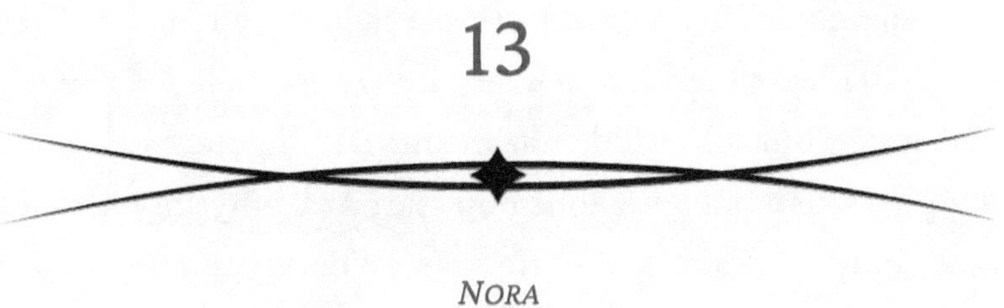

I STOOD IN the lobby of the movie theater feeling awkward. The teenager at the ticket counter had already given me several weird looks, but Cal insisted I let him buy the tickets for us, so I held my conspicuous ground in the middle of the confetti-printed purple carpet. Checking my phone for the dozenth time revealed no new messages.

Ten more minutes and then I'll just go in.

I rocked back on my heels and studied the Coming Attractions movie posters adorning the nearest wall. Two rom-coms, a thriller, the latest superhero flick, and a feature-length version of some kids' show.

I fought the urge to look at my phone again.

He just hit traffic. It's not a big deal. There's lots of traffic at two-thirty in the afternoon on Saturdays...

Letting out a gusty sigh, I debated nixing my self-assigned time frame and just heading into the movie alone. I had seen plenty of movies by myself in the past, and considering there were only a handful of other movie-goers at the theater just then, it's not like there was anything to be embarrassed about.

I was sure Cal's absence had nothing to do with the event he attended the previous night. That was just a work thing, anyway.

He did say it was a work thing, didn't he?

An uncomfortable feeling twisted in my gut as I realized I had no idea what kind of event it was. He called it a meet-and-greet, but what did that mean? Did he meet his board members, or some gorgeous pop star? And why shouldn't he meet gorgeous pop stars? He was a young, attractive, and insanely wealthy man. Exactly the type you'd see on the cover of a tabloid, strolling around Hollywood arm-in-arm with some A-lister.

I grimaced at my self-destructive spiral of thoughts. Cal didn't deserve my ire. He'd been a good friend to me from the start, and even if our relationship never went further than that, he deserved to have a happy life.

Even if it is with a pop star...

I peeked at my phone a final time before digging out my wallet and approaching the ticket counter. The attendant looked confused, like he would have given up and gone home by now. I gave him a self-deprecating smile. "I guess it's just me today."

The entry doors banged open, drawing the attention of the attendant and me, both. Cal hurried across the lobby toward us, a frown on his face. I opened my mouth to make some lame joke about his tardiness, but he jumped in before I could say anything.

"I'm so sorry! I got held up with some paperwork Mother insisted I look at today and then I forgot my phone at home and couldn't call you. I hope I'm not too late."

The look he gave me was so earnest I couldn't help melting a little inside. "Well... I guess I don't *completely* hate you." I crossed my arms and gave him a stern look. "But I'll have you know, you've made me miss my favorite part of the movie. I can't stand not knowing what new movies are coming out in the next six to eighteen months."

For a moment, he looked worried, but then realization dawned, and he smiled in relief. "My sincerest apologies. I'll gladly buy you tickets for every showing this afternoon so you can have your pick of previews to watch." He coupled his offer with a courtly bow, making me giggle and ruining my mock indignation.

The ticket attendant looked at us like we were nuts but refrained from commenting. Cal bought our tickets and steered us toward the concession stand when I made to bypass it. After an obscenely expensive popcorn, soda, and candy purchase, we found our seats just in time for the opening scene.

"I especially liked when the guy jumped out of the helicopter and tackled the other one off the roof of the building, but still managed to not even sprain an ankle. Or muss his hair," I laughed over an appetizer of chips and salsa.

Cal had talked me into an early supper after the movie as a further apology for being late. The hole-in-the-wall

Mexican restaurant apparently wasn't very popular at this hour, but had some amazing salsa. I applauded Cal's choice.

"That was really impressive. I bet it makes for a good resume entry: 'I regularly perform death-defying stunts and never become rumpled.'" Cal framed his hands in the air as though recounting a news headline.

I snorted into my iced tea and nearly had a coughing fit.

He grinned at my amusement, his eyes dancing.

"You sound a bit jealous. Are you going to put that on your resume, now?" I asked once I caught my breath.

"Oh no, I could never claim that. I frequently become rumpled."

"Is that so?" I snickered. "I didn't realize working in an office was such a strenuous activity."

"You clearly haven't been frequenting the right sort of offices," Cal said, sipping his water with a lofty air.

"I'm thinking you just frequent the wrong sort, actually."

Expecting further banter, I was surprised at the odd look Cal gave me. "Perhaps so," he said after a brief pause.

Before I could question the awkward moment, our waiter arrived, and we spent the next few minutes complimenting the food and trying each other's entrees. Conversation moved back into lighthearted topics ranging from the movie we'd seen, to Rachel's latest swooner of a chapter, to a hilarious recounting of the previous afternoon in Cal's office when his secretary had apparently laid into some bootlicking bigwig.

By the time the check came (Cal insisted he would pay the bill *and* the tip so I'd better put my wallet away if I knew what was good for me), I was feeling overly full and very content, in more ways than one.

He makes me feel happy—about life and *about myself. Would a relationship really be so bad?*

Thoughts of attending all his public appearances crowded my mind, but for once, they didn't feel like such a deterrent. If "normal" life would be like this, what did a few uncomfortable outings matter? Besides, I knew Cal would do everything in his power to make any stressful situations easier for me.

Totally living up to expectations, Cal returned from paying the cashier and pulled out my chair as I stood. He offered a chocolate mint candy from the counter and politely gestured for me to proceed him through the maze of tables. When we reached the door, he stepped ahead of me to open it. I gave him what felt like an embarrassingly dreamy smile as I passed through, but I couldn't help it.

Cal flashed his gorgeous smile in return, albeit looking a little bemused at my expression.

A trio of college-aged girls rounded the corner from the parking lot, chattering animatedly. Cal, gentleman that he was, held the door for them. I moved aside and just managed to reign in my starry eyes.

The group filed into the restaurant, murmuring thanks to Cal, until one of them let out a loud gasp.

"Oh my gosh, you're Caliban Vasile!" the girl squealed.

Her two friends whipped around to join her in gawking at Cal, who smiled and tipped his head politely while still patiently holding the door for them.

"I can't believe this! We literally just saw you on a magazine cover. This is the greatest day of my life!" the first girl gushed.

The two friends giggled together as one whispered to the other loudly enough for everyone to hear, "He's even *hotter* in real life!"

Cal didn't visibly react, and I wondered what he thought of the attention. I shifted my weight from one leg to the other, but I might as well have been invisible for all the notice I received.

"Can we take a picture with you?" The ringleader was already pulling out her phone and moving closer to Cal.

"Of course." He stepped back onto the patio to make room as the girls crowded around him. He gave me an apologetic smile, which I weakly returned before starting toward the parking lot, intending to wait by the car, my embarrassment drowning out all the previous gooey feelings I had.

"Nora."

I turned back to meet four sets of eyes. Cal stretched out his arm for me to stand next to him, dislodging one of his fans from her perch against his shoulder. The girls looked like they would gladly toss me into the nearest snake pit. My face heated, and I debated refusing, but Cal's expression was so warm and genuine, I couldn't bring myself to care what they thought.

This was exactly the kind of uncomfortable situation I was thinking of earlier. If I couldn't even face three snooty coeds, then I had no business furthering this relationship.

Lifting my chin, I took my place at Cal's side. The heat in my cheeks increased when he slid his arm around my waist and angled me even closer, leaving me with nothing to do with my hand except put it against his side.

I tried very hard not to notice his toned stomach muscles.

Fangirl #1 pulled a selfie stick out of somewhere and had her phone mounted and ready to go in a matter of seconds. "Say cheese!" she sang as she pressed into Cal's other side.

After snapping half a dozen photos, the girls gave Cal a chorus of over-enthusiastic thanks before we could finally leave.

"Thank you for bearing with me through that," he said as he opened the car door for me. "I promise they're not always so...overbearing."

"Oh, I'm sure they are," I joked.

He grinned in return. "You may be right."

As he circled to the driver's seat, I realized the experience wasn't as bad as I expected. Not once I focused on what mattered instead of fixating on my discomfort, anyway.

Cal hopped in and gave me another flutter-inducing smile. "Thank you for today, Nora. I really enjoyed my time with you."

Unable to hold his gaze, or match his unabashed sincerity, I turned my attention to the windshield and resorted to sarcasm. "Does that mean you've reached the end of your enjoyment, and you're going to hate the drive back to the theater? I told you I could have brought my own car."

He was clearly becoming accustomed to my sense of humor. "Certainly not. I told you before, I would be a gentleman and drive you to the restaurant and back, and I will stick to that promise. Even if it *is* unbearable."

I laughed, delighted with his bantering.

Cal pulled out of the parking lot and reached over to wrap his warm fingers around mine, resting his wrist against my thigh. Cheeks scorching, I risked a peek at him. He kept his eyes on the road, but squeezed my hand gently. I looked back out the window, unable to fight a sappy grin.

When we reached the movie theater, he gave my hand another squeeze before releasing me and jogging around the car to open my door. "My lady," he said, bowing and offering his hand to help me out.

I giggled and accepted, adopting a breathy British accent. "Why, thank you, kind sir! I don't know how I would have managed without you."

He grinned and played along, still clutching my hand. "My lady is too modest! I'm certain she possesses unknown depths of grace and ability."

"You flatter me, sir," I breathed, fanning my free hand at my face. "I'm afraid you might be the type of charmer my mother warned me about."

"Oh no, madam. I'm the plain, reliable sort mothers tell their daughters to look for *instead* of falling for one of those handsome, charming rogues."

I laughed at the ridiculous line coming from the mouth of possibly the most handsome, charming man I'd ever met.

As I smiled up at him, I suddenly realized how close we were standing. Something shifted between us.

Cal took a tiny step closer, his expression intent. Feeling heat crawl up my neck, I chewed the inside of my lip nervously. It was apparently the wrong move (or the right one?) as his gaze immediately dropped to my mouth. My heart rate felt like it tripled, and I suddenly had trouble swallowing around my dry tongue.

As he dipped toward me and my eyes slid closed, Lina's voice suddenly jumped to mind: *"I do believe honesty is the best policy."*

My eyes popped open, and I took a quick step back. "I'm sorry, I can't!"

Disappointment chased hurt across Cal's face before he schooled his features into something more neutral. He stepped back as well, dropping my hand. "There's nothing to be sorry for. I apologize if I made you uncomfortable."

Panic overtook my guilt. I moved toward him again, reaching out vaguely. "No! No, you didn't make me uncomfortable!" Dropping my hands, I groaned. "I'm sorry, I'm handling this so badly. I didn't mean I don't want to kiss you, because I really do!" My cheeks were likely crimson by then, but I soldiered on. "I just remembered something Lina said. Not that I was thinking about Lina during... *Anyway,* she made me realize I shouldn't start anything with you without being honest and open about my circumstances."

I expected Cal to look relieved that I wasn't rejecting him, or maybe confused by my rambling. Instead, he wore the same strange look he'd given me at dinner. I suddenly felt a little less sure about myself. "Um—do you not agree?" I asked.

Does he want this to be more casual than I thought? The idea made me want to shrivel up after my outburst.

He sighed. "I do agree. Completely. Actually, something happened at that work event last night—"

It was *a work event! I knew it!*

"—and I've been debating how to tell you."

Oh.

I couldn't fight my rising apprehension. The only connection I possibly had to his work event was Cal himself, and there weren't a lot of things that could have happened to him that would affect me. Unfortunately, the few possibilities were all things I wasn't eager to hear.

"I met someone at the party," he began.

My blood suddenly felt like ice in my veins. He was telling me this *after* taking me out on a date? After trying to *KISS* me?! I felt like I was caught in a horrible movie moment.

"A vampire," Cal continued. "A member of the Circle of Elders, actually. He told me some…*disturbing* things. I'm still not sure I should even tell you, but I feel it's not my right to withhold something that concerns you."

Wait, a vampire? A *he?* …Not what I was expecting.

"Okay," I said slowly. "What does it have to do with me?"

Cal grimaced. "It's Loralai," he said. "She—that is, Kael told me—" He broke off with a frustrated sound.

I was getting worried again. "What about Loralai?"

He gave me a look so full of sympathy I couldn't decide whether to feel warmed by his concern or terrified of what he was about to say.

"Kael, the vampire, said—*implied*, really—that the Circle of Elders was going to kill Loralai as part of some ritual last night."

Huh?

Shock consumed me. A young couple with a pair of excited kids raced past us toward the theater, but I hardly noticed.

A warm hand covered mine, startling me out of my daze.

"Are you alright?" Cal asked gently.

Letting out a somewhat hysterical laugh, I dropped my face into my hands and rubbed my eyelids until I saw stars. "I don't even know what to think right now," I groaned. I peeked at him between my fingers. "What would you do?"

His expression twisted. "Honestly? I don't know. I'm so sorry, Nora. I knew you would have a difficult time with this, which is why I was nervous about telling you. It's an impossible situation. On the one hand, it's a horrible thing to contemplate, but on the other, it brings a lot of positive aspects to your life. As callous as that is to say," he added, noting my grimace.

He was right. A Loralai-free life was almost impossible to imagine after all these years, but would I even be capable of enjoying it now without feeling some measure of guilt?

14

WHEN MY ALARM went off Monday morning, I was already awake. I had been for a few hours, actually, and had become well-versed in the pattern of shadows on the ceiling of my bedroom. When the upbeat jingle came trickling out of my phone speakers, I rolled over to silence it with a groan before returning to my contemplation of the ceiling shadows.

What now?

The textured drywall had no more answers for me than it did the first dozen times I asked.

I finally worked up the gumption to get out of bed. An embarrassing amount of time later, I stood in the bathroom brushing my teeth, dressed and hair combed, still with no actual idea of what I was doing.

By the time I exited the elevator to Jensen Publishing, I had finally decided I was just checking things out. Testing the waters, as it were. I would go about my day as usual and see what happened. Besides, I had the meeting with Dad's lawyers that afternoon—I might as well go to work if I was going to be downtown, anyway.

From what Cal told me of his work event, it didn't seem likely any of my coworkers would have heard what happened yet, so the day would probably be the usual quiet affair, like it always was when Loralai was out of the office.

I arrived at my desk with nothing more eventful than a friendly nod to Rebecca, whose cubicle was next to my own. After a last look around the quiet floor over my gray fabric office walls, I felt satisfied things really were peaceful and calm. Sinking into my desk chair with a relieved sigh, I began unloading the laptop and accessories from my bag.

A touch on my shoulder nearly sent me leaping out of my skin. Whirling around, I found myself staring into Charna's deep red eyes.

"Hello, Nooora," she purred, squeezing my shoulder gently. I'm not sure how she maintained her grip during my freak-out.

"Uh," I stammered. "Hello. Charna." I may have also gulped.

"How are you this morning?"

"I'm…fine." I stared at her blankly.

She held my gaze with a vaguely pleasant expression.

The moment stretched out, and I realized she was waiting for me to uphold my half of the conversation.

"Um, how are you?"

"I'm very well, thank you." She smiled in a half-friendly, half-calculating manner.

"That's…great. Um. Did you need something?" I was hyperaware of her hand still on my shoulder.

"Oh, no. I just wanted to visit with you. Did you have a nice weekend?"

Did I not actually wake up this morning? Am I still in bed and this is all some bizarre dream?

"Yeah, I did." Her expectant look prompted me to continue. "How was your weekend?"

"Mine was very nice. I got my nails done." She finally took her hand off me to flaunt her fancy manicure. I had to admit the style was pretty, but no amount of pink and glitter would ever make those talons appear anything less than deadly.

"Oh—wow. They look really, uh, nice."

"Thanks. I tried a new place and I'm pleased with the results. We'll have to go together next time."

I felt my mind crack a little as I smiled at her blandly.

"So... Did *you* do anything special this weekend?" She gave me a knowing look, and I suddenly felt like an animal being herded toward a trap.

"Uh, not really. I just went to a movie on Saturday."

"Oh, that sounds like fun. I love going to the movies. Did you go with your friends?"

I stared at her for a few moments, but her slightly challenging expression never changed.

Did she take over Loralai's job and Item One on the Vampire Universal Agenda is "Torment Nora"?

"I went with a friend, yes."

She leaned marginally closer and lowered her voice. "Was he nice?"

This time I know I gulped. I also couldn't look away from her eyes. Why had I started looking at them in the first place?!

"Yes," I whispered.

She blinked, releasing her hold over me. I fell back in my chair with a gasp. She smiled and straightened. "Good."

The elevator dinged and Charna turned toward the sound, her usual distasteful expression returning as she watched whoever it was approaching.

My brain hadn't fully reformed from whatever had just happened, so when Loralai, still perfectly undead, stepped into my cubicle doorway, my mind completely shattered, sending little shards of Nora's Former Sense of Reality clinking around the inside of my skull.

"Charna. Shouldn't you be working?" Loralai's voice sounded raspy, like she'd spent the evening screeching at a sporting event. She was also wearing a long-sleeved turtleneck. In June.

Rather than snarl or test out the durability of her new manicure, Charna re-affixed the disconcertingly pleasant smile she had used on me a moment before. "And how was *your* weekend, Loralai?" She leaned in until the two were practically nose-to-nose. "I hear you finally got that introduction to the Circle you've been panting after. How *lucky* for you." She waved over her shoulder as she strolled out of the cubicle. "See you later, Nora."

Loralai watched her go with a murderous expression, but didn't make a sound. Before I could contemplate the vamp's attire and apparent laryngitis, she whirled around and stomped over to my chair, pulling a magazine out of her purse. Slapping it down on my desk, she shoved my face into it, her fingers gripping my hair so hard my scalp screamed. "Explain yourself," she growled.

I was too close to the magazine to see what it was, but somehow didn't think Loralai would accept that excuse. I peeled it out from under my face and angled it awkwardly to read the cover. A current edition of *Entertainment Today*, it was festooned with neon colors and gossipy tidbits, including a small headline in the bottom right corner proclaiming "Sorry, Ladies! Caliban's Taken!" I stared at the snapshot of myself plastered to Cal's side, my horror growing by the second.

"Well?" The question was accompanied by a further painful wrench to my scalp.

Half a dozen excuses sprang to mind, none of them believable. I couldn't even claim I had just been out with friends and ran into him as the magazine had helpfully cropped the other three girls out of the photo.

"We had classes together in college. I didn't know who he was!"

My forehead throbbed where it was being ground into the desk.

"This picture is dated from two days ago!" Her raspiness did nothing to lessen her menacing snarl.

I silently cursed the inventor of timestamps.

"I know; it was on Saturday. I was out with friends and ran into a group of old classmates. Ca—*Mr. Vasile* was with them. You can see the other people at the edges of the picture!" I waved the magazine frantically. "I don't know why they cropped it like that—I never even talked to him in college!" Not a total lie, but would she believe my misdirection?

Loralai gave my head a final, painful squeeze before releasing me, her nails catching on my hair and ripping out several strands. I stayed down, afraid of what would happen if I dared make eye contact. The magazine was still shaking in my grasp. As she reached out to snatch it, Loralai's sleeve slid up, revealing a thick, white bandage around her wrist.

Maybe Cal wasn't wrong about what happened. He just misunderstood the extent of it.

A crinkling sound told me Loralai was probably stowing the magazine back in her purse. I continued to lie on the desk.

"I will never see a photo like this again," she said matter-of-factly. "This is your only warning."

As her heels clicked away, I stared at the wall of my cubicle and pondered the point of my existence.

"Nora."

At the whisper, I peeled my head off the desk and met Rebecca's gaze as she peered around the corner.

"Are you okay?"

No. I'll never be okay.

"I think so," I said, rubbing my eyes to discourage the threatening tears. "Maybe I should have taken those days off like Mary suggested."

Rebecca didn't laugh. She grimaced, her eyes darting nervously toward Loralai's office. "Maybe you should," she whispered before retreating to her own cubicle.

Maybe I should.

I returned to staring at the wall, my emotions flattening out into a dull ache in my chest. A buzz from my phone rattled through the desk. I sighed and dug it out of my bag.

Cal: Good morning. How are you today? I hope you have a relaxing day planned!

I forgot I told him I was taking some time off. After the bomb he dropped on Saturday, we never got around to having that talk that Lina suggested, either.

I stared blankly at my phone for probably a minute before tapping out a reply.

Nora: I'm at work. Loralai is here. There's a picture of us on the cover of entertainment today. She's not happy about it.

He must not have been very busy at work. My phone lit up again almost immediately.

Cal: What?? How is that possible? Are you alright?

I wasn't sure which part he was referring to. Maybe all of it. Another text came in before I thought of a reply.

Cal: Can I call?

I guess he really isn't busy.

Bitterness welled up in me.

He could be in the middle of a meeting for all I know. HE can do whatever he wants!

The anger left as suddenly as it arrived, leaving only numbness in its wake. Being upset with Cal wouldn't change anything. At the end of the day, it was my own wretched life that held me captive, not his.

Nora: It isn't a good time.

I turned my phone to silent and returned it to my purse, then got out the filing project I'd been working on Friday afternoon.

An hour later, I spotted Loralai entering the elevator as I returned from the records room. I lingered out of sight until the doors closed, then turned the corner to see which floor the counter stopped on.

The ground floor. She was leaving the building, but for how long?

I hurried back to my cubicle and sent a quick email to HR before stuffing my belongings into my bag. I was taking that time Mary suggested. If I was lucky, Loralai would fire me—heavens knew she'd never accept a resignation letter. Not without personally escorting my mangled corpse from the premises, that is. If I was gone, maybe she'd just forget about me and that would be that.

I was nearly back to the elevators when a sudden, blistering realization stopped me in my tracks.

Charna.

She knew I was out with Cal and hadn't just run into him like I claimed. She obviously had no love for Loralai, but cared about humans even less, as evidenced by the nastiness she'd shown me and everyone else in the office since the day she arrived.

Until today.

But was that just some weird new form of torment she was trying out? It was impossible to know, but I had to take the chance that she was at least somewhat sincere. And if she wasn't, she was going to rat me out to Loralai anyway, so talking to her first wouldn't change anything. Except maybe how quickly I needed to leave the country.

I approached her desk cautiously, unsure how to begin. She was reclining in her chair, her purple stilettos propped on the corner of the desk, as she thumbed through a fashion magazine.

"Um, Charna?" I stood an awkward distance away, clutching the strap of my bag like a lifeline.

She immediately lowered the magazine and smiled at me. "Oh, Nora! I didn't hear you arrive!"

The strangeness of the statement made me suspect she had, in fact, heard me arrive.

She pulled her feet off the desk and leaned forward, turning her magazine around to display a leggy model clad in an expensive-looking gold cocktail dress. "What do you think of this? Would it suit me?"

Once again taken aback by her strange behavior, I could only stare dumbly at the ad.

"Hm." She turned the page back around and studied it closely. "You may be right. I'll have to keep looking for something for the gala." She sighed wistfully before laying the magazine aside and smiling at me again. "Are you headed to lunch? Do you want a companion?"

What was this, *Invasion of the Body Snatchers?*

I couldn't help glancing at the clock. 9:15. "Uh...no. I actually wanted to talk to you about something."

She clapped her hands gleefully and bounced out of her seat to perch on the edge of the desk, beckoning me closer. "Oooh, I love a good gossip session! Is it about that Richard in the accounting department? He's very attractive. I plan to have him over for dinner sometime soon."

I felt faint. *Don't work late, Richard.*

"It's actually about…well, what we were talking about earlier. About this weekend."

"I see." She smiled conspiratorially and leaned toward me. "How was he? I've heard he's quite *experienced*."

Heat flooded my cheeks, and nausea churned in my gut. I swallowed thickly, attempting to ignore the envy and insecurity suddenly rampaging through me. "You may have seen the picture of the two of us in the newest *Entertainment Today*."

She screwed up her face in an overly dramatic expression of pondering. "No, I don't think I'm familiar with that."

She was lying. And she wanted me to know she was lying. I didn't have time to puzzle out what her angle was, so I pressed on. "Well, there was one. Loralai saw it and assumed—um, assumed we're *together*. She was upset about it for some reason, so I told her I just ran into him while I was out with other people."

Charna's smile turned predatory. "She was upset, was she?"

It's now or never.

I took a fortifying breath. "Yes. So I would appreciate it very much if you wouldn't tell her otherwise."

She stared at me so long I was on the verge of fleeing for the elevator when she finally spoke. "Of course, Nora. I would never share our private conversations with someone else. What are friends for?"

Just when I thought I couldn't be more confused about this…

"Um. Right. Thank you." I started edging backward. "I, uh, need to step out for a while. Have a good morning."

I turned and was halfway to the elevator when she called after me in a cheery voice, "Goodbye, Nora! I can't wait to see you again!"

Unease was crawling up my spine by the time I reached the lobby. I couldn't trust Charna and she was going out of her way to make the fact obvious, but why not just continue with her previous hostile behavior? Why this new "besties" charade? It seemed to have something to do with her antipathy toward Loralai, but I didn't understand how I could be a pawn for her in that game.

Pushing thoughts of the confusing vampire to the back of my mind, I searched the lobby for Loralai before darting across the expanse and out into the bright sunlight. Despite it still being somewhat early, the temperature was already uncomfortably high. I was sweating by the time I reached my spot in the parking lot across the street.

I envisioned a relaxing soak in the bathtub at home as I unlocked the car door and was just starting to breathe easier when a sinister growl froze the blood in my veins.

"Where do you think you're going?"

15

THIS WAS IT. I'd squirmed out of her clutches once too often before and now it'd finally caught up with me. I clenched my car key tightly—if I was extremely lucky, it might make a serviceable shiv—before turning to face my perfectly coiffed executioner.

She stood barely an arm's length away, hands balled into fists and eyes blazing. I was careful to focus my gaze on her forehead. Her flawless, sweat-free forehead. She opened her mouth and raised her claw-tipped fingers toward me, but before she could take a single step, a hand wrapped around my forearm, scaring the wits out of me and causing me to drop my pathetic "shiv."

So much for my street cred.

In my panic, I instinctively struggled against the grip, desperate to break free and dive for my car. Maybe I could even get the door open before Loralai gutted me.

"Ms. Jensen." The male voice sounded amused.

I froze and peered up at my captor. A familiar teasing glint lit his blood-red eyes, and I could have wept at the sight.

"I apologize for startling you, Ms. Jensen, and also for my delay," said AJ. "Thank you again so much for your willingness to assist me while my secretary is on maternity leave. This case is extremely important, and I don't know what I would have done without you." He smiled pleasantly and released my arm.

"And who are you to waltz in and steal my employee?" Loralai attempted to look down her nose at him despite being several inches shorter.

"AJ Hunt, of Reese, Parker, and Hunt, Attorneys-at-Law. You may be familiar with our office. We've represented the Vasile family for several generations." He politely held out his hand, but his voice carried a threatening undertone that Loralai seemed to grasp better than I did.

She accepted his greeting but snatched her hand away as soon as could reasonably be deemed proper. "I see. But I'm afraid I must deny your request for Nora's use. My office requires her attendance."

I barely kept from scoffing. And if AJ was truly who he said, I was amazed at her brazenness in refusing him, especially after I'd witnessed her pandering to Cal and his lackeys.

"You misunderstand me, Ms. Evans." Loralai's eyes flashed at AJ's address. "My request has already been approved. I'm sure you'll find the memo in your inbox." He turned to me, putting his back dismissively in Loralai's face, and bent to retrieve my keys. "Now, Ms. Jensen, we must be going. We have a meeting at V-Corp Central that we cannot be late for."

I accepted the keys shakingly, unsure what to say, if anything. It suddenly occurred to me that Loralai could simply wait for me to turn my back before pouncing. I gulped and stayed where I was.

AJ suddenly pressed close, eliciting a nervous squeak from me. Reaching around me, he opened the car door and guided me into my seat with a gentle but insistent hand on my wrist. Waiting until I stowed my bag behind the passenger seat, he closed the door and turned back to Loralai.

"A pleasant day to you, Ms. Evans. Please alert my office if you require a temp in Ms. Jensen's absence."

I suddenly had a clear view of Loralai's seething expression. My fingers twitched toward the door lock button, but AJ beat me to it. I didn't even hear the passenger door open; he was suddenly just *there*.

As the lock clicked and I stared at him in shock, he gave me a wry expression. "I would prefer not to damage my suit today." He gestured toward the road. "Now, if you don't mind, I'm afraid I really do have a meeting at V-Corp."

I fumbled my way through starting the car, a quick glance showing me Loralai had already disappeared. We left the lot and were halfway down the block before I finally found my voice. "What was that? Since when am I supposed to be your assistant? And why didn't you tell me you're a partner in your firm and you work for the Vasiles?"

"That was me assisting you out of a precarious situation. I believe thanks are in order." He smiled at me blandly, that same infuriating gleam in his eye.

He was right, of course, but I still struggled not to scowl. "Thank you. Now how 'bout you answer my other questions?"

He chuckled at my disgruntlement. "My secretary is, indeed, out on maternity leave. I rather suspect she won't be returning to work at all, actually. Not that I blame her." His tone took on a wistful note for a moment, making me wonder what it was he envied. "Anyway, I do require a new assistant," he continued, "but no, I didn't request you to fill that role, though you are welcome to it if you choose. And yes, my firm represents the Vasiles. I didn't mention my position because I didn't believe it to be vital information. Do you find me more desirable now that you know I'm a partner?"

This time, I didn't contain my scowl as he smirked at me. "If this is how you talk to your secretary, I'm not surprised she doesn't want to come back."

"Certainly not. My secretary is happily married while you, my dear, are most assuredly not."

I glared at him as we waited at a red light, furious at his rudeness, even if it was the truth.

Wait, does that mean his teasing is actually flirting?!

My jaw nearly dropped in shock at the outrageous thought, but I couldn't help a nervous sideways glance at him as we continued on toward V-Corp's main campus. He watched the traffic, a self-satisfied grin plastered on his handsome face. I was suddenly struck by the absurdity of the situation: a suave, expensive-suit-wearing vampire lawyer being chauffeured to an important meeting with one of the most powerful companies in the world by a frumpy girl in a dirty, dented-up Toyota. I couldn't help snickering.

AJ looked over, a sincere smile replacing his smug grin. "I'm glad to hear you laugh, Ms. Jensen. It proves you won't let your circumstances defeat you."

I was surprised yet again, this time by his kindness, as I realized all his teasing and flirtations were simply a welcome distraction. I smiled to myself, and we maintained a comfortable silence as I pulled into the V-Corp parking garage and found an open spot. It wasn't until after I turned the car off that I realized I probably should have dropped him at the front door.

"Sorry," I said. "I'm not used to chauffeuring. Do you want me to take you around to the front?"

"This is fine," he replied, then opened his door. "Are you coming in?"

"Uh—do you want me to?"

He stood next to the car but leaned back down to eye level. "That depends on if you want the job or not." He winked and closed the door, heading toward the nearby elevator.

Did I want the job? I obviously couldn't go back to Jensen Publishing. At least, not until I had definite answers about my dad's will and knew how to deal with Loralai without winding up in the trash compactor. In the meantime, I could either sit at home or try to find a new job—and here was a perfectly good one, practically gift-wrapped and dropped in my lap.

And working for AJ might provide a safer avenue to figuring out what, exactly, was going on with Miroslav and the rest of the vamps.

I snatched my bag out of the backseat and hurried after my new boss.

He held the elevator for me, another smug grin on his face. "Apparently, it *does* make me more desirable," he drawled.

I debated smacking him.

We were off to a fantastic start.

———

"Do you need help with that?" AJ asked.

I hefted the banker's box of paperwork and quirked an eyebrow in challenge. "I'm the assistant. I'm supposed to carry the stuff."

The clerk looked between us with a bemused expression. AJ's important meeting turned out to be nothing more than an information gathering errand related to setting up Cal's succession as the new CEO of V-Corp. As the Vasile's lawyers, AJ's office was responsible for writing up the paperwork related to the change of leadership, as well as making all the necessary adjustments to the various wills, trust funds, and charities associated with the family.

As we returned to the elevator, I couldn't help wondering if Cal was in the same building. Remembering my cold brush-off of his concern earlier that morning, I inwardly cringed and resolved to call him as soon as I had time. I'd been nervous about the possibility of seeing him when we first arrived, but our errand had taken us to the subfloor archives rather than any corporate offices, and I sincerely doubted *Mr. Vasile* would be lurking around the basement.

Speaking of which…

"Why did *you* need to come get these files?" I asked. "Why not send a courier for them?" I knew for a fact the building housing Jensen Publishing and AJ's office kept a staff of half a dozen couriers for the use of the on-site businesses. Loralai regularly tasked them with bringing her fresh supplies from the local blood bank.

AJ quirked his eyebrow in imitation of my earlier expression. "Am I not allowed to get out and stretch my legs? Perhaps I have a secret affinity for dark, musty environments."

I rolled my eyes at his nonsense. "Maybe you should return to your crypt, then," I muttered.

"Only if you promise to return with me, my lady."

I tried and failed to stifle a smirk. *What a ridiculous flirt. Rachel would love him.* I gave him an amused sideways glance as I imagined inviting him to the next movie night.

He met my gaze and grinned back. "Actually, if you're not in too much of a hurry, I would like to make one more quick stop while we're in the building."

"It's a bit hard to be in a hurry when I'm going back to *your* office."

"Indeed. Then I guess you won't mind." He smiled and pressed the button for the top floor.

I attempted to look unconcerned even as I felt heat crawl up my neck. By the time the doors opened, I was supremely grateful for the box in my arms, as it gave my trembling fingers something to occupy them.

I followed AJ out into a stark, gleaming lobby. Floor-to-ceiling windows lining the wall behind the reception desk had me blinking uncomfortably against the light.

"Make yourself comfortable, Ms. Jensen," said AJ, gesturing to a ritzy-looking waiting area. "I'll only be a moment." He headed down the right-hand hallway with nothing but a wave to the receptionist.

They must be pretty used to him coming here.

Perching on the edge of a white upholstered couch with chrome legs and accents, I balanced the file box on my knees and settled my hands on top, afraid of leaving dust smudges on anything. I was busy appreciating the view from the additional wall of windows bordering the waiting area when the receptionist stepped in front of me.

"Can I get you anything while you wait?" she asked politely. "Coffee, water, something to eat?"

I nearly refused, but realized I was a bit thirsty. Toting the heavy file box around wasn't helping.

I should have just let AJ carry it.

"Water would be great, thank you," I replied with as grateful an expression as I could muster. I imagined she got enough imperious orders in a job like this that I wouldn't add to it if I could help it.

Her smile turned more genuine in return. "Of course! I'll be right back with that." She disappeared in the direction AJ had gone, but was back just a few moments later. They must have had a kitchenette or break area right around the corner. "Here you are, miss. Let me know if you need anything else," she said, handing me a chilled glass of water. She left an additional bottle on the glass coffee table in front of me. After setting it down, she paused briefly and glanced at me with an odd expression before hurrying back to her desk.

"Thank you!" I called after her. I took a cold, delicious sip, then shifted to the side so I could set the glass on the table without upending the box still on my lap. My fingers were already cold. The bottle she brought was one of those fancy ones with a brand name that makes people like me think it's a type of wine. I tried not to wonder how much it cost and vowed to drink every last drop—I didn't want to waste their money. I deposited the glass and wiped my damp fingers on my skirt, glancing at the array of magazines spread across the table.

Then I noticed a very familiar one lying directly next to the bottle of water.

Oh no.

I looked at the receptionist, but she quickly ducked behind her monitor and pounded away on the keyboard. I could only hope she wasn't sending out some office-wide invitation to come gawk at Tabloid Girl. By the time AJ strolled back around the corner, I was seriously considering heading back to the car to wait. He snatched the file box off my lap as I started rearranging my bag to fit the water bottle in. Tucking it easily under one arm, he gestured toward the elevator with a casual smile.

"What should I do with my glass?" I whispered, holding it up.

His smile grew. "I believe you can leave it there and Leanne will take care of it," he whispered back loud enough for the receptionist to hear.

"Oh yes, don't worry about that, miss!" she chirped from her desk.

"Thank you," I called again, narrowing my eyes at AJ as I followed him to the elevator.

"What?" he asked after pressing the call button. "Would you have preferred I take you to the kitchen so you could wash out your glass and put it away?"

"Maybe," I grumbled. Then I remembered the magazine and the receptionist's behavior and was grateful he hadn't.

We were stepping into the car when a feminine voice called out behind us, "Hold the elevator, please!"

I pressed the Door Open button at the same time AJ blocked the door with his foot. I was about to ask if he expected me to polish the scuffs out of his expensive loafers when an extremely tall, extremely gorgeous woman stepped into the car with us.

"Thank you." She also had a slight Hispanic accent.

I had never felt so small and plain before.

She gave AJ a stunning smile, her eyes lingering, and he returned it with a sly grin. I was thankfully distracted from their silent flirting by the fact that she was obviously also a vamp.

How was every new person I met these days a vampire? Were they secretly multiplying in hopes of outnumbering us? And why were they all so dang good-looking? Were attractive looks one of the main criteria for being Turned? Maybe all the decrepit old vampires got tired of looking at each other and wanted some pretty faces around for a change.

I was busy glowering at my reflection in the door and nearly missed when the woman turned her smile my way, then did a double take. "I know you!" she exclaimed.

"Uh," I responded intelligently.

"I saw your picture in *Entertainment Today!* All the girls upstairs are talking about it, but Mr. Vasile has been very tight-lipped about his beautiful mystery woman. Were you here to visit him?"

"No..." I gave AJ a helpless look, my cheeks burning.

He stepped in once again, much to my relief, offering his free hand to the vampire. "AJ Hunt, at your service." He gestured to me after releasing her hand. "Ms. Jensen is kindly assisting me on a legal project. She's here at my behest and wouldn't dream of barging in on Mr. Vasile unannounced; she has entirely too much class for that. In fact, I had to beg her to come with me, as she was so concerned about causing a distraction for the poor man."

I blushed harder than ever and wished the stupid elevator would hurry up. There was no way anyone would believe that load of rot. I couldn't wait to see the news of Caliban Vasile's desperate, pathetic stalker plastered all over tomorrow's tabloids.

To my shock, the woman pressed her hands to her chest as if she might swoon. "Oh, my goodness, that's so incredible! I've only talked to Mr. Vasile a few times, and one of them was when he was taking my job away—"

What?!

"—but he's always been so kind. He even went out of his way to make sure I received a position just as good as the first one. He's truly an extraordinary man."

I felt more insecure the longer she talked. Paranormal or not, if *this* was the kind of competition I could expect, what chance did I have?

"He's so lucky to have found someone as special as you," she sighed, completely flooring me.

I replayed her words in my head a few times to be sure she'd said what I thought. Adding to my confusion was the fact her kind expression looked completely genuine. She actually thought I was special, and that *Cal* was lucky to be with *me*, rather than looking down her perfect nose and proclaiming the opposite.

AJ, too, was smiling at me, the teasing glint missing from his eyes for once. "He is a truly lucky man," he murmured.

I blushed again and dropped my gaze, unable to continue looking at either of them. After a moment, AJ turned back to our companion. "So, you must be Sandra," he said.

"He told you what happened?" she gasped.

"Word got around."

"Well, it wasn't exactly how I expected my first day in the new position to go," she laughed.

The bell chimed, and I stepped out first, smiling to myself as they continued chatting. I *was* meeting a lot of vamps these days, but at this rate, the decent ones might soon outnumber the monsters.

16

"THIS IS REESE'S office. He is a vampire. And this is Parker's office. She is not. The conference room is next, followed by a breakroom, and the restrooms are at the end of the hall." AJ finished his tour and turned to me with an expectant look. "Questions?"

I glanced back the way we'd come, running the information over in my mind. Now that I wasn't sneaking around trying to pry secrets out of AJ, I realized the office was much more welcoming than I previously noticed, with lots of windows and well-tended houseplants. My new desk, in the anteroom of AJ's office, was across from half a dozen legal aide workstations. It seemed the firm pooled their personnel resources with the other law office on this floor, and so maintained a robust library and cubicle area to serve the various aides that came and went.

"Not about the layout," I replied. "Will I be able to get help from the other assistants or legal aides if I can't figure something out? I don't have a law degree, you know."

"Oh dear, how will I possibly cope?" said AJ dryly. He beckoned me to follow him back to his office. "I really only need you as an assistant on a personal level."

I narrowed my eyes, and he huffed a laugh. "Fine. A professional level, then. But the only help I'll need from you on legal matters will involve making copies or sending memos. Speaking of which! I need you to send a memo to Loralai." He grinned wickedly as I felt myself blanch.

"What sort of memo?" I asked, my voice wobbly. Maybe this was a mistake after all. The last thing I needed was Loralai running down here and snapping my neck in front of everyone.

AJ's expression softened a bit. "Don't worry, I'll compose it. I just need you to proofread for me and dig up her email address. The software we use here is great for collaboration—you'll see."

Deciding to trust the vamp for some unearthly reason, I settled in at my computer as AJ headed into his office. He popped back out a moment later. "Oh, and you're welcome to use your cellphone as you like. Just tell me if you need to step away to make a call, so I know to answer the phones."

He disappeared again, leaving me to ponder the differences between Jensen Publishing and the apparently much more relaxed environment at Reese, Parker, and Hunt. Something as simple as the ability to check my phone without peering over my shoulder shouldn't have felt like such a monumental improvement, but Jensen was the only employer I'd ever had. It'd been a happy, supportive workplace once upon a time, but somewhere along the way I got so used to the cloud of fear and anxiety spreading over everyone that I must have forgotten it wasn't supposed to be like that.

I grimaced as I suddenly remembered one of my professors in college describing the Boiling Frog Syndrome, where a frog put into a pot of lukewarm water wouldn't know it was in danger until it was too late—provided the water was heated gradually enough.

Apparently, my experiences weren't anything new.

I turned my attention to the computer, determined to make the most of this unexpected opportunity. A sticky note hanging from the monitor provided the default login information. After following the prompts, I found all the programs and settings were already configured, including my own company email. It seemed the IT guy AJ had waylaid when we first returned to the office did quick work.

A sudden chime startled me. A pop-up notification in the corner of my screen announced a new chat request from AJ.

A Hunt: Miss me?

I rolled my eyes.

N Jensen: Don't make me turn in my resignation already.

"I won't accept it!" AJ shouted from his office, making me snicker.

The message window chimed again.

A Hunt: Here's the memo for Loralai. It will open in your email; you just need to fill in her address and send it when you're done. It will still show as being sent from me.

A new message popped up before I even clicked on the link.

A Hunt: In case you're considering adding anything *special* to the message, you should know it sends me a copy, too.

Somehow, I didn't get the feeling AJ was telling me *not* to add anything. I shook my head at the strange vamp and opened the memo.

Ms. Evans,

It was brought to my attention that you did not receive notice of my request to employ Nora Jensen as my executive assistant for the foreseeable future.

I instructed my previous assistant to send notice of my intentions to all relevant parties last week and received confirmation that she completed the task. It seems you were regrettably overlooked.

I apologize for accidentally misleading you during our conversation earlier today. I am informing you now so as to maintain my good name as a fair and honest man.

Sincerely,

AJ Hunt

"'Fair and honest man,'" I scoffed under my breath. I noticed he didn't even include a standard signature box with his information. I pulled up the network address book and found Jensen Publishing listed. Apparently, the firm liked to keep close tabs on the V-Corp subsidiaries. After finding Loralai's address and sending the message, I stuck my head into AJ's office. "I didn't add anything to your memo. I don't think I could have made it any more ridiculous if I'd tried."

AJ gave me a look of pure innocence. "That memo was the height of professionalism."

"Uh-huh," I deadpanned. "Is this more of your version of honesty?"

"Ms. Jensen, I'm beginning to feel you don't believe I'm the upstanding person I know myself to be."

"To be frank, you make it a little difficult."

"How so?" Much to my chagrin, he looked genuinely confused.

"Well, for starters, that whole email was a flat-out lie," I replied dryly.

"Was it?" The corner of his mouth twitched suspiciously.

"Of course! You just told Loralai what you needed to so she wouldn't murder me in the parking lot."

AJ left his desk and strolled toward me, shaking his head in pity. "Oh, Ms. Jensen. You must give me more credit than that. We lawyers pride ourselves on our excellent strategy and timing. Loralai's behavior this morning simply provided the opening I needed."

I stared at him in shock. "You were *planning* this? Since when?!"

"Since it seemed necessary." He shrugged. "Now, I'm headed to lunch. Are you going out to eat or staying here? If you go out, you should plan on going with me until the situation is a bit more settled."

Still trying to wrap my mind around the fact he had made legitimate plans to rescue me from Loralai, I shook my head absently. "No, I brought lunch."

He was already heading for the elevator when I realized he was also offering to take me to lunch for as long as Loralai was lurking nearby. "Thank you!" I called after him, surprised, yet again, by his thoughtfulness.

He waved a hand over his shoulder without turning around. "Just don't get yourself killed. The carpets are the devil to replace."

I frowned but couldn't bring myself to actually be annoyed. Gathering my Tupperware of leftovers, I found my way back to the breakroom. It seemed not everyone kept the same hours as there was only one other person in the room. The girl was engrossed in a book, so I did my best not to disturb her as I heated my food and quietly settled at a different table, pulling out my phone to text Cal.

Six new messages. Five missed calls. Three voicemails. *Yikes.*

One of the calls and voicemails was from Dad's lawyers. I dealt with that one first. Thankfully, it was nothing but a courtesy call from the receptionist reminding me of my appointment with them that afternoon.

Two of the remaining calls were from Cal. The other two were from Lina and the city library. Lina's voicemail was brief, but worried. Apparently, Cal had looked up her work number after not being able to reach me. She had tried me on the library's phone immediately after hanging up with Cal, which explained the other call. Two of the text messages were also from her, seeing if I was okay and asking me to call or text her back as soon as I could. And also informing me Cal was worried out of his mind for me. Nothing like a little extra guilt... I typed out a quick reply letting her know I was fine and would fill her in after work.

The next new message was from Izzy.

Izzy: Lina called. Are you still alive?

I smiled at my friend's concern and endearing bluntness and responded with a text similar to the one I sent Lina.

My finger hovered over Cal's voicemail. I took a deep breath and steeled myself before opening it.

Nora, are you alright? I know I've already texted a bunch and I'm really sorry if you're just busy right now, but I'd much rather annoy you than find out something terrible happened. If I don't hear from you by lunch, I'm coming to your office to make sure you're okay. Please call me or text me back!

I frantically backed out of the voicemail and punched the button to call him, nearly choking on leftover noodles in my haste. It rang several times—sending my anxiety through the roof—before he answered.

"Nora! Oh, thank goodness." He sounded as keyed up as I was.

"Cal, you can't come down here! Please tell me you're not already here!" Book Girl gave me a weird look, but I ignored her.

"I was heading there now. I just stepped off V-Corp's elevator. It's actually lucky I received your call—my phone service gets screwy when I'm around the elevator here."

That explained why it rang for so long. I nearly collapsed on the table in relief.

"What's going on? Are you alright? I can still come down there."

"No! No, it's okay. I'm alright. I'm sorry I didn't answer you sooner; there was just a lot going on. I'll explain everything to you, but I don't think right now is the best time." I lowered my voice to a murmur as a man and another woman entered the breakroom. "Can I call you when I get home tonight?"

"Would you mind if I come over instead? I've been worried all morning—I'd really like to see you."

I flushed at his words. "Okay; if you really want to." Remembering my appointment, I added, "I have to meet my dad's lawyers at five, though, so I probably won't be home until at least six."

"I'll plan to be there at six, then."

"Alright. I'll let you finish your lunch break. I hope you have a good afternoon."

"Well, I'm sure it can't be any worse than this morning," he replied in a teasing voice, making me cringe a bit in guilt. *"See you soon."*

I said my goodbyes and returned to my now-cold lunch, feeling much more at ease.

When AJ returned, I was already back at my desk. An aide hurried up to him before he entered his office, asking for clarification on a task he apparently assigned her. He sent her off with an explanation, but not before the encounter inspired a question of my own.

"Am I supposed to call you Mr. Hunt?" I asked as he turned to his office, referring to the address the aide had used.

"You may if you like." His expression turned suggestive. "You may also call me devilishly handsome."

I grimaced. "Did you people even *have* sexual harassment training?"

He shrugged. "We did. The presenter asked me out to dinner afterward."

"Figures," I muttered.

He waved cheekily and sauntered off to his desk, the picture of nonchalance.

The afternoon passed quickly as I worked on a simple data entry project for AJ. When 4:30 rolled around, he let me leave early for my appointment with nothing more than a token threat to fire me.

"I haven't even filled out new hire paperwork yet," I said. "I doubt it would affect my resume too much."

"Good point." He pretended to consider before shaking his finger at me in a grandmotherly way. "Well, it seems I'll have to keep an eye on you, young lady. I don't want any shenanigans in my office."

I smirked. "I'll do my best, *Mr. Hunt.*"

After arriving for my meeting with Dad's lawyer, I was waiting in the reception area when it occurred to me—I'd spent more time in law offices today than in the entirety of my life to this point.

Not quite how I saw things going...

A door opened and a familiar salt-and-pepper-haired man beckoned me in with a smile. I followed him into his office and settled on one of the comfortable lounge chairs set before his desk.

He sat across from me and tapped a file laying before him. "It's nice to see you again, Ms. Jensen. What can I do for you today? You told my secretary it was about your father's will?"

I nodded, trying to appear more confident than I felt. "It's nice to see you, too, Mr. Barnes. Yes, I had some questions about Jensen Publishing."

He opened the file, passed me a copy of the paperwork within, and donned a pair of reading glasses. Taking up his own copy, he thumbed through a couple of pages. "Ah, here it is—page three."

I followed his direction and saw a heading with Jensen Publishing listed beneath it. The content of the paragraph made me pause in confusion over more than the complicated legal jargon. "Wait, this makes it sound like I'm supposed to inherit the company."

He gave me an odd look over the rim of his glasses. "Well, yes, of course. Was that in question?"

"Yes. It was." I was tempted to shout. "Why didn't anyone tell me?"

Putting the papers down, Mr. Barnes took off his glasses and peered at me with a thoroughly confused expression. "Ms. Jensen, I'm afraid I feel a bit lost. You signed the paperwork acknowledging your father's wishes and accepting his bequeathment of the company."

A chill ran down my spine. "No," I said, my voice sounding very small. "No, that can't be right. The only papers I signed were for the house and Dad's accounts."

Frowning, he flipped to the last page in the packet. He squinted at it briefly before turning it toward me. "Right here," he said, pointing to a signature line. "The wording on the first papers you signed accidentally omitted Jensen Publishing, so we had to make up this addendum, remember? We faxed it to you at work."

I had never in my life received a fax addressed to myself, at work or otherwise. I stared at the paper in disbelief before turning to the same page in my own packet. The words swam before my eyes.

"Mr. Barnes," I stammered. "That's not my signature."

Below the forgery was a line reserved for whoever officially witnessed my signing. The stark lines and curving loops seared into my mind.

Loralai Evans.

17

I DRUMMED MY fingers on the hood of my car, telling myself once again I was *not* worried. I was simply looking forward to seeing Nora.

Yes, that was it. Eager, not anxious.

I checked my watch for the umpteenth time. 6:37. Any minute now...

Sighing, I ran my hand through my hair. It wasn't the first time I'd given in to the nervous urge, and I was sure I looked a mess by then.

My phone rang, and I practically leaped off my perch on the hood to pull it out of my pocket.

"Hello? Nora?" I realized I hadn't actually looked at the caller ID.

"Uh, no, it's Lina."

"Oh, I'm sorry, Lina. I'm waiting for Nora, but she's running late, and I guess I'm just a little wound up after everything today."

There was a pause. Enough to halt my attempts to calm down.

"Actually, Cal, that's why I'm calling. Nora was in an accident. We're down at Central Memorial now."

A sudden ringing in my ears nearly drowned out Lina's voice.

"An *accident?* What—I mean, how did—is she alright?!" I could barely spit out the words. My hand was fisted in my hair again, but this time I thought I might yank out a chunk.

"It's alright, Cal. She's okay, just a few bumps and bruises. They're checking her over, and then they're planning to send her home."

My breath left me in a whoosh of relief. I leaned back against the car, my legs suddenly wobbly. "Thank goodness." I ran my hand over my face. "Is there anything I can do?"

"Yes, actually. I wondered if you might be able to come down here and bring her home when they're done? My sister got stuck on a double shift at work and I really need to get home to take care of my uncle."

I was already in my car by the time she finished. "Yes, I'm on my way now. I'll be there as soon as I can."

———

I entered the hospital lobby at a fast clip, making a beeline for the reception desk. There were two people ahead of me and by the time it was my turn, I was practically bouncing on my toes with impatience.

"I'm looking for Nora Jensen. She was just brought in this afternoon." I realized I had no idea when her accident happened. Had she been there since we spoke, and I never knew?

"Let me look." The receptionist tapped on her keyboard for a few moments, murmuring to herself. "Ah, yes, here she is. Room four-fourteen. The elevators are around the corner," she said, pointing past me. "Fourth floor. It'll be a left when you exit and then a right at the end of the hall. The nurses can direct you from there."

"Thank you!" I called, already turning away. Following her directions, I found myself at a nurse's station in the center of a large square of rooms. People bustled around the area and machines beeped. I stepped up to the counter, intending to get someone's attention, when my eyes drifted across the space and fell on room number 414.

"Can I help you with something?"

I met the eyes of the eager-looking woman. "Thank you, no. I see where I need to go now." Ignoring her disappointed expression, I circled the station and knocked on the room's closed door.

Lina answered it a moment later, giving me a grateful smile. "Cal! I'm glad you're here." She stepped to the side and beckoned me into the room.

I entered, feeling apprehensive. Lina had assured me Nora was fine, but still—the drive into the city hadn't been kind to my nerves. I moved around the curtain separating a bank of equipment from the rest of the room and saw her. She was sitting in a chair under the window, putting her shoes on. No hospital gown, no awful tubes and wires. I let out a breath I hadn't realized I was holding.

She stood and brushed off her skirt, her hand moving nervously to the bandage wrapped around her left forearm.

There was another peeking out of her short sleeve, a mottled bruise on her cheekbone, and dirt streaked through her hair.

She had never looked so beautiful.

"Hi," she murmured, plucking at the strap of her bag.

I stepped forward and took her gently in my arms, as I'd longed to do since that first movie night. She let out a quiet sound of surprise, and I smiled into her hair, tightening my hold only a little, wary of any unseen injuries. Her hands slid around my waist, making my heart soar.

Several long moments passed before she patted my back and whispered, "I'm really okay, Cal. You can let go."

"No," I replied, matter-of-factly. "I need this."

Unfortunately, the doctor that bustled into the room had other ideas. "Good news, Ms. Jensen—we didn't find any sign of concussion. It looks like the nurses are finished patching you up, so you're all good to go."

Aching to know what happened but resolved to wait until the time was right, I took a firm hold of Nora's hand and, snagging her bag from her shoulder, headed toward the hallway. I led her toward the elevators, politely ignoring the smug look Lina gave us as we passed.

Once we reached the lobby, Lina embraced Nora gently and murmured a few words to her. I did my best not to eavesdrop. Stepping back, Lina smiled. "I'm so glad you're okay. Call me if you need anything, alright?" Turning to me, she added, "And thank you, Cal. You really are our knight in shining armor."

Nora made a sound of protest, but her friend just waved as she walked toward the main entrance. I waited while Nora settled her account, then we stepped out into the warm evening air. I offered to bring the car around to the front so she wouldn't have to walk all the way to the lot, but she refused.

"I'm not dying," she grumbled, attempting to snatch her bag from me.

I held it out of reach and recaptured her hand, turning us toward the parking area. "I can be a gentleman without the lady in question lying on her deathbed."

She muttered something that sounded like "Stupid Cinderella," before following me with a sigh. I smiled to myself, feeling as though I'd won some small victory. The feeling grew when we reached the car and she let me help her into her seat.

I waited until we left the lot and were on the road back to her house before asking what happened.

"It was so dumb." She snorted in a self-deprecating way. "I was leaving my meeting with the lawyer and got clipped by a cyclist as I crossed the road. I guess I hit my head and passed out, because I woke up in the ambulance."

I squeezed her fingers where I held them on her lap. Now that she seemed to be getting used to the display of affection, I wasn't about to relinquish it. "I'm so sorry—that sounds awful. But I'm relieved it wasn't worse. When Lina called me and said you were in an accident, I thought *I* was going to pass out. I was terrified."

"Really?" Her voice sounded so small.

I met her uncertain gaze briefly, giving her the most reassuring smile I could manage. "Yes. That's what happens when you care for someone." Another glance revealed two pretty spots of color blooming on her cheeks as she ducked her head, and I realized with a jolt that *care* didn't seem quite an adequate word... I shook my head at myself. She was finally coming around; I couldn't risk spooking her off now.

Something to examine later.

We traveled in comfortable silence for a while before I got the sense that she wanted to say something. I waited, but she didn't speak. Rather, she seemed more and more uneasy, shifting in her seat and fidgeting with the seat belt. Finally, she pulled her hand from mine and wiped it against her skirt. I hadn't been uncomfortable holding her hand, but the gesture suggested she was.

I suddenly felt uneasy, myself. My thoughts returned unbidden to our almost-kiss in the movie theater parking lot. It'd hurt when she pulled away from me, but she claimed it wasn't for the obvious reason. Once I confessed my news about Loralai, Nora was so distracted she never explained her hesitance. I knew she had a lot to deal with and wanted to keep from adding to her burden with my own insecurities, but it didn't stop me from wondering. Those same questions came to mind now, coupled with the one I'd been trying hard to repel ever since Lina's call.

The growing worry, combined with Nora's fidgeting in my peripheral view, proved too much. "Why didn't you call me?" I blurted. It seemed I was committed now. I met her confused look with a sideways glance. "I know Lina's your close friend and you've known her a lot longer than me, but I would have come, you know. I *want* to be there for you."

I longed to reach for her hand again, but feared she would withdraw further.

"Cal—"

I braced myself for whatever was coming.

"I didn't call Lina."

What?

I gave her a puzzled look. Her expression was now faintly amused. Better than pitying or indifferent, at least.

"She's the emergency contact listed on my driver's license. I changed it after Dad died. By the time I woke up, the paramedics had already notified her. When she got to the hospital, I asked her to call you."

I was quiet for a moment, letting her words soak in. It may not have answered my questions about the movie theater, but it banished a few of the fresh worries trying to creep in. I gave her a relieved smile and tentatively reached for her hand. She smiled back and entwined her fingers with mine, swelling my heart once more.

After a moment, she cleared her throat. "I need to tell you something. Or a lot of somethings, really. I should have told you sooner, but I kept being afraid it wasn't my place to say anything since you're kind of my boss—"

I scoffed.

"—and I guess I was just scared in general." She squirmed a bit.

Concern pulling at my features once more, I pressed her hand and nodded for her to continue.

She took a deep breath and let it all out at once. "Loralai—she's been abusing me. Ever since Dad died."

Anger prickled, but I stayed quiet, waiting for her to find the words.

"She would say nasty things when no one was around before Dad passed, but after that it's like she didn't care who heard or saw anymore. It started mostly with the brain-bending but then it turned into physical stuff, too—pushing me around, pulling my hair, things like that."

She wiggled her fingers, and I realized I was clenching her hand. I loosened my grip, and she continued.

By the time we pulled into her driveway, I was fuming. I turned the car off and sat staring out the windshield, unseeing.

After witnessing the vampire's behavior during my tour of the subsidiaries, and hearing occasional, vague details from Nora, I believed the woman to be a harsh, domineering person.

I had no idea.

The things she's done... What she attempted to do only this morning!

A slight tug drew my attention. "Are you okay?" Nora asked meekly.

I wasn't sure whether I wanted to laugh or cry. After recounting an unbelievable list of atrocities committed against her, Nora was concerned for *my* well-being.

"I think...I think I need to focus on something else for a while. Otherwise, I might do something rash."

She gave me a sad-looking smile and nodded before turning to the door. I hurried to exit and help her out of the car, tucking her bag under my arm once more.

Sighing exasperatedly, she yanked on my hand. "My keys are in there, you know. I'll need to unlock the door."

"Fine," I replied archly.

When we reached the front stoop, I held out her bag so she could dig through the contents without having to hold it.

Her mouth twisted, but she shook her head in good humor. Pulling out the keys, she unlocked the door, and I followed her inside.

After removing my shoes, I turned to find her eyeing me with an air of uncertainty. "Thank you for driving me home. I imagine you need to be getting back soon."

"Nonsense. What I need is to make sure you're comfortable and taken care of." Putting a hand on the small of her back, and trying not to focus on how perfectly it fit there, I steered her toward a couch in the living room. I put her bag on the coffee table and went to the kitchen.

"You'd better not think about cooking for me," she said sternly from the doorway.

"You're supposed to be resting," I replied as I perused the contents of the refrigerator.

"I rested the whole way home. Get out of the fridge."

I narrowed my eyes. "How about a compromise: I won't cook, and you can sit at the island instead of in the living room?"

"Bossing me around my own house," she muttered, but settled on one of the stools.

I returned to the fridge.

"Hey, you said you wouldn't cook!"

"I'm not cooking," I said, selecting a few takeout cartons. "I'm microwaving."

A few minutes later, Nora directed us to the back deck, plates full of an odd combination of Chinese and breakfast food. Thanks to the longer summer days, we enjoyed a vibrant sunset as we ate. After we were both stuffed and had abandoned our plates on the wicker patio table, Nora reminisced on times spent in that very spot with her parents. Her stories matched the beauty of the scene and I felt humbled she allowed me to share it with her.

The time passed entirely too quickly. Before I knew it, Nora was bidding me goodnight as I stood on the doorstep. I tried to convince her to let me stay longer, but she flat refused.

"I draw the line at you tucking me in!" she declared.

I might have protested harder if I hadn't also wanted to ensure she got plenty of sleep after her disaster of a day.

"Thank you again," she said, leaning against the doorframe and stifling a yawn. "The first part wasn't awesome, but this turned into a really nice evening."

I smirked. That was a bit of an understatement. *On both accounts...* "You're very welcome. I'm sorry I couldn't do more."

She lifted her head to give me a narrow-eyed stare. "You fixed dinner, washed the dishes, *and* watered the houseplants. I think you did plenty."

"I could tuck you in."

She laughed. "No!"

I chuckled. Then wondered...did I dare? Nora had shared so much with me that evening, but I wasn't positive they were the things that held her back on Saturday.

I took a tentative step forward.

Her eyes widened marginally and her posture tensed. It wasn't a rejection. Not yet, anyway.

Another step. She still didn't shy away.

So slowly I might have been attempting to soothe a wild animal, I reached out and wrapped my hands around her waist. She resisted briefly then allowed me to draw her closer. Her hands fluttered a bit before settling softly on my arms.

"Nora," I whispered, dipping toward her. "You're so beautiful."

She gasped softly as our lips met, the sound sending heat coursing through me. My arms tightened instinctively, and her hands fisted in my sleeves.

I tried my best to keep the embrace gentle, mindful of her injuries as well as her trepidation, but when she threaded her fingers through my hair and angled her head to deepen the kiss, I lost it.

Desire roared through my veins, and I practically crushed her to my chest, desperate for more. I raised a hand to run my fingers through her thick, silky hair, every sensation eliciting a heady new response.

She suddenly hissed and flinched to the side, knocking some much-needed sense back into my addled mind. I loosened my hold immediately and drew back, not quite bringing myself to release her entirely. "I'm so sorry, I didn't mean to hurt you!" I searched her face, seeking a hint of what bothered her, as well as perhaps a bit of reassurance that I hadn't erred in more ways than one.

She smiled softly, setting my fears at ease. "It's okay. The bump on my head is just a bit sore, still."

I removed my hand from her hair with another apology, while mentally kicking myself. *You couldn't have touched the other side of her head?*

Nora gently pushed my arm from her waist. "I really should get some sleep, and you still have to drive home," she murmured in a tone that spoke to opposite wishes.

Fighting unsuccessfully against a goofy grin, I tucked a piece of her hair behind her ear on the non-injured side and stepped back onto the porch. "Goodnight, Nora. Thank you for a lovely evening."

She blushed. "Goodnight, Cal."

She waited until I returned to my car, a ridiculous spring in my step, before closing the door. If she'd kept watching, she would have seen me sitting in the driveway, grinning like a fool, for a full five minutes before finally leaving.

———

It wasn't until I returned home that my thoughts circled back to Loralai. Although the notion of being Nora's boss felt utterly laughable, Jensen Publishing *was* a subsidiary of V-Corp, meaning I supposedly had some measure of power over the management of that company.

A calculating smile crossed my face.

18

I LEANED AGAINST the inside of the front door for what simultaneously felt like an hour and no time at all. As soon as the heat in my cheeks started to cool, I would consider a new aspect of our kiss and start blushing all over again.

At some point, I heard Cal's car start and pull away. Apparently, he needed to take a moment, too.

Eventually, I peeled myself off the door and staggered to my bedroom, my nerves still tingling all over. I'd known before that I wanted to kiss Cal and was pretty sure the experience would be really nice, but *wow*—talk about an understatement. I couldn't stop smiling as I readied for bed and crawled under the blankets.

I lay looking up at the ceiling for a few minutes but was way too jittery to sleep, so I rolled over and grabbed my phone off the nightstand. I'll admit, I was tempted to text Cal, but managed to restrain myself. Instead, I found several new messages from my friends in our group chat.

Lina wanted to be sure we made it home safely, and I was settling in okay. Her empathy was a bit undermined by the inclusion of a winky face. She had also caught Izzy and Rachel up on what was happening while we were still at the hospital, and I had messages of concern and well-wishes for a speedy recovery from both of them.

Unfortunately, Lina's winky face set Rachel off in a whole different direction.

Rachel: OMG, Cal took u home??? Did he carry u inside?? Is he spoon feeding u?? SEND PICS!!

Rachel: Is he still there? Dont leave me hangin Nora!

Rachel: NORA! I NEED TO KNOW!

Izzy: Shut up, Rachel. She's busy smooching.

Rachel: !!

Lina: Please forgive me, Nora...

I laughed at my friends' antics, even though Izzy's comment was embarrassingly accurate. I typed a vague response but paused over the Send key.

Why shouldn't I tell my friends what happened? I was happy, and I knew they'd be happy, too, so why bottle it up?

Maybe changing my life didn't have to require huge, terrifying shifts, but simply a long series of small, bearable nudges instead.

I erased my message and started over.

Nora: He's gone now. He didn't carry me inside or spoon feed me, but he did heat up some dinner for us and stay to eat. It was nice. There wasn't any smooching. At least, not until the very end ;)

Rachel must have been staring at her message app already as her reply onslaught was immediate.

Rachel: OMG WHAAAT???????

Rachel: How was it?? Was it AMAZING???!!!!!

Rachel: Omg I think Im hyperventilating

Lina: I don't think she needs to tell us any details, Rachel... But I did tell you so, Nora :)

Rachel: Speak for urself! I need deets!

Izzy: The two of them smushed their lips together. There. Deets.

Rachel: Blech ur so BORING Izzy!

I couldn't resist joining in the teasing.

Nora: Izzy summed it up pretty well.

Rachel: Uuuughghghghgh ur the WORST! Fine. Im working on a new chapter anyway. If u wont tell me anything good Ill just have to immortalize how I imagine it for all my fans!

Izzy: You mean all 3 of us will have to hear about it again on Wednesday?

Rachel: RUDE!

Laughing, I said my goodnights, once more refusing to provide any juicy details, and turned out the light. As I smiled into the darkness of my room, feeling very content, I realized the empty house didn't feel quite so lonely that night.

"What happened?" AJ looked more serious than I'd ever seen him.

I wore a long-sleeved button-down to work, but there wasn't much I could do to hide the massive bruise on my face. To make things even better, it had transformed into some truly spectacular colors overnight.

"I got clipped by a bicycle yesterday when I was leaving my appointment," I replied sheepishly. The story was going to get nothing but more embarrassing as time went on.

Expecting a laugh, or at least an annoying smirk, AJ startled me by grabbing my arm and dragging me into his office. He closed the door behind us and turned to me with a frown, his arms crossed. "What really happened, Nora?"

I stared at him in confusion. "I just told you what happened."

"Really. You were leaving your lawyer's office and just *happened* to get run over by a cyclist."

I huffed and crossed my own arms, feeling a flush rising up my neck. "Yes, AJ. I really did get into the stupidest accident possible."

"What did he say?"

"Who?"

"The cyclist, obviously."

I threw up my hands in frustration. "He didn't *say* anything! I stepped off the curb, and a bicycle crashed into me. The guy flipped over, I hit my head and passed out, and I woke up in the ambulance. That's about the extent of it."

AJ remained unmoved in the face of my outburst, like a dog on the trail of an imaginary scent. "Did he go to the hospital, too?"

His question tripped me up. "I—I don't know. Maybe? It looked like he landed harder than I did." Why hadn't I wondered about it before?

"He didn't find you in the hospital to make sure you were all right? Or to exchange information?"

"What, am I supposed to date the guy, now that he ran me over?" I was growing more confused by the moment.

AJ rolled his eyes. "Personal injury lawsuits are extremely common. If he thought he was at fault, it would be in his best interest to make amends with you privately to avoid ending up in court. If he thought *you* were at fault, then there's a good chance he'd want to track you down to sue you."

Oh. "No, I didn't see him again. So, I shouldn't need to worry about it, right?" I asked nervously. I had enough on my plate already.

He considered my question. "Probably not. At least, not about that."

"What does that mean?" I was definitely anxious now.

"It means it seems like an awfully big coincidence for such an unlikely thing to happen only a matter of hours after someone has made a serious threat against your life."

It took me a moment to catch up with his train of thought. "You think *Loralai* had somebody run me down with a *bike*?" I wanted to laugh, but he looked so serious I didn't dare.

He stared back at me.

"But—that's ridiculous! Even if she decided not to snap my neck or drain me in some dark alley, why wouldn't she just push me out into traffic? That seems a lot more effective."

"Unless her goal isn't to end your life."

"But you just said she was threatening my life!"

"She implied as much," he conceded. "But she never explicitly said it."

"Do most vampires explicitly say when they're planning to murder you?" I asked in a flat voice.

"No, not especially. Only marginally more so than a human might."

I was tempted to throw up my hands again. "Is this supposed to be helping somehow?"

He took a deep breath and looked at the ceiling, as though praying for patience—like *I* was the one being difficult!

My defensiveness stopped in its tracks when AJ stepped forward and took me gently by the upper arms. I noticed distantly that he was especially careful with my left arm, despite not being able to see the bandages. "Nora, I'm not trying to confuse you. I told you the first time we met, you could trust me. However, you need to understand that there are many of my kind who revel in the manipulation of humans."

I opened my mouth to remind him I was *well aware of that fact,* but he continued before I could say anything, releasing me to hold up his hands in a placating manner.

"I know you know all about manipulation. But it's more than that. Even though it affects the mind, vampiric compulsion is essentially a physical ability for us, like a bully pushing someone around the playground. It's an easy, brutal kind of power.

"But to truly manipulate a person's mind, to make them believe a lie with every fiber of their being, and to ultimately not need the extrasensory influence to continue believing it—that is something many vampires devote lifetimes to perfecting.

"Holding another in thrall simply by the nature of your existence is a power that has been sought after since the dawn of time—by humans as much as paranormals.

"We all come in contact with it numerous times during our lives. The school jock strutting the halls in his letterman jacket pretending to be unaware of the crowd of sycophants trailing in his wake is no different from the office gossip playing the part of a friend in order to wheedle out the next juicy tidbit."

I thought uncomfortably of Charna's behavior the day before.

"In the end, it's all about power. And there's nothing a vampire loves so much as power." AJ wore a rather bleak look by the time he finished.

"And here I thought you loved blood the most." I hoped the weak joke might lighten the mood a bit.

He smiled, but it was grim rather than amused. "Blood is the very life-force of a creature. What greater power is there on Earth?" He wandered away to look out the window but didn't seem to expect a response.

I pondered his words. I had known for years that Loralai hated me, but lately had begun to believe she was just biding her time before killing me. She never seemed to have any qualms about telling me as much, either.

Or did she?

Wracking my brain, I couldn't think of a single instance where she told me, point blank, that she would end my life.

Save one.

I turned to where AJ still stood before the window. "Loralai told me once that when Miroslav awakened, she was going to peel the flesh from my bones. Actually, she said she would 'be free' to do it, but I'm not sure that makes a difference. I guess that's still not the actual 'I'm going to kill you' phrase, but it doesn't seem very open to interpretation."

AJ, having faced me when I started speaking, regarded me from across the room. "For a vampire, everything is open to interpretation. You're right, though, that is fairly direct." He narrowed his eyes. "But you're wrong about the other. The wording *does* matter."

"How so?" Following this other, seemingly random, train of thought felt marginally safer than stopping to consider AJ's confirmation of my impending death.

He sat at his desk, gesturing for me to take the chair opposite. I settled into the comfortable seat and gave him an expectant look. He leaned on the desk and drummed his fingers on the polished wood for a moment before responding.

"If she had simply said 'when Miroslav awakens, I'm going to kill you,' it would have been a much more neat and tidy comment to unpack."

"I don't see much *neat* about it," I muttered under my breath.

The brief quirk of his lips told me he heard me perfectly, but he didn't deign to comment. "As it is, wording it as 'I'll *be free*' to do this thing adds a lot more nuance to the situation." He drummed his fingers again. "She seems to be implying that she not only is aware of the circumstances of Miroslav and his apparent resurrection, but fully expects to be in a favorable position with him and, presumably, the Circle, whenever that event occurs."

I thought I was starting to catch on. "So...if she had phrased it the first way, it could have just been bragging that she knows about it?"

"Right. Judging by our interaction yesterday, she seems to be the type to cling faithfully to the vampire hierarchy. Although that seems rather self-defeating, given her age."

"Her age? What does that have to do with anything?"

He gave me a wounded look. "Dear Ms. Jensen, don't tell me you've already forgotten our first meeting? And here I was clinging to it as the glorious foundation of our great romance."

If I rolled my eyes any harder, I would've given myself a headache. "Yes, I remember our first meeting." But somehow, I had never applied the newfound knowledge to the vampires in my workplace. "Her eyes are pretty bright— you said that means a vampire is young, right?"

"Correct. I imagine she's no older than fifty."

"Wow. She must be raiding her daughter's closet."

He smirked. "I can't imagine the flattering things you must say about me when I'm not around."

"At least you don't wear leather skirts and five-inch heels."

"Indeed. My calves are sculpted enough as it is."

I laughed outright. "Okay, okay, let's get back to the important stuff," I said, shaking my head. "Loralai is apparently a baby vamp, but thinks the hierarchy is important. I assume it must be based on age?" AJ nodded. "So, she doesn't rank high but must have some kind of in with important people. At least, enough to believe she's gonna warrant notice from Miroslav when he shows up." I leaned my head on the back of the chair and chewed on my lip, trying to make sense of things.

"After our previous rendezvous, I made some inquiries. I haven't heard from all my sources yet, but the information received so far indicates the Vampire Elite are preparing for something big. Something that's expected to happen very soon—even by human standards." AJ gave me a weighted look.

"That's gotta be Miroslav, then. Even the news has been talking about some unusual stirrings in the vamp community," I said, remembering the headlines I had seen weeks ago. I stood and paced in front of the desk. I felt like we were still missing some crucial piece of information. "Charna mentioned Miroslav once, too, but she was using it like a threat *against* Loralai. One of them must have a better grasp of the situation than the other one, but how do we tell which?"

"Or neither does, and they're both relying on opposite sources of unreliable gossip," he replied in a dry tone.

"Possibly. But if the gossip was that prevalent, wouldn't you have heard something, too?" Perhaps a tad insulting, but he didn't seem like the type to get his feathers ruffled easily.

He nodded in a manner that suggested I'd made a fair point.

"Although I think there would have to be a fair bit of gossip involved, regardless," I went on. "I don't know much about Charna, beyond the fact she seems to despise Loralai, but she doesn't strike me as someone that would be much farther up the totem pole than her, either. Although that still doesn't explain how they seem to know so much that you don't, and from what you said to her yesterday, am I right in assuming you've got a lot more pull than Loralai?"

"You are, in a way. I've never spent much time catering to the Elite, but I do have more status than her purely by nature of my age. My connection with the Vasiles gives me an added boost as well."

That gave me pause. "Loralai practically worships the ground Cal walks on, but he's a human. Does she think V-Corp's connection with the vampires will make them excuse any atrocities the vamps are planning to commit once Miroslav's back? They can't exactly shield anyone from the repercussions if vamps start going on murder sprees." For the first time, I began to wonder why she'd been so obsessed with taking over some unimportant local publishing house.

AJ narrowed his eyes. "Or she believes the Vasiles are directly connected to Miroslav himself and wants to stay in their good graces."

"Is that even possible?" How would a regular human family, regardless of how rich they were, have ties to the father of all vampires? Especially considering he had apparently been in a coma for centuries.

And, more importantly, wouldn't Cal have told me if they did?

19

I DIDN'T GET a chance to ask Cal about Miroslav before the PLS meeting on Wednesday. We talked on the phone Tuesday evening, but I felt like it was something that needed to be said in person, so our conversation was lighthearted, if slightly awkward, instead. Awkward in that I didn't know how to broach the subject of what had happened between us the previous night and wasn't sure if I should, anyway. He seemed to be content to follow my lead on the matter, resulting in a sort of hesitant dance around the topic.

Wednesday evening arrived and my friends and I were once again sprawled around my living room, this time in tank tops and shorts, with the air conditioning blasting through the lingering swelter of the day. Even Izzy managed a goth summer look, with a purple and black bustier and matching skirt.

Only Rachel was unaffected by the heat. She sat at her desk in a cozy-looking sweater, as chipper as ever. *"So, then she starts talking about how much she misses her hairdresser and how the cut never turns out quite right."* Rachel rolled her eyes. *"I'm positive I could do an awesome job, if she would just let me try again!"*

Rachel's mom had apparently made the mistake of letting Rachel help cut her hair early in their underground tenure. She'd been forbidden from coming near her mother with scissors ever since.

I'd always wondered how someone on a first-name basis with their hairdresser wound up as an extreme end-of-times prepper.

"Maybe you should practice on the cat first," suggested Izzy, draped over the arm of the blue lounger.

"I'm not allowed near Tam with scissors, either," sighed Rachel sadly.

Lina coughed and met my gaze, her eyes full of mirth. "I'm sorry, Rachel," she said. "What if you cut your own hair sometime? Show your mom you can be trusted with it?"

"She insists on cutting it for me... But maybe I can do it after she goes to bed! Then she'll see my awesome new style as soon as she wakes up!" Rachel warmed to the idea quickly, while Lina appeared to regret the suggestion.

"Oh, I don't know if that's a good idea—"

"It's brilliant, Lina! Hold on, I'll be right back!" Rachel ran off before Lina could say anything else.

Our poor friend gave Izzy and me a mournful look. "You don't think she'll tell her mom it was my idea, do you?"

"Only if it turns out awful," Izzy reassured her.

Rachel returned with a dog-eared copy of a dated hairstyle magazine. I thought I remembered seeing the same issue when I went to the salon to get styled for my junior prom. She waved it at us before thumbing through the pages excitedly. *"Now I just need to find the perfect look!"*

As she searched for hair inspiration, occasionally holding up options for us to critique, I debated about the best way to broach the Miroslav topic. I hadn't told Lina any more about it since I first approached AJ.

I finally decided there was no tactful or non-abrupt way for it. "Do you guys remember learning about Miroslav in school?"

Izzy flopped her head toward me on the armrest of her chair. "Wasn't he some old vampire?"

"Oh yes, he was the Original Vampire, the father of the entire race!" Rachel replied, surprising the rest of us. Considering her mother moved them underground entirely because of the paranormals, she didn't seem like she'd be an expert on the topic. She shrugged at our expressions. *"I can do a web search."*

Izzy snorted.

"Have you found out more about him coming back?" Lina asked.

I nodded as Rachel squealed, *"What do you mean, coming back?!"*

After filling them in on what I had previously told Lina, I recounted the events of the last week, ending with the conversation I had with AJ the day before.

Everyone was quiet for several minutes.

Rachel was the one to break the silence. *"Um, congratulations on the new job, I guess?"* She cringed even as she said it.

I chuckled. "Thank you. It seems a lot less life-threatening than the last one, so that's always good."

"The news has been talking about the vampires a lot lately but trying to stay low key about it. This really is happening, isn't it?" Izzy actually sounded slightly worried.

"I think so," I replied, grimacing. "Even if AJ is able to find out for sure, what do we do? Are we supposed to warn people?"

"*What if we do and the vampires come after us first?!*" Rachel voiced a fear we were probably all feeling.

"Have you talked to Cal yet?" Lina asked quietly.

"No. We're having dinner tomorrow night."

My friends were silent again.

"*What if...*" Rachel hesitated. "*What if he* does *know about it?*"

The thought felt like a kick in the gut. "Then, I'll try to find out everything he knows, and we'll go from there," I said decisively, my voice only wobbling a little.

Rachel and Lina gave me sympathetic looks.

"He might not know. He still hasn't even taken over V-Corp yet. Something like this probably qualifies as one of those dirty little secrets people only find out once they're in up to their ears," Izzy pointed out.

"*If they call this a little secret, I'd hate to see one of the big ones,*" Rachel muttered.

I was grateful for Izzy's reassurance but tried not to get my hopes up. If I prepared for the worst, I couldn't be too let down.

––––––––––

Driving to the restaurant the following evening, I kept up a steady stream of mostly ineffective "positive" self-talk. AJ still hadn't heard from his other sources, and I became increasingly more anxious throughout the day at the thought of having to talk to Cal about it. He wanted to pick me up for dinner, but I didn't think I'd be able to bear the car ride, either before or after the conversation. Instead, I made a lame excuse about needing to run an errand in that part of town anyway and said I'd meet him there.

I arrived at the place, a fancy Italian restaurant I'd only ever driven past. I parked in a cheap lot down the street rather than embarrassing myself with the valet parking and hurried up the block, already regretting the heels I'd chosen to wear. Comfort should have overruled whatever the restaurant thought of my style, especially if I wound up needing to make a weepy getaway.

Cal met me outside the entrance with a brilliant smile and a beautiful bouquet of pink lilies and red roses interspersed with wispy ferns and baby's breath.

I swallowed hard past the sudden lump in my throat. "Thank you," I managed, giving him a weak smile in return.

He ducked his head toward me as he offered the flowers and I, in my anxiety-riddled state, noticeably startled and turned my cheek to his kiss. Internally wincing, I made a show of smelling the bouquet, hoping to cover the slip. He thankfully didn't comment on it, although his smile was more subdued as he opened the door for me.

The maitre d' paraded us through the entire restaurant, giving ample opportunity for every swanky-looking patron there to get an eyeful, and for me to seriously regret ever agreeing to come. No matter how the conversation went, there was guaranteed to be a crowd of witnesses.

We were finally seated at a relatively private booth. At least I wouldn't have to worry about anyone else overhearing, though I'd still have to face the sea of overly interested diners if an abrupt exit became necessary.

Cal took the bouquet from me and laid it on the end of the table—a thoughtful gesture, albeit one that took away one of my objects of distraction. I clenched the strap of my purse instead, my palms already turning clammy.

Cal, unaware of the true source of my unease, gave me an apologetic look. "I'm sorry for all the looks. I wasn't expecting this many people on a Thursday evening."

I glanced around, noting the occasional head still turned our way. "Maybe you should have reserved the whole place."

He laughed. "I'll be sure to do that next time."

My answering smile was more of a grimace.

His forehead creased, and he reached across the table to take my hand. I reluctantly allowed the gesture. "What's wrong? You've been subdued all week. I know a lot has happened lately, but I thought maybe, after Monday night..." A bit of color appeared on his cheeks, and he cleared his throat. "I just thought we were on the same page now."

I tugged my hand away and picked at my nails, unsure what to say or how to say it, trying hard to ignore Cal's crestfallen expression and the heat building behind my eyes.

Why does everything in my life fall apart?

The waiter chose this opportune moment to arrive. When asked if we were ready to order, Cal looked to me, seemingly giving me the opportunity to end the night before it even began.

I picked up my menu with trembling fingers. "I'm still looking," I mumbled, waving away the offer of something other than water to drink. Cal opened his own menu, and we sat in silence until the waiter reappeared.

Since I hadn't been able to focus on a single word while hiding behind my menu, I selected an entree at random and sat quietly, trying to bolster my nerves, while Cal ordered. "Should I ask them to put it in a to-go box?" he asked, once the waiter was out of earshot.

Ignoring the pang his comment caused, I squeezed my eyes shut and took a deep breath. "Cal, is your family connected to Miroslav?"

Obviously taken aback, he seemed to flounder for a moment before comprehending the abrupt question. He shook his head, closing his own eyes briefly. "Miroslav...the Original Vampire?" I nodded at his inquiring look. "I don't believe so. One of my cousins is a vampire, and I think there might be a shifter somewhere among my more distant relatives, but I don't know of any connections to Miroslav himself."

His answer didn't provide the overwhelming relief I'd hoped for. Izzy's comment about Cal not knowing for sure rang in my ears. Was it possible the information had been kept from him and he was about to become unknowingly immersed in the situation through his inheritance of V-Corp?

"Why do you ask? Is that what's been bothering you?" He looked more confused than I'd ever seen him.

Now I was even more unsure about what to do. Should I confide in him and hope his family wasn't about to feed him a completely different narrative, putting him in some kind of split loyalty predicament? Or should I keep quiet and try to distance myself from the whole situation?

Remembering my friends' fear, and even AJ's worry, decided for me. Whether or not I had a future in his life, he deserved a fair warning.

"I met someone at work," I began and immediately kicked myself for the choice of words. Cal's eyes widened, and I winced as I remembered his own use of the phrase and my reaction to it. "Not like that," I amended, giving him a wobbly smile. He returned it with evident relief, and I continued. "I ran into him in the elevator one night as I was leaving, and he told me some interesting things about vampires."

I told him what I'd overheard from Loralai and Charna about Miroslav, as well as the sort-of investigation into it that AJ, and now my PLS friends, were helping me with. I kept a few tidbits to myself that didn't seem relevant, like AJ's good looks and constant flirtation.

I also didn't tell him I had left Jensen Publishing and was now working for the vamp or that AJ was one of Cal's family lawyers, although I wasn't quite sure why I chose to omit it. By the lack of recognition of the name, I assumed AJ must have only interacted with Cal's mother.

"Wow. That's a lot to take in." Cal rubbed his chin in thought. "Now that you mention it, I remember seeing some of those news articles, although I can't say I've paid much attention to them."

"Same here. I didn't even realize there were more of them than usual until just recently."

Cal nodded absently. "So, this AJ, he suspects my family has something to do with Miroslav's return?"

"Well...not exactly." When he phrased it like that, it sounded like we were preparing to bring charges against him or something. "We were trying to figure out Loralai and Charna's behavior, and I wondered about their awe of you since they obviously don't like humans in general. AJ thought maybe *they* believe you have something to do with him."

"Ah."

The response wasn't exactly illuminating, and I began to feel nervous for a whole new reason. Did Cal believe I'd been snooping around in his affairs with the help of some random other guy, all while he'd been gallantly trying to woo me?

I swallowed hard. *Not a flattering portrayal of myself.*

"Cal, I—" I wasn't even sure what to say. He gave me a carefully neutral look. "I wasn't looking into you or anything. We were just trying to find out about Miroslav. This was the first time it had anything to do with you, so I knew I had to ask you directly."

His expression didn't change.

The waiter arrived with our orders and Cal busied himself with his food, studiously avoiding eye contact. Unease twisted in my gut. I had obviously screwed up, but I wasn't sure how or where, or even how to start making amends. If I said I was sorry, what were the odds he'd ask me what for, leaving me in the awful position of admitting I didn't know and thereby making everything worse?

I picked at my own plate, my appetite gone.

Maybe he's upset because you were right about his family and Miroslav, but he was never going to tell you.

The sinister, unwelcome voice in the back of my mind made me want to pound my head on the table. Even Loralai's brain-bending had never made me feel so confused and anxious before.

The meal seemed to last for ages, although I could tell Cal was eating as quickly as could still be considered polite. It felt like a vise had taken hold of my heart and was tightening with each long minute of silence that passed.

By the time our plates were removed, and Cal requested the check, I wondered if I could even make it to the door without completely falling apart. Thankfully, the waiter processed the payment in record time. Distantly, I noticed he didn't seem to be waiting on any table besides ours.

I stood and, at Cal's gesture, preceded him back through the restaurant, doing my utmost to ignore the judgmental looks from all the people we had arrived after and were now leaving before.

When we stepped outside, I turned to say goodnight, desperate to get away from this disaster, and saw he brought the flowers from the table. In my fog of emotion, I'd forgotten them. Truth be told, even if I had remembered, I would have expected him to just abandon them on the table at this point.

"Where did you park?" he murmured.

"Down the street." I gestured vaguely over my shoulder.

He nodded and stepped away from the entrance in the indicated direction. "I'll walk you to your car."

I flushed. "That's not necessary."

"Of course it is. It's getting late—"

It was still light out.

"—and I'd never forgive myself if I didn't walk with you and something happened."

Considering I'd been run down by a bicycle a few days prior, I could hardly argue the point. Narrowing my eyes at the shamelessly eavesdropping valet attendants, I accepted and set off down the street, wishing once more I'd opted for sensible shoes.

Cal, despite politely placing himself between me and the street, didn't say another word for the duration of the walk. Granted, it was only half a block down and then part way up the first ramp of the parking garage, but it might as well have been across the country for how shot my nerves were by the time we arrived. I quickly unlocked my car, intent on leaving as soon as possible.

The sound of a throat clearing halted my flight. Reluctantly, I turned around. Cal held out the bouquet, his face still an unreadable mask. Slowly, I wrapped trembling fingers around the stems. He didn't let go.

We stood frozen, staring at each other, for an endless moment.

"Nora." He spoke so quietly I nearly didn't hear him. "Will you ever be able to trust me?"

"I-I do trust you," I stammered, taken aback.

He gave me a mournful look that caused a painful twinge in my heart.

"You said you weren't looking into my family. That you told me as soon as something came up that involved me."

I slowly nodded, feeling like it was somehow the wrong response.

"You were assaulted. Your life was threatened—and, apparently, the lives of humanity at large. But you don't believe any of those are things that might concern me?"

I flushed hot and then cold. "No! I mean, yes! I mean..." My fingers tightened convulsively around the flowers, jerking them toward me.

Cal retained his grip and followed the bouquet a step nearer. "If you had withdrawn into yourself, hiding what was going on and trying to work through it alone, I would have at least understood. But instead, you turned to a complete stranger! Someone who could have been tied up in this mess already and decided you were getting too nosy for your own good. And then what? I certainly wouldn't have had any idea what happened. Would Lina, or Izzy, or Rachel? Would your coworkers even know?"

The obviousness of his point hit me like a bolt of lightning. As far as I knew, AJ had worked in the same building as Loralai for years. The fact that they weren't even acquaintances suddenly seemed very strange.

The odds of AJ being the same kind of sick psycho as Loralai were much higher than the calm, level-headed person he turned out to be. So why had I never even *thought* to tell anyone until just a couple of days ago?

A memory of my father suddenly washed over me.

"Do you have any plans this weekend, Nora?" he asked.

I laughed as I fluffed the pillows around him. "You know I don't, Dad."

"Why not? Don't tell me you've already turned down all those poor boys on campus."

"Hardly." I rolled my eyes. "Besides, I'm too busy to date. Between classes and homework and my job and keeping you company, when would I ever have time for a boyfriend?"

Dad shifted into a more comfortable position, a pained expression briefly crossing his face at the movement. I suppressed a wince of my own. I knew he didn't like it when I worried. "Well, you could start by keeping me less company," he said in a mock annoyed tone.

I smirked. "Is that so?"

He nodded archly. "I'm perfectly content here by myself. Besides, I'm an old man. I've already had my fun."

I didn't bother to point out that forty-seven was hardly old.

"You're just starting your life, sweetheart," he continued. "You need to get out there, make new friends, go on adventures, find someone wonderful to love." He sighed happily, no doubt remembering his own adventures with my mother.

I smiled at him. "I will, Dad. But you need to get better first so you can properly intimidate whoever the unlucky guy turns out to be."

He chuckled and patted my hand where it lay near his side on the bedspread. "I think you mean completely lucky. No one who catches my daughter's eye would be anything less."

I blushed.

He laid his head back and closed his eyes. "When are you going to bring your friends over again? I like those girls—especially that Rachel."

"I can ask them any time you like, Dad," I replied with a chuckle. "Rachel actually had the idea of us getting together to work on our writing after this class ends."

Dad squeezed my hand. "I think that's a great idea. Everyone needs a family to love and support them, Nora. Just remember: family often has nothing to do with blood."

I gasped and choked on a cry. Covering my mouth with both hands, I felt my knees buckle. Cal was suddenly there, his arms wrapped around me, murmuring against my hair as wracking sobs overcame me.

Some amount of time later, once my tears had mostly turned to sniffles, I reluctantly pushed away from his shoulder. Appalled by the wreck I'd made of his shirt, I apologized and tried to step out of his arms, mortified by my display.

He just smiled and gently pressed my waist, drawing me back against his chest. One hand traveled to my hair, guiding me to his dry shoulder this time. "Don't worry," he whispered as he began smoothing my hair over my shoulder in gentle, relaxing strokes. "It's machine washable."

I gave a watery chuckle as I leaned against him, still feeling a bit dazed. "That's good," I murmured back. "I'd hate to run up your dry-cleaning bill."

I felt him smile against my hair as his arms tightened briefly.

Pulling back enough to look at him, I dabbed my eyes. No doubt what little makeup I'd been wearing was an utter disaster. "I'm sorry," I whispered. "I never meant to hurt you. And you're right, I've been handling everything so stupidly. It's a miracle nothing worse happened."

Cal's expression turned a wry. "I would definitely never call you stupid. And I forgive you. As much as I want to be here for you, I want you to be safe and happy even more. If you don't feel you can have that with me, that's okay—I never want to make you feel pressured or anxious. If I can't help ease the burdens you already have in your life, then it's better if I just remove myself rather than make things worse for you."

"Oh, Cal." I felt fresh tears welling up. "You've never done anything but be kind and supportive." My dad's words replayed in my mind, hitting home even harder. I sniffled loudly. *"I'm* the one that keeps screwing everything up."

Cal's fingers brushed my chin, gently raising my face until my eyes met his. "If by 'screw everything up' you mean introduce me to the most wonderful woman I've ever met and make me hope for a life I never even dreamed possible, then yes, you definitely have irreparably screwed everything up."

I gave a breathy laugh, and his smile softened in return. Leaning forward, he gently pressed his lips to mine. The tender kiss lingered, spreading warmth all the way to my toes. While it lacked the heat of our first, it seemed to contain something else instead. A promise, maybe? Something that made the future suddenly appear much brighter and my obstacles much less daunting.

Dad's advice was spot on. I needed a family. It was time I stopped running from the one right in front of me.

20

"I FOUND HIM!" AJ slapped a folder down on my desk, startling me out of my chair.

"Found *who?*" I glared at him, attempting to get my heart rate back under control.

He tapped the manilla cover and gave me a smug grin. "Miroslav."

I gaped for a moment before plopping back into my seat and opening the file. An assortment of newspaper clippings, memo-style documents, and web print-offs greeted me. AJ pulled a chair around from in front of my desk and sat by my side, scooching as close as possible and jostling me in the process. Ignoring my exasperated look, he started pulling items out of the file and arranging them on the desk.

I examined the papers closest to me while I waited for him to finish.

Market Report Shows Substantial Increase in Stock Purchases Made by Vampire Elite.

Opinion: Vampires Consolidating Political Power to the Local Region.

Woman Claims Vampires Abducted Husband for Satanic Ritual.

"What is all this? What's it have to do with Miroslav?"

"It's the breadcrumbs that are going to lead us to him." AJ finished laying out the papers and sat back to view the final product.

"I thought you said you already found him," I said as I continued to look over the seemingly random pile of information.

"It requires a fair bit of reading between the lines. And I'm still working on what he's planning. Or what the Circle is planning for him."

I studied the pages with increased interest but couldn't discern any obvious clues pointing to Miroslav's location or scheduled reemergence. "Okay—care to share it with the rest of us?"

"Of course! You only needed to ask." I rolled my eyes at his smirk but leaned forward eagerly as he pointed to the first paper on the top left of the grid. "This one got me started in the right direction. It's a pretty dry account of a local homeowners association meeting from a few years ago. Lots of drivel about yard maintenance and leash rules, but then there's one tiny part during the questions portion where some old lady wanted to know why the vampires that owned the house behind hers didn't have to follow the HOA rules. She complained they had a generator that violated the 'Noise' and 'Beautification' statutes. The board brushed it off, but right at the end, she said if they don't do something about it, she's going to move; said she's listened to the generator for the last *seventeen years* and she can't take it another day."

"Wow. That really sucks for her, but what does it mean for us?"

AJ's eyes flashed eagerly, all traces of his usual teasing and smarminess lost in excitement. "It means there's a hibernating vampire in that house."

He pulled several more pages toward us while I attempted to understand his logic. "How could you possibly know that, though? Maybe the owners just have lousy wiring and don't want their food to go bad during an outage."

He shot me an amused look. "Maybe, except for a few more clues." He tapped a paper that appeared to be a property deed. "The house in question was purchased by a member of the Vampire Elite in 1922. I did a little social networking and determined several members of the Circle have lived there ever since."

He paused to lay a new paper on top. "Poor old Mrs. Gimmel, who just wanted a little peace and quiet, moved into her house seventeen years before that HOA meeting."

"So, the generator was already there when she moved in," I said.

"Right. The HOA didn't keep very good records until more recently, but *utility* records," he switched papers again, "tell us the thing has been in operation ever since it was first installed in 1986." He briefly pointed to a stapled collection of pages. "The individual unit has been replaced periodically, but there has been some kind of generator connected to that house for several decades now."

"Okay... But I still don't understand what a generator has to do with a hibernating vampire."

"We need very specific environmental conditions in order to hibernate at all, and to do so for an extended period makes everything even more difficult to maintain. The stories about crypts and such came about because keeping everything adequately dark and cool is much easier underground. If the vampires fashioned some kind of sealed environment in the house, a generator would ensure the conditions were always ideal."

"That makes sense." I gestured for him to continue.

Stacking those papers to the side, he picked up a photocopy of a newspaper article titled *Local Residence Drives Ice Market*. "This was printed in the 30s. Even if there were half a dozen iceboxes in that house, they wouldn't need this much ice. Hibernation requires a dry environment, so they would need to essentially build a room within a room and fill the space between with ice, thereby keeping it cold enough without producing too much humidity."

Apprehension was forming a knot in my stomach. "Okay," I said again, drawing out the word. "So, it's most likely a hibernating vampire. But how can you be sure it's Miroslav?"

"That requires a bit more deduction, unfortunately. Because of his age, and the obvious secrecy of our race, we'll never find something that specifically says what happened to him or when, without having a direct line to the Circle of Elders. With that in mind, let's begin with the fact that there is not a vampire in our known history who has survived hibernation for longer than fifty years."

I gestured toward the ice article. "Until now."

AJ nodded. "Exactly. Vampires have long mourned the fact that we are seemingly unable to hibernate for long stretches. Many get bored with day-to-day living and would prefer to just wake up every so often and experience the amusements of a brand-new world for a decade or two. If someone had figured out how to hibernate for the past hundred years, we all would have heard about it."

I studied his profile for a moment. "Would *you* prefer that?"

He smiled and bumped my shoulder with his own. "No. I learned what's important in life a long time ago and intend to enjoy it for as long as I'm able."

I smiled in return before turning back to the collection of papers. "Okay. What's next?"

"So. We have an unknown vampire that's been secretly hibernating for at least a hundred years in a house populated by a portion of the Circle of Elders. The Circle being responsible for, if you didn't know, the affirmation of devotion and subservience to our creator, Miroslav."

"Really? I thought they were, like, your Parliament. That sounds more like a religious thing."

He shrugged. "It's a combination of the two. I never concerned myself much with them." His expression turned teasing. "My mama taught me to say my prayers and go to church on Sunday."

This was so completely contrary to every legend ever told about vampires, I couldn't help but gape at him.

Ignoring my bewilderment, he went on, "Even though we can't say with absolute certainty that it's Miroslav, we can get a few more clues from another direction."

Adding several pages to the discard pile he'd made to the side, he spread the remaining documents out before us. They consisted largely of financial reports and records, with a few random tabloid type pieces thrown in.

"After going through these, especially once I noticed the connections between them, I believe the Elite are preparing for something major to occur. They've been consolidating a lot of assets, buying up more investments, solidifying their positions with numerous holdings within the government and private sector, both." AJ pointed to the various pages as he spoke. "I'm not exactly a financial expert, but it appears as though they are doing all of this in a way that actually narrows the major spheres of power within the vampire community. Why else would they suddenly start consolidating their networks of influence even as they snatch up more power within human society unless they were preparing a place at the very top of our hierarchy for *someone* to step into?"

Why, indeed? "And this only recently started?" I asked.

"Within the last five years," AJ confirmed.

Five years wasn't exactly overnight for a human, but with the news stories increasing in frequency, paired with the comments from Loralai and Charna, it seemed likely whatever the vampires were planning would be soon.

I gestured to the article I'd noticed earlier about the abducted husband. "What about this? It just looks like the usual tabloid nonsense."

"It does, and it's probably complete fiction, but the ritual they describe is very similar to something I heard about when I was much younger. With everything else we're discovering, it seemed unlikely to be a coincidence. I haven't been able to track down any more information on it yet, but I'm still looking."

I skimmed the paper, pausing to read through the description of an occult ritual apparently designed to strip away a human's soul to allow for demonic possession. I shuddered and quickly added the page to the discard pile.

AJ gave me a half-smile. "Not to worry—vampires can't actually possess anyone."

"Well, *that's* something," I responded dryly as I helped him gather up the papers and return them to the file.

We sat in silence for a few moments afterward, both seemingly lost in our own disquieting thoughts. At least, I know I was.

"What should we do?" I murmured, thinking back to the conversation with my friends. "What *can* we do?"

The vamp returned his chair to its place in front of my desk and stood quietly, examining the small potted plant sitting next to my computer monitor. "I'm not sure," he said at last. "I don't know what the Circle is hoping to accomplish by this, but I do know the lore surrounding the first dominion of Miroslav." He gave me a grave look. "It's not something I want to see repeated."

I swallowed hard and nodded, unsure what else there was to say. If a vampire as confident as AJ was expecting the worst, what hope was there for us puny humans?

"Do you mind if I tell my friends what you've found?" I asked. "They've been helping me research, too."

He shook his head, and I turned away to dig my phone out of my bag. After the conversation with Cal, I was determined to uphold my newfound dedication to the little family unit that had formed around me when I wasn't looking. I'd started a new group text with the girls and Cal in order to keep everyone up to date on the Miroslav situation and wanted to share AJ's information as soon as possible, so I didn't forget anything.

"Nora." AJ's voice close behind me startled me once again. I swiveled my chair around to peer up at him. "I know this is a lot to understand and accept. But no matter what happens, I promise to do my best to keep you safe through whatever is coming."

My mouth worked for a moment, but no sound came out. "Why?" I finally blurted.

"Because your survival is important." He didn't wait for a response this time, instead heading back into his office and leaving me staring after him in confusion.

I shook off the odd moment and returned to my phone, resolving to puzzle through his peculiar behavior later.

Nora: Found out a bunch of new info on Miroslav. Can we meet up tonight to discuss?

Lina: I have a couple hours free after my shift ends.

Cal: Definitely! Do you want to meet at your house again?

Izzy: Okay.

Rachel: Absolutely!! I printed a ton of stuff off the web too!!

Nora: Are any of the meeting rooms available, Lina? It'd save everyone the drive out to my place.

Lina: Yes, there's only one booked so far. I'll sign us up for 5:30.

Nora: Perfect, thanks. See you there.

Cal: Can't wait!

I blushed a bit at Cal's response, and sternly reminded myself we were going to discuss serious—possibly deadly— things, not get all mushy.

"Myself" didn't listen very well.

A separate text that arrived a moment later helped.

Rachel: U cant make out in the LIBRARY Nora!!!

A slew of angry, disappointed, and possibly haughty emojis followed. Since the bunker didn't get regular cell reception, Rachel used a web application to text and seemed to have a never-ending supply of new and exciting animated faces to bombard us with.

I chuckled before responding with a shrugging emoji, knowing it'd leave her in a tizzy.

Sure enough, she responded promptly.

Rachel: Dont SHRUG about this! Dont u even care about ur relationship?? It needs care and devotion so it can thrive! Meeting up w/ friends to talk about dead people and the end of the world ISNT care and devotion!!!!!

A follow-up appeared immediately.

Rachel: Unless ur Izzy....

I snorted to myself but couldn't deny it. Only a man who could discuss death and decay like a connoisseur would turn our dear Izzy's head. I tapped out a reply and returned my phone to my bag.

Nora: You make it sound like Cal's a houseplant. Besides, you're the romance writer—don't the best relationships thrive in adversity? I've gotta get back to work. See you tonight.

21

SHORTLY BEFORE MY shift ended that afternoon, I organized a copied set of AJ's information to help me remember everything I wanted to tell Cal and the girls. I initially asked the vamp if he would just go with me and explain everything himself, despite the thought of him and Cal meeting causing me a bit of apprehension, but he had a prior engagement already scheduled for the evening.

I was thumbing through the pages and repeating the information to myself a final time when I heard my phone vibrating from inside my bag in the desk drawer. Pulling it out, I saw there was an incoming call from an unknown number. The area code was local, so I answered.

"Hello?"

"Nooora, dear! How are you?"

"Uh—Charna?"

"Of course! I've missed you at work these last few days—I hope you've not come down with something..."

With everything else going on, I'd nearly forgotten about Charna's strange behavior on Monday. "Oh, um. No, I'm not sick. I'm actually working for, uh, another company. Temporarily." I felt uncomfortable telling her I was still in the same building. I might have been surprised Loralai didn't say anything about my leaving with how angry she was, but having seen how much the two vamps hated each other...it didn't seem that surprising after all.

"Interesting! HR said you were going to be gone for a while, but I thought you were just taking a vacation. Did someone else poach you away from us?"

"Not exactly. They just need me for a temporary project. Loralai approved it." I smirked at the blatant lie.

"Oh, I understand now." I could hear the answering smirk in Charna's voice. *"Are you enjoying your time there?"*

I glanced through the door toward AJ's desk. He was reading over the case files I'd collected for him a half-hour prior. "Yes, I am. Everyone here is nice, and my boss is very understanding." I realized a moment too late how that statement might sound to my former coworker, but didn't try to backpedal. I still had no idea what game Charna was playing, but figured I might as well be brutally honest. If nothing else, maybe it would startle some honesty out of her in return.

"I'm so glad to hear that! I'm afraid your talents were terribly wasted here at the publisher. You deserve a position where you can shine and prove your worth to the world."

I felt uncomfortably suspicious she wasn't talking about work at all. "Um. Thank you."

"You're very welcome. You're probably wondering why I called."

More than anything. "A bit, yes."

"Do you remember that dress I showed you in the magazine? The one I was considering getting for the gala?"

"Uh...I think so. It was...gold?" *How did I get suckered into this conversation?*

"Right! I knew you would remember—you're so thoughtful like that."

I had to satisfy myself with giving my phone a bewildered look. "Okay... So, what about the dress?"

"Well, you know I decided against it. But I just saw that the shop is having a sale tomorrow. You should come with me! I'd love your opinion on their other options. We can get lunch, too."

I couldn't bring myself to say anything for several long, awkward moments. Charna waited patiently, as if she expected this response. *The weirdo probably did.*

It suddenly occurred to me I might be able to ask her about Miroslav, and possibly find out where she and Loralai were getting their information. AJ had found a ton of useful stuff for us, but there were still a lot of unanswered questions. Maybe Charna could clear some of them up.

"Sure, Charna. That sounds like fun. But would it be okay if a friend of mine comes with us? I promised to spend some time with her this weekend."

"Absolutely! A girls' day out sounds divine! Let's meet at La Rosé for lunch at noon and then we can do our shopping afterward. See you there!"

The line clicked, and I massaged my forehead. I definitely needed some aspirin after that.

"She sounds like fun."

I jumped in my chair. "AJ! Stop doing that!" Gripping my head harder, I complained under my breath about vampires and their annoying sneakiness.

"My apologies. I'll endeavor to walk more noisily in the future."

I glared at him, but he just grinned back, entirely unrepentant.

"So, that's Charna, huh?" he asked.

"Yeah—wait, you heard our conversation?"

He shrugged. "Maybe you should take your phone calls in the parking lot."

I'd have to if Cal ever decided to call me at work. I couldn't bear the teasing AJ was sure to inflict. "Not that you need me to tell you, but she apparently wants to hang out tomorrow, for some unimaginable reason."

"I take it you agreed in hopes of ferreting out information on Miroslav?"

I nodded.

"Taking someone with you is a smart move. Just be careful. Two humans aren't much better than one when facing off with a vampire."

"Thanks for the pep talk," I grumbled. "Maybe I should just take you along on our girls' day out."

"Maybe so. Feel free to call if you need me to charm the information out of her," he said with a flirtatious wink, before sauntering off down the hallway. "Have a good weekend, Nora. See you on Monday."

Thanks to Charna's ridiculous phone call throwing me completely off kilter, it was five-forty by the time I rushed up the steps of the library.

Lina, Izzy, and Cal were all in the meeting room and Rachel's feed was already connected. "Sorry I'm late!" I gasped, dropping my belongings in a chair and pulling out the folder with AJ's findings.

Before I could say anything else, Cal stepped forward for a hug and to drop a quick peck on my lips. Cheeks flaming, I awkwardly cleared my throat and turned to face the smirks on my friends' faces. Rachel contributed a few catcalls.

"Right, um. Anyway." I brandished the folder and began laying the papers out on the table. "AJ gave me a copy of all the stuff he found. I'll try to explain it like he did, but I might forget a few things." Clasping my hands, I launched into it as best I could. Cal stood beside me with an arm around my waist, nodding encouragingly whenever I faltered.

"AJ believes whatever the vampires are cooking up is going to happen really soon. He said he's looking into this ritual thing but didn't say why exactly he thinks it's important," I finished. "Maybe it could help us pinpoint when or where Miroslav is going to wake up?"

My friends had gathered close to the table while I talked and were presently examining the various papers. Lina was holding a sheet up to her laptop's webcam for Rachel to read.

Cal tipped his head toward mine. "Thank you for including me in this, Nora," he whispered before planting a kiss against my temple. He stepped away and picked up one of the documents himself.

I fluctuated between trying to discern further clues to our mystery and melting into a puddle of goo from Cal's affection.

Izzy held up the *Satanic Ritual* page. "If AJ *can* find out when and where, could we stop it from happening?"

"Ooo great idea, Izzy!" Rachel exclaimed. *"We could be like the Armageddon crew, saving the world from certain annihilation!"*

"Didn't most of them die in that movie?" Cal stage whispered to me.

Lina stifled a laugh, and Rachel rolled her eyes dramatically. *"Well, not* exactly *like that,"* she said. *"But still—all heroic and stuff!"*

"Heroics aside, I think you guys might be right," I replied. "If we can figure it out, wouldn't it be better for everyone if we could somehow prevent it? AJ's proof that even some of the vamps don't want him back."

Everyone nodded thoughtfully.

Lina spoke up for the first time since I started my presentation. "But how would we stop it? All of us together couldn't overpower *one* vampire, much less a whole group of them. And I don't imagine they'd be very happy about us barging in on their ritual."

I grimaced. For the first time in my life, I somewhat regretted being a mere human.

"We'd have to leave that part to AJ," said Cal. "None of us would be anything but a hindrance in a situation like that."

Rachel looked supremely disappointed, while Lina seemed a bit relieved. Izzy displayed her usual zero amount of emotion.

"But there will probably be things we can do to help him when it comes down to it," Cal continued, much to Rachel's evident delight. "Maybe even just creating a distraction."

"I can do that! Mom says I'm an expert at distraction!" Rachel announced gleefully.

"From your computer screen?" Izzy asked, effectively tossing a bucket of cold water over Rachel's enthusiasm.

"Maybe not the distraction part," said Lina in a kindly tone. "But you're really good at research. I bet you could help narrow the search a lot faster if AJ could give you some ideas about what to look for."

Rachel nodded, her eyes lighting up once more.

"I'll give him your contact information," I said. "I need to talk to him about this whole idea anyway and figure out what we should be focusing on first."

"Finding out where Loralai is getting her information would probably help," said Izzy.

"Um, yeah, speaking of that." I wet my lips nervously. "Charna called me. She wants to go out together tomorrow for lunch and shopping. I agreed—"

There was something of a collective gasp of disbelief.

"—but said I was bringing along another friend." I gave Izzy and Lina both apologetic looks. "Could one of you do me a huge favor here? I'll pay for lunch."

They exchanged a skeptical glance.

"Are you sure that's a good idea?" asked Cal. "With her behavior lately, Charna sounds like a loose cannon. You'd be putting yourself in a lot of danger for potentially no payoff. She's not likely to tell you anything useful about Miroslav."

"I know," I said, reaching out to grasp his hand. "But if we don't get ahead of this, we're all going to be in a lot of danger. I feel like we can't afford to pass up the opportunity."

"I'll go," said Izzy. "I want to buy new boots, anyway."

Although I wasn't sure a store that sold the glittery dress Charna showed me would also stock platform combat boots, I was immensely relieved. "Thank you! Can I pick you up, or—"

"I'll meet you there," she said quickly. It wasn't lost on the rest of the PLS group that Izzy was extremely private about her home life, to the extent none of us even knew where she lived. I didn't press the issue.

"Okay. Charna wants to meet at La Rosé at noon. I think that's downtown, right?"

Cal nodded. "It's just around the corner from V-Corp Central. Very expensive. My mother loves it."

Great—another place to not fit in. At least I'd have the unwavering support of Izzy's total lack of caring what other people think.

"If you see any celebrities, be sure and take pictures!" Rachel added.

"Sure, Rachel. Maybe Charna will hold the camera for us," I chuckled as I started gathering up the papers.

"You never know," Cal said with a grin, handing me the ones from the far end of the table. "It sounds like she's very accommodating these days."

————

The next day at 11:58 am, Izzy and I stood in front of La Rosé, bolstering our nerves. Or at least, I was—Izzy probably could have faced a firing squad and not batted an eye.

Taking a deep breath, I pushed my shoulders back. "Ready?"

"I was ready five minutes ago," she said blandly.

I chuckled, further easing my nerves. "Sorry. Let's get it over with, then."

We marched inside, immediately drawing horrified looks from the host and hostess manning the reception. They didn't go as far as whispering to each other, but I could tell they wanted to. I had opted for a simple sundress and sandals since I assumed the place wouldn't accept shorts, but it was way too hot out to try for anything higher maintenance. Izzy was eye-catching in her black and green corset dress, fishnets, and spiked choker. It was hard to tell which of us the staff was more appalled by.

Before they had a chance to refuse us service, Charna's voice rang out across the restaurant. *"Nora!* You made it!" She waved from a table directly in the middle of the room.

The host and hostess gave each other significant looks but didn't say anything when we headed toward the table. Charna was dressed to the nines in a slinky red dress and towering stilettos, but didn't bat an eye at our outfits. "I'm delighted you're here," she said as we sat down.

"Um, yeah. Me too," I fibbed. "This is my friend, Izzy."

Charna turned a megawatt smile on her. "Izzy! It's so nice to meet another friend of Nora's. I'm Charna. I'm sure Nora's told you all about me." She turned a sly look my way, and I tried to keep from fidgeting.

"Sure," replied Izzy, totally unfazed. "You're one of the vampires she used to work with."

"The important one," Charna added smoothly.

Izzy responded with a blink before picking up the menu left in her place setting.

I followed her lead and was horrified to find everything was written in French. "So...um. Do you eat here often, Charna?" I asked, with an admirable lack of nervous squeak in my voice.

"As often as I can. The *coq au vin* is one of my favorites," she replied airily, perusing her own menu.

Izzy spoke up before my anxiety could get too out of hand. "Yeah, the chicken is good, but it's kind of heavy for how hot it is today. I think I'll keep it simple and get the *jambon-beurre*. A ham sandwich sounds good right now." She spoke casually, but gave me a pointed look as she laid her menu aside.

I could have kissed her. Seizing the opportunity, I plopped my menu down, too. "That *does* sound good. I'll get the same."

"You're probably right. It is a bit warm out." Charna closed her own menu and held out a hand to accept the wine glass a waiter offered. The contents seemed suspiciously thick to be red wine. "We'd like three orders of the *jambon-beurre*," she said and flicked a dismissive hand before the poor man could say anything.

Thankfully, there was already a pitcher of water on the table. I poured Izzy and myself both a glass simply to give my hands something to do.

"So. Izzy. Are you attending the gala as well?" Charna took a dainty sip from her glass, her manicured brows raised inquiringly.

Izzy flicked her eyes to me briefly. "I haven't decided yet."

"We must find a gown for you today, as well, then! In case you decide to go." She gave Izzy an indulgent smile.

I wondered what kind of minefield we'd waded into. I hadn't the faintest idea what this gala was the vamp kept talking about and, from the quick look she shot me, I didn't think Izzy did, either.

Izzy shrugged. "If I find something I like."

My attention wandered around the restaurant and snagged on an older woman wearing a fox fur stole. *What on earth? It's the middle of June!*

I nudged Izzy and nodded toward the strange sight.

She smirked. "How many times do you think she's dropped the thing's tail in her soup?" she murmured, making me snort a laugh.

"Why is she even wearing it while she's eating?" I whispered back.

Charna followed our gazes and wrinkled her nose. "Ugh. She's probably using it to soak up sweat. That's all the good a fake thing like that would do."

"You can tell it's fake?" I asked, surprised.

"A scent doesn't lie," the vamp replied with a predatory smile.

A delightful reminder that she probably knew exactly what all my emotions were doing as soon as I did.

"How do you single out the scent from across the room?" Izzy asked.

This was apparently the perfect thing to ask, as Charna launched into an explanation of her heightened vampire abilities with obvious relish.

Our plates of baguette-and-ham sandwiches arrived while she was describing how to home in on a scent ("It's similar to how you can force your eyes to focus on one small point and ignore everything around it."), and I shot a grateful look toward Izzy, both for her non-embarrassing help in ordering and her effective distraction of Charna.

A bonus to our simple fare turned out to be the speed with which we all finished our plates and were ready to leave. When the waiter returned, Charna insisted on paying for all of us. "No, no," she said, when I tried to ask for the bill to be split. "I invited you out today, so it's my treat. You can pay next time." She waved a credit card at the waiter and gave me a challenging look.

I hoped with all I was worth there wouldn't be a next time.

We left the restaurant, and Charna directed us down the block, her long legs and painful-looking heels setting a rather brutal pace. I was a sweaty mess by the time she led us into an upscale boutique on the next street over.

A fashionable saleswoman sashayed over and greeted Charna warmly, giving Izzy and I only the tiniest odd look. *A real professional.*

"These are my dear friends, Nora and Izzy." Charna gestured to us like she was presenting the grand prize on a game show. "We're all here to find something for the gala."

That seemed to clear any confusion about our presence right up. The woman whisked us off to a plush seating area situated around a changing room and called for two more associates. They grilled the three of us on our sizes and styles and then rushed off. Someone else brought a tray of refreshments while they were gone. Pop music pulsed overhead while I nibbled on a cracker and mused about the fact that places like this existed outside movies.

Charna lounged comfortably, perusing her cellphone. Izzy bumped my shoulder and tipped her head toward the vamp. She was right. With the saleswomen around, I might not have another opportunity to ask about Miroslav.

"Charna," I began. She immediately put her phone away and gave me a winning smile. "Um. I wanted to ask you about something you said a while back. Well, something you and Loralai both said."

She scowled at the name. "I can't imagine we said something in agreement."

"No, nothing like that," I hurried to assure her. "Just on the same topic, is all."

Her expression cleared. "Alright. Ask away."

I glanced at Izzy. She gave me a tiny nod. "It's about...Miroslav." I realized I wasn't sure how much I, as a human, would be expected to know about the Original Vampire. Less seemed to be the safer bet. "I've heard you both say that name, and I was just curious who it is."

She narrowed her eyes slightly, but it seemed to be more calculating than suspicious. "Of course. Humans are curious by nature, after all." She adjusted her expression into nonchalance. "Miroslav is the leader of the vampiric race.

Those who practice religion even worship him. He is the most powerful of us all and we look to him as our guide and mediator in all things."

"Oh," I said lamely, sharing another look with Izzy. Charna spoke like Miroslav had been awake the whole time.

"Does he live here?" Izzy asked.

The vampire smirked. "*Live* isn't quite the word for it. He exists in stasis."

"Stasis... I think they taught us a little about that in school," I said, keeping my tone vague. "Isn't that where a vampire sort of sleeps for a long time?"

She nodded. "An oversimplification, but yes, that's one way to describe it."

"How does he guide you if he's asleep?" Izzy was nailing all the important questions. I was more grateful she'd agreed to come than ever.

"That's part of the problem with the oversimplification. He's not *awake*, per se, but he's also not asleep. His body is dormant, but his mind remains active and aware of his surroundings. He is able to send small indications of his thoughts to his representatives so that they might carry out his wishes."

"Is that the Circle of Elders?"

"How quick you are!" Charna gushed. "It is, indeed. The Elders have long been his trusted lieutenants and are experts at interpreting his instructions."

It was Izzy's turn to look at me. It was likely as much confirmation as we would get that the house AJ researched did, indeed, contain Miroslav's comatose body.

"That's really interesting. I had no idea a vampire could be in stasis like that for so long. Have you ever gotten to talk to him?" I asked.

She laughed. "Certainly not. Only Elders are allowed into our Lord Miroslav's presence."

"That's too bad," replied Izzy. "It would have been cool to hear what it was like."

"I'm sorry to disappoint." She leaned forward with a conspiratorial look. "But my father is one of the Elders and he loves bragging about his interactions with Miroslav."

Her father?

"He's told me the chamber itself feels heavy with the sheer power Lord Miroslav emanates," she continued.

I stifled a grimace.

"Wow, that must be really impressive." Izzy actually managed to sound slightly impressed. "But why has he been in stasis all this time? Wouldn't it be easier to lead the vampires if he was awake?"

Charna leaned back in her chair. "Apparently, he's been waiting for the right moment." Her smile made me deeply uncomfortable. "Father says that moment will be any day now."

The saleswomen bustled back in, each carrying an armload of garment bags. They quickly set us up in changing rooms where we spent the next hour squeezing into disgustingly expensive gowns and tottering around on sky high heels while the employees all *oohed* and *ahhed* over us. The minutes dragged by as I itched to pull my phone out and text everyone.

We finally left the store with a dress for Izzy, a promise from me to "think about it," and a whole pile for Charna. Money clearly wasn't an issue for her, especially since the checkout lady understood perfectly when the vamp instructed her to "send them to the house."

Charna hailed a cab and blew us a kiss goodbye, and Izzy and I practically sprinted back to our cars, chattering the whole way about what we'd learned and how we could find out more.

When we reached Izzy's car, I watched her lay her new dress carefully in the backseat, belying her usual detached attitude. "Do you know what this gala is?" I asked.

She looked uncomfortable for a moment, further surprising me. "I think she's talking about the Solstice Festival."

I'd never heard of it. "Should I be familiar with that?"

"Probably not. It's this ritzy, invitation-only event. They don't advertise it at all. My stepmom is part of the planning committee."

"Oh." The word seemed inadequate for the amount of personal information she'd just revealed. "So, you *are* going to go?"

She shrugged. "I've only gone once before, when I was a teenager. It's not really my scene."

I smiled. "I imagine not. Thanks again for coming. I couldn't have done it without you."

"You would have figured it out," she replied as she opened the driver's door. "I'll let you send the messages."

Laughing, I waved goodbye and hurried to my own car, eager to share our news.

22

"CHARNA'S FATHER IS *one of the vampire Elders? How does that even work?"* asked Rachel.

It was Saturday evening. Nora arranged a video call to tell the rest of us how her and Izzy's afternoon had gone and what they'd learned from Charna.

"I texted AJ about it. He said male vampires can still, uh, have babies." Nora blushed adorably. *"But only with humans. Apparently, female vamps can't. He thinks the guy probably Turned Charna when she grew up, so he'd have sort of an extension of power in their society."*

"Yuck."

I agreed with Rachel's sentiment. I imagined watching your child grow old and die while you remained ageless would be heartbreaking, but to turn them into nothing but a tool in your eternal quest for power... That was something else entirely.

"So, we're fairly positive the Elders are keeping Miroslav in that house," said Lina. *"With how excited Charna seems about*

this gala, what are the odds the vampires are planning to revive him before that?"

It was a depressing possibility—the Solstice Festival was less than a week away. "Miroslav attending the event would definitely cause an uproar. They'd be hard-pressed to find a more prestigious way to reveal him, and it would ensure all the most affluent humans in the area are made aware of him and his standing within the paranormal community."

"But this area isn't anything special." Nora looked like she was trying to convince herself it wouldn't happen.

I could hardly blame her. I kept hoping it wouldn't happen, no matter the setting.

"You're not wrong," said Izzy. *"But a lot of people from other places fly in to attend the festival. The planners have contacts all over the world and they always make sure the event is well-known among their elitist friends. Short of holding some kind of massive press-conference or attending a red carpet premiere or something, this really is one of the best ways to get Miroslav's name and reputation back out into the world. At least, among those who 'matter.'"* Izzy rolled her eyes in tandem with the air quotes. Her opinion of the ultra-wealthy wasn't hard to discern, even if she, apparently, was part of the same social circle.

"So...there's no chance Charna is just excited to attend a fancy event?" Rachel asked hesitantly.

Izzy scoffed. *"Not likely. The festival is organized and hosted exclusively by humans. She probably sees it as the equivalent of a tea party with a two-year-old. The only way she'd be excited about the event itself is if she was planning to murder everybody there. I imagine she'd be furious if she got blood on her new outfit, though."*

"Oh." Rachel visibly wilted in her chair.

Although difficult to reconcile tea parties with mass murder, I understood Izzy's sentiment. Nora's past stories about Charna made it clear the woman had no love lost for us mortals. Flaunting her superiority in front of a room full of humans seemed like a waste of time for her.

"Something still doesn't make sense, though," said Lina. *"Like Izzy said, Charna clearly doesn't give two figs about humans. So why would parading Miroslav around a human event be all that special to her? She's obviously excited for the festival itself, but I would think Miroslav waking up would be way more important."*

Understanding seemed to strike us all at once.

"Maybe they—"

"What if—"

"Oh, my gosh!" Rachel's shriek drowned out the rest. *"They're going to wake him up AT THE FESTIVAL!!"*

We all gaped at one another.

It was just speculation, of course, but the more I considered it, the more sense it made. Why settle for a splash when you could make the headlines and history books in one go? It was exactly the kind of power move the vampires would plot.

"You said Charna didn't seem to know when he was waking up," said Lina. *"Is it possible she's lying?"*

Nora nodded. *"Definitely. She's told me obvious lies before and acted like she wanted me to know that's what she was doing. It's almost like some weird game to her."*

"In this case, she's probably smart enough to realize if any leaked information was traced back to her, she'd be in serious trouble with the Circle," I said.

"Okay, so we agree this makes the most sense. Is there any way we can confirm it?" asked Lina.

"AJ'll probably have to weasel his way into someone's confidence," replied Izzy.

"I'll message him as soon as we're done," said Nora. *"The sooner he can confirm it, the better."*

"How are we supposed to stop them in the middle of a fancy party? Izzy's the only one even invited," said Rachel.

"Actually…" I was tempted to squirm as everyone's attention shifted to me. "My mother and I attend every year, along with several of the V-Corp board members."

Nora looked shocked, and I winced a bit. Rachel perked up, Lina narrowed her eyes in contemplation, but Izzy wore the same neutral expression she usually did.

"I'm sorry," I said, focusing on Nora. "I planned to tell you. Actually, I, uh, planned to invite you as my guest…" She blushed again and broke eye contact. I definitely *hadn't* planned to tell her in such a public setting.

Before things could get too awkward, Lina spoke up again. *"Okay, this might actually work out really well."* She flashed a rather wicked grin, surprising me thoroughly. *"We're going to plan a bit of a heist."*

As it turned out, mild-mannered Lina had a talent for strategy and subterfuge. It probably served her well in writing the complicated fantasy novels Nora told me about.

Following my assigned role, I paid a visit to my mother the next afternoon.

"Caliban! I wasn't expecting you." She beckoned me inside and led the way to the front sitting room. "Visiting would be much easier if you hadn't moved out of the house, you know."

I didn't take the bait. "Probably so, but having my own apartment has been very enjoyable."

Thankfully, she didn't press the issue. "Very well. To what do I owe the honor?"

"I came to tell you I'm bringing a guest to the festival on Friday."

"Really?" She looked a bit shocked. "You've never taken a date before."

"I know, but I want to this time. Her name is Nora. We had classes together at the university and we recently reconnected." Somewhat misleading, but I didn't want Mother snooping too much before the festival.

"I see. Is this the young lady from the magazine article?"

Suppressing a grimace, I nodded.

She gave me a speculative look. "Did you reconnect with her, or she with you?"

I sighed and slouched in my chair. "Technically, she contacted me, but she only wanted to hire me to illustrate her book—she didn't even know my last name for the first month. She's not angling for money or fame," I said, recalling Nora's discomfort with public attention. That she was willing to face her fear for my sake was incredibly humbling.

Mother looked contemplative but held up her hands in a gesture of surrender after a moment. "Alright. You can't blame your mother for being concerned about the welfare of her child. Especially after the previous women."

This time I did grimace. Having my own mother witness my past naivety in believing social-climbing gold diggers were actually interested in me as a person was its own special brand of humiliation.

"You're welcome to bring Nora to the festival, but since this is the year you're officially taking my place at V-Corp, I want you to escort me that night."

I opened my mouth to protest, but she held up a commanding hand. "No arguments. Nora is welcome, but if you think it would make her uncomfortable to arrive with us both, I can request a separate invitation be sent to her, and she can meet you there."

I still wanted to argue. I wanted Nora glued to my hip for the evening, both to keep her safe and (a small, silly part of myself admitted), so I could show her off. But, despite my wishes, Mother's offer made sense. Nora would likely be much more comfortable arriving with her friends, I begrudgingly conceded.

The plan was for Izzy to take AJ as her plus one, provided he agreed. I volunteered Alden to escort Lina, but she surprised us all with the announcement that she already had an invitation. Or rather, her uncle did. Apparently, the organizers sent him an invitation every year in recognition of his contributions to the scientific community. He could never attend because of his health, so Lina planned to elect herself as his honorary representative. If it didn't work, Alden or I could step in and make sure she was admitted.

It all hinged on AJ confirming our suspicions, of course, but it would also be easy to call off if he discovered otherwise. A part of me hoped our theory *would* be disproved, if only so I could spend the evening enjoying Nora's company rather than attempting to stop a paranormal apocalypse.

"You realize choosing to take this girl to the festival, especially in the year you're announced as V-Corp's new leader, is going to send a strong message. The public will see her as your official significant other, even if the two of you only consider the relationship to be casual. If you choose to stop seeing each other, it won't remove her from the public eye. If anything, she'll probably receive even more scrutiny and criticism." Mother softened her warning with a sympathetic look. "You've never shown serious interest in anyone before and, knowing your preferences, Nora is probably a very sweet girl. I just don't want either of you to get hurt, dear."

The thought had occurred to me before. Taking Nora to dinner and the movies was one thing, but to parade her past all of society's elite would be an unmistakable snub to every eligible young lady around. Nora would become the subject of a great deal of envy and disdain. I trusted the depth of my own feelings and felt no hesitation publicly announcing my attachment to her, but if she didn't feel the same way... To strip away her privacy, possibly indefinitely—and all for the sake of *maybe* foiling a plot—would be utterly cruel.

To be fair, this plot, if allowed to unfold, could very well lead to the downfall of humanity, rendering any social scandals rather inconsequential. But I couldn't bank Nora's future on that—I needed to talk to her privately before we went ahead with our plans.

"I know you're trying to look out for me, Mother, and I appreciate it. I, for one, am completely willing to shout it from the rooftops," I said, causing her eyebrows to raise, "but you're right. This affects more than just me. I'll speak to Nora and make sure she understands the ramifications before anything is finalized. I'll call you when I know whether we'll need the extra invitation."

Mother nodded and leaned over to pat my knee. "I know it's difficult, but you're doing the right thing."

She walked me to the door shortly after, chatting animatedly about the old friends she was looking forward to seeing at the festival. I embraced her in parting and was halfway down the front walk when she called out.

"Cal!" Her use of my nickname stopped me in my tracks. I turned back to find a warm smile on her face. "If it's any consolation, I hope you *do* need that invitation."

Feeling bolstered by Mother's approval, I opted to call Nora when I reached my car rather than giving my nerves a chance to kick in.

"Hello?"

Her sweet voice never failed to bring a smile to my face. "Hello, Nora. I just spoke to my mother about our part of the plan. She doesn't have a problem with me bringing you as my date, but I'd like to talk to you about it a bit more first, if you don't mind."

"Oh, um, okay. What did you want to talk about?"

"Actually, I was hoping we could speak in person. Do you have plans this evening?"

"*No—just doing some things around the house.*" She sounded hesitant.

"Would you mind if I come over? I can bring dinner." Although I would rather take her out for something fun, our previous dinner date taught me the dangers of trapping us both in an uncomfortable situation. Without being sure of Nora's reception, I preferred to avoid a repeat performance.

"*Alright. Maybe six? You can pick the food.*"

"I'll be there."

I drove home, purposely brainstorming takeout options to avoid overthinking the way the evening might go. Nora and I seemed to have reached a real understanding after our previous date, but it was still difficult not to imagine the worst. She highly valued her privacy, after all, and likely envisioned our relationship progressing at a much more gradual and comfortable pace than attending the festival would allow.

She was still well within "scaring off" territory.

I shook my head to dispel the thought. All I could do was my best. I would be honest and genuine and show her just how much I cared for her. If that wasn't enough... My mind briefly pondered trying to go through with the "Foil the Vampires" plan if Nora and I were on the outs.

That certainly wouldn't do anyone any favors.

I'd just have to accept whatever her answer was as graciously as possible and do what I could to help the cause, while hopefully not ruining the new friendships I'd forged.

When I arrived back at my apartment building, I was surprised and pleased to find Alden lounging beside my door.

"Roger let me in," he said, referring to the energetic young doorman.

"Did you accept his invitation to see his band as thanks?"

My friend shuddered theatrically. "Heavens, no. I tipped him a fifty."

I laughed and let us into the apartment. "So, what are you doing here? Don't you usually have to pencil me into your schedule at least a month in advance?"

"For my best friend? Of course not. Two weeks is all it takes."

Shaking my head, I grabbed a couple of bottles of water from the fridge, tossing him one as he lounged comfortably on my couch.

He caught it easily and took a lazy swig. "*Ahh*. This summer is really shaping up to be brutal."

"Seems that way. You came over to discuss the weather, then?"

He chuckled. "No, I didn't come to discuss the weather. Actually, I wanted to talk to you about the festival. Have you asked Nora yet?"

I realized I had been so busy with everything going on recently, I'd never filled Alden in on any of it. "Sort of," I replied, anticipating his less-than-impressed answer.

"'Sort of?' What, did you say 'hey, Nora, I'm going to this thing this weekend. It'd be super cool if I happened to see you there?'"

"Does that actually count as asking someone to go with you?"

He shrugged. "I thought so when I was a lad."

"Not always quite so smooth with the ladies, huh?" I laughed. "No, I didn't say that to her, but it wasn't much better."

"Do tell."

"Well, it's actually kind of a long story…" I filled Alden in on everything that had happened recently, from my ups and downs with Nora to our plan to stop Miroslav.

"Huh. So, you never even asked her to the festival at all," he said once I finally finished.

"Uh." I immediately felt like a fool. "No, I guess I didn't."

He nodded sagely. "You and Young Me would have gotten along well."

"Is that really the most important thing you took from all that?" I said, somewhat defensively. "Not the vampires angling to take over or the potential apocalypse? Not even that I tried to assign your plus one for the festival?"

"You're right. I am a little hurt that you didn't ask before offering up my invitation."

I rolled my eyes. "You're impossible."

"The stuff about Miroslav sounds serious," he conceded. "But it also sounds like there's really nothing I can do about it at the moment. I'll help however I can, of course, but I imagine we mostly just need to keep things under wraps until the festival, right? Not go shouting it out to everyone on the street?"

He was right. "Sorry," I said. "It's all just a bit overwhelming. I'm going to see Nora tonight to talk over the public outcome of her attending it with me, and to give her one last chance to back out of it. I guess I'm more nervous about it than I'd like to admit."

"I get it. It's a lot to deal with. And trying to cope with your relationship issues at the same time as planning to thwart a potentially world-altering plot probably isn't great for your mental health." At my grimace, he snorted. "Not a good pep talk?"

"Maybe you should leave that skill up to coaches and self-help gurus," I replied with a chuckle.

He nodded and stood, grabbing his keys from the side table.

"Wait, did you really just come to see if I'd asked Nora to the festival?" I asked.

"Well," he said, walking backward toward the door, "I actually came to see if you would use your sway to help me convince your old assistant Sandra to go with me, but it sounds like we've got bigger fish to fry. Besides, bringing a vampire to the scene of a hostile vampire takeover might not help our case. Now go get cleaned up and get to wooing Nora. I expect to see you both there on Friday."

23

THE HAND ON the clock was moving unbearably slowly. It had been 5:43 for at least twenty minutes. I huffed an annoyed breath and yanked my fingers out of the tangle of hair they'd twisted themselves into. I didn't even know why I was so nervous. Cal and I had reached an understanding.

Maybe because you're only going to the festival with him because Lina assigned you to—he never actually asked you. And now he needs to talk after telling his high-society mother about you...

The minute hand crawled to 5:44. I wanted to scream.

A knock at the front door sent me flying down the hallway, a flush climbing my neck as my nervous energy escalated. I stopped in the entryway and ran a hand over my hair, hoping I hadn't knotted it up too horribly. Steeling myself, I opened the door.

Cal stood on the porch with a bag of Styrofoam takeout containers and a full drink tray. "Hello," he said with a warm smile. "I hope I'm not too early—the order came out faster than I expected."

"No, it's fine," I replied, stepping to the side and beckoning him in. I didn't bother to tell him I'd sat on the couch staring at the clock for the last half-hour, anyway.

Kicking off his shoes with an enviable amount of grace, Cal led the way to the kitchen. I padded after him in my bare feet, fighting the urge to wring my fingers.

"I saw Alden this afternoon," he said, setting out containers of cheeseburgers and fries and a variety of separate toppings. "He, apparently, wanted my help to talk my old assistant into going to the festival with him. I told him about the plan, and he decided maybe taking a vampire as his plus one wasn't a good idea after all."

I laughed nervously as I loaded up my burger. "Is he going to help us, then?"

"He will." The look he shot me was sly. "He also wanted to know if you and I are going together."

"Oh?" I met his eyes for a moment before focusing on the food again.

He nodded. "He's very invested in our relationship."

"I can't imagine why," I said, adding another pickle to my burger. "He's never even met me."

Cal shrugged. "He sees that I'm happy, and that's good enough for him."

And your mother?

Once my burger was loaded with toppings, I finally accepted there was nothing more I could do to avoid giving Cal my attention.

When I raised my gaze once more, he held out the drink tray. "Chocolate or strawberry?"

Surprised, I took a moment longer than necessary to decide on the pink-tinged milkshake. "Thank you."

He took the chocolate and picked up his takeout container, directing us to the back deck. "I thought burgers and ice cream would be a nice way to end a hot summer day."

We settled into a comfortable silence as we ate. The sun was still well above the horizon, but the park below us was quickly falling into shadow as the treetops turned golden. The temperature had reached a comfortable level and pleasant scents wafted from my neighbor's freshly tended lawn and flowerbeds.

I was picking at the last of my fries when Cal pushed his empty container aside and turned to me with a deep breath. My nerves returned with a vengeance.

"I wanted to talk to you about us going to the festival together and, well, what it will mean for both of us."

"Okay..." I set my container aside, too, and instantly regretting the loss of something to fiddle with. I settled on the weave of my wicker armrest.

He clasped his hands together and studied them for a moment, his elbows resting on his knees. "Nora, I care about you very much," he said, raising his head to meet my gaze.

I waited for him to continue, but he just looked at me, his eyes roving over my face. The knot in my stomach tightened. "But?" I murmured.

He smiled gently. "No 'buts.' I care about you. I know we've had some difficulties and misunderstandings already, but it's all been worth it to get to know you and spend time with you."

Warmth spread over me at his words, but it warred with my confusion. "What about the festival?" I asked, needing a straight answer before the rising butterflies made whatever bad news he had even harder to bear.

He grimaced, causing a sort of bleak resignation to wash over me. "I'm so sorry about this whole thing," he said. Standing, he walked over to lean on the porch railing, looking out at the park. "I had this grand plan to invite you to go with me. I was going to take you out to dinner, and then go for a stroll through the park. Maybe get down on one knee to present you with the invitation." He turned back to face me with a chuckle. "It didn't quite turn out the way I hoped."

"No," I agreed, picturing the way Lina had handed out marching orders like a general.

Cal smirked, possibly thinking of the same thing. "Even though I didn't get to ask you like I wanted to, I was still thrilled when you agreed to go with me."

Was?

"But when I spoke to my mother this afternoon, she brought up something I've thought a lot about myself."

Great, he didn't even need *his mom to tell him he can do better.*

Cal hesitated a moment, running a hand through his hair with a nervous expression.

I suppressed a sigh. Of *course,* he would look even more attractive with mussed hair.

A part of me wanted to save him the discomfort and just back out of going to the event. The bigger part wanted to know why, after all this time and all his reassurances, *this* was the thing that changed his mind. So, I stayed quiet and waited for him to work up the nerve to tell me.

At last, he pushed off the railing and returned to the chair beside me, sitting forward to reach for my hand. I accepted his hold but kept my grip loose—apparently my body was already prepping for fight-or-flight mode. As though sensing this, Cal's fingers tightened around mine, anchoring me there beside him.

"Nora, going to the festival together will change everything."

Right. All his family's rich friends will see me. I tried to pull my hand away, but he kept a firm hold. My eyes started to burn. "You don't have to say it," I whispered, unable to meet his gaze. "I understand. I won't go. Lina and the others will be fine without me."

Silence stretched out awkwardly until his hand abruptly clenched mine to the point of hurting. Startled, I looked up to find him staring at me with a shocked and mildly angry look. "You think I don't want you there?" he demanded.

"I..." I trailed off. I'd expected him to be relieved, not upset. "Isn't that why you wanted to talk? Because your mom reminded you I don't belong there?"

Whatever response I might have expected, it certainly wasn't for him to lean over and yank me forward into a firm kiss. I yelped in surprise and didn't even remember to close my eyes before he broke it off and glared at me. He was sending some seriously mixed messages.

"How could you possibly think that, Nora?"

I gaped at him. "How could I *not* think that?!" I exclaimed, my hackles rising. "You're *Caliban Vasile*. There's probably not a person in the whole country who hasn't heard your name!"

His mouth twisted in discomfort. "Even if that were true, I don't see what it has to do with this."

I wanted to roll my eyes. "It *is* true, and it has everything to do with it! Do you really expect me to just wander around acting like everything is totally normal when people trample each other to take your picture? When girls throw themselves at your feet everywhere you go? I'm not some high-society princess, Cal—that stuff is never going to be normal for me!"

"I know it's not normal," he said. "And I know it's not something you'll ever be comfortable with. But that's a good thing! I like that your head isn't turned by all the fame and flattery. I like that you see me as more than just a headline on a tabloid. I love that I can be myself with you."

"But it's like you said—going to the festival will change that," I replied resolutely. "It won't be just us anymore. Everyone will be looking, and it won't take long for them to see I don't fit in. I'll never be the person you need."

He was shaking his head before I finished speaking. "You're wrong—you're exactly who I need! Whatever anyone else thinks doesn't matter."

"You might think that now, but, eventually, you'll realize someone from your own world is better for you. Someone who understands the pressure you're under and won't make embarrassing mistakes when everyone's watching." I swallowed down the lump in my throat.

"Someone you won't have to constantly guide through every social interaction."

He stared at me for a long moment before sitting back in his chair and rubbing a hand over his face. "Is that really how you feel when you're with me?" he asked at last.

No. Most of the time, I felt cherished and seen. Understood and appreciated. Being with Cal made me feel happy in a way I hadn't felt since long before the death of my father. Could I really give that up?

I have to. It'll be so much harder if I wait until he sees I was right.

Tears pooling in my eyes, I nodded miserably, my gaze locked on the deck boards.

He didn't say anything for several agonizing minutes.

When I was sure I couldn't bear it any longer, he stood. "I'm very sorry I made you feel uncomfortable," he murmured. "It's the very last thing I wanted." He strode across the deck but paused at the door. I still couldn't bring myself to face him. "I'll make sure you receive a separate invitation. And I'll let Lina know about the change of plans."

The door closed quietly behind him, and I fell apart.

Some indeterminate amount of time later, a call roused me from my malaise. I half-heartedly felt around the bed and found my phone buried under a fold of blanket. The screen displayed Lina's name.

Sighing, I accepted the call. "Hello?"

"Cal said you decided not to go to the festival with him. What happened?"

"We broke up, I think." I wasn't sure if we were technically together in the first place.

"Why?! I thought you guys were finally getting everything worked out!"

"He talked to his mom today about taking me to the festival. He said it was going to change everything."

"Okay...and he decided that was a bad thing?"

"Not exactly, but it got us talking about how different our lives are and how it's never going to be comfortable for me to deal with all the public scrutiny that being with him comes with."

"He said that?!" she gasped.

"Um...I did, actually."

There was a long silence.

"So, you broke up with him? For being a public figure?"

I cringed. I'd already been berating and second-guessing myself since the moment he left. "Yes," I whispered.

"Oh, Nora," she sighed. *"Why do you do this to yourself?"*

I puffed up defensively for approximately half a second before groaning and burrowing deeper into my bed. There was no use pretending—Lina could read me too well. "I don't know," I intoned. "Maybe I'm just too used to everything in my life sucking. I can't handle anything good."

"Maybe that's something you need to tell Cal," she suggested gently.

I vacillated for a moment before answering. "No. I might have sabotaged myself, but it doesn't change that I'm not a good fit for him. There's no way I could be any help to him with V-Corp, and all his friends would be laughing behind his back at every embarrassing thing I do. It's better this way."

"There's no way to know any of that for sure without at least trying. And you know him better than that; you know he wouldn't be friends with those types of people. Don't you think he deserves to make up his own mind about this?"

She let me mumble a few incoherent excuses before cutting me off. *"Think about it, okay? Whether or not you two are meant to be together, you'll eventually have to learn to let yourself be happy. There are still lots of good things in the world, Nora—you just have to be willing to open yourself up to them.*

"My sister is about to leave for work, so I need to go, but please call me if you need anything. You know I'm always here for you. And think about what I said. I know your father wanted you to be happy more than anything, and so do your friends."

I murmured a goodbye and tossed the phone back onto the blanket mound. Rolling over, I pillowed my arms under my head and stared at the framed photograph on my bedside table. My mom and dad posed together in front of the lion enclosure at the zoo. I was perched on Dad's shoulders with a huge gap-toothed smile, pink sneakers and matching ball cap, my tiny hands plastered to Dad's forehead. He held me fast with a firm hand on my knee, his other arm wrapped affectionately around Mom's waist.

The only thing I could remember about that day was dropping my ice cream cone on the ground as soon as Dad handed it to me. He laughed, and Mom elbowed him before hugging me. She was warm and soft, and her hair tickled my nose. We sat at a picnic table and Dad shared his ice cream with me.

The memory caused a teary smile. Dad *did* want me to be happy. Mom did, too. But Lina was right—I had no idea how.

24

DESPITE MY HEARTACHE and indecision, the days passed quickly. My invitation to the Solstice Festival arrived on Tuesday. It was the fanciest piece of paper I'd ever seen. I wouldn't have been surprised if the glitzy lettering was made of actual gold.

AJ agreed to his part of Lina's plot without much fuss. I think he was more concerned with confirming our theory than who would be on his arm that evening. He also readily accepted Rachel's help with research, much to her delight. She threw herself into the effort wholeheartedly and proved adept at sniffing out even the most minute details online.

On Wednesday evening, we met once more in the library's meeting room. AJ accompanied me this time, but Cal, to my silent relief, was absent. Lina had been providing updates to our group text, so he already knew the part he had to play.

"Alright," said Lina, passing around bundles of paper. "I printed off a list of people we need to be on the lookout for on

Friday. Rachel sent them to me this afternoon. I believe AJ knows about them, too?" She sent him an inquiring look.

He nodded in return. "I was able to provide some direction and add a few more details to a few of the profiles, but Rachel did most of the digging." He flashed a stunning smile toward her screen. She beamed back. They'd proven to be a much more effective team than I think anyone expected.

I thumbed through my packet as AJ continued, "I've been able to confirm a fair number of vampires who plan to attend the festival—more than normal by far—but unfortunately, I haven't found proof that the Circle plans to revive Miroslav that night. Without knowing for sure, our safest bet is to assume the worst and plan accordingly."

I nodded my agreement along with the others as I turned a page and blanched at the photo of Loralai glaring up at me. It wasn't surprising, considering she was the one who'd put me on this path in the first place, but facing her in the midst of everything else made the whole event suddenly seem a lot more daunting.

Lina, obviously aware of the direction of my thoughts, gave me a commiserating look. "Some of these people we're already familiar with, but quite a few of them are going to be complete strangers to all of us, even AJ. Rachel was thankfully able to find at least one photo of each of them, so we'll have a bit of a leg up."

"Some of the pictures are old and kind of blurry, though— sorry!" Rachel chimed in.

"It's better than nothing," said Izzy as she studied the papers. "Are these all vampires, then?"

"The majority are, but several of them are human," said Rachel.

"Human-esque, anyway," said AJ. "Some paranormals are almost impossible to tell apart from regular humans."

I grimaced. Were those the "lesser" beings the vampires once mentioned?

"Do we need to be concerned with the difference?" asked Lina.

"Unless you're dealing with a shifter, no," replied AJ. "The differences between humans and beings like hobgoblins or gnomes are negligible. They're the equivalent of a particularly fit human male—strong and fast, but not abnormally so."

Lina frowned.

"So, we're at the same amount of disadvantage, then," Izzy said dryly.

AJ looked around at all of us, as though just noticing we were nothing but a bunch of average young women. "You have the same chances, especially if you aim to defeat them the same way you would a human man." He smirked. "Choose higher heels and lower necklines, and you shouldn't have much trouble."

I flushed and glared at him. So much for making a good first impression. Lina, her cheeks bright red, cleared her throat and nervously shuffled through the stacks of papers. Izzy just gave him a flat look.

"I wish I could go," sighed Rachel dejectedly. *"You guys have all the fun."*

"Yes—the risk of disembowelment is so fun." Izzy rolled her eyes.

It didn't seem as much of a deterrent to Rachel as it was to Lina and me.

"Right..." Lina coughed. "You mentioned shifters, AJ? Is that also something we should expect?"

"Unless the Circle of Elders has become radically more progressive in their old age, I would say no. Most vampires prefer to only work with those they can easily subjugate—shifters are too much our physical equals for comfort. It's why we don't usually cooperate with other vampires outside our immediate circles, either. Trust isn't particularly common in our society," he added dryly.

"Why do you call them shifters? Do they not like being called werewolves?" asked Rachel.

"As far as I know, werewolves don't mind their name," AJ said with a chuckle. "But there are many more kinds of shifters than just those."

That was certainly news to me—and to the others, judging by the looks on their faces.

"Alright, so there's obviously a ton about paranormals that we don't know," I said. "But since you don't think any of it will seriously affect our efforts on Friday, then maybe we should just try to focus on the plan for now. If it all goes well, you can give us a crash course in paranormal life afterward."

Everyone agreed, and we settled in to hash out the final details.

As we packed up our stuff an hour later, Lina reminded us to study the bios Rachel made. The more key people we could keep an eye on that night, the better. Especially since we'd need to point them out to AJ if he didn't see them first.

I struggled not to snicker when the vampire met with an impressive amount of disinterest after asking Izzy for her phone number. They would need to coordinate, of course, as they were attending the festival together, but I couldn't help wondering if Izzy would be able to bring AJ's ego down a few notches while they were at it. Either way, it provided a welcome distraction from the insane situation we were facing.

"See you all Friday! We've got this!" Rachel sang in farewell before Lina turned off and stowed the laptop.

Izzy gave us a resolute nod and headed out, AJ trailing after her with a stream of questions she thoroughly ignored.

Lina and I walked to the parking lot together. "How are you doing with all of this?" she asked.

I tugged on the strap of my bag. "I'm okay. I'll be glad when it's over."

"Me, too. But I was talking about more than just Miroslav."

"Yeah," I sighed. "I figured."

Lina chuckled and nudged my arm. "So?"

"I don't know." I kicked a pebble. "I have no idea if I made the right decision or not. I regret it, of course." I gave a self-deprecating huff of laughter. "But I'm afraid I'll wind up falling in love with him and it just won't work out down the road. I'm not from his world, Lina. He's about to become the CEO of a global corporation! I have no idea how to even act around people like that."

"It's not like you crawled out of some hole in the ground and don't have the first clue how a business works. Your dad founded and ran a successful publishing company, and you've been involved with it since the beginning!"

"Lot of good it did me," I grumbled. "I barely made it out of the mail room, and he didn't trust me to take it over after he died."

Lina gave me a sympathetic look. "You talked to the lawyers, then?"

I nodded and willed myself not to cry. I was sick of crying.

"I forgot all about it with your accident, and then this Miroslav stuff. I'm so sorry, Nora." I forced the lump in my throat down as Lina embraced me. She gave me a few comforting pats on the back before stepping away. "Well...at least now you know, and you can start making plans for your future without this hanging over your head."

"You're probably right. Honestly, I wish I'd left the company years ago. Maybe even moved away. I kept wanting a fresh start but could never bring myself to actually go for it."

"You're much braver than you give yourself credit for. But I won't pretend we wouldn't miss you a ton," she said with a smile. "Besides, if you *had* left, you wouldn't have met Cal. Is that something you want?"

Rather than feeling like a guilt trip, she seemed genuinely curious.

I thought back to the beginning. My embarrassingly bad first meeting with Cal. My embarrassing attempt to invite him to the movie night. My embarrassing run-in with him at work...

There seems to be a pattern here, I thought with a cringe.

Our other moments together replayed in my mind. His thoughtfulness and genuine interest in my writing, and his kindness to my friends. His caring and supportive nature throughout all my blunders and breakdowns. Our playful flirtations and bantering.

I blushed as I recalled a few other pleasant memories.

Lina squeezed my hand, bringing me back to the present. "It doesn't look like you regret your time with him," she teased, causing my cheeks to darken further.

"No," I murmured. "I don't think I do."

"Good." She turned toward her car. "Now you just need to figure out what you're going to do about it."

I smiled and returned her wave goodbye.

What *was* I going to do?

———

Friday afternoon saw me sitting at my desk, bouncing my heels and staring at the clock. I think AJ would have understood if I'd called in, but I knew I'd go crazy waiting for the time to pass just sitting at home. I suspected it was the same reason he was there, anyway—he certainly didn't seem to be accomplishing much as far as his lawyer duties went.

He *did* take me to lunch, which was nice, but he insisted on referring to it as "the last supper," which made it less nice. There was supposed to be food at the Solstice Festival, but I was sure I wouldn't be able to eat anything with my nerves like they were. Last supper or not, I was grateful to have something in my stomach.

"Nora." AJ popped his head out of the office. "Would you mind running downstairs to meet the delivery man with my dry cleaning? They always refuse to bring it upstairs, but

Parker has us scheduled for a conference call in a minute, so I can't go down there myself."

"Oh, okay." I stood up, glad of the distraction.

"Just a heads up," he added. "I never tip them since they make me come downstairs. Don't take their attitude to heart!"

I glared after him as he waved and returned to his desk. "Jerk," I muttered. Of course, he'd make *me* face the disgruntled delivery person.

When I arrived in the lobby, I immediately saw the guy in his bright purple Speedy Clean t-shirt chatting with Alistair. Apparently, AJ opted to use the cheap place downtown rather than one of the nicer cleaners in the suburbs. No wonder he wasn't worried about tipping and the cleaners weren't refusing his service. For the first time, I wondered where the vamp actually lived.

"Hello," I said, smiling at Alistair and the delivery guy both. "I'm here to pick up those clothes."

"Hello, Ms. Nora! It's been so long since you stopped by for a chat, I've been missing you!" Alistair beamed at me like a proud grandfather.

My cheeks warmed. "I'm sorry, Alistair. Things have been kind of crazy lately. I'll be sure and stop more often."

He nodded happily.

"If you work for Hunt, I'm not surprised it's crazy," the delivery guy griped, handing me the plastic covered bundle. There were only two hangers, so I figured AJ must do at least some of his own laundry. I thanked him and turned pointedly to Alistair, hoping to avoid most of the awkwardness of not tipping. Sure enough, the guy groaned and marched away, grumbling loudly about stingy paranormals and lousy jobs.

I winced and gave Alistair an apologetic look. "Sorry about that. AJ apparently refuses to tip them."

The old man laughed. "Not to worry, Ms. Nora. I've seen that young man receive his fair share of strongly worded complaints."

Of course he had. Alistair had been the front lobby attendant for as long as I could remember. He probably knew more about the people in the building than anyone.

"I'm not surprised," I laughed. "Thanks, Alistair. See you later!" Waving, I headed back to the elevator. I pushed the call button and carefully laid AJ's clothes over my arm while I waited. I couldn't see much through the semi-opaque plastic, but it looked like a suit—I wondered if it was his outfit for the festival.

The bell chimed, and I found myself face to face with Loralai.

"Nora." She smiled nastily and made a show of looking me over. "Moving up in the world, I see."

"Yes, Mist—" I gritted my teeth against the instinctive response. "Hello, *Ms. Evans.*"

Loralai's eyes flashed and the tips of her elongated canines jutted over her lip. She reined in her anger after a moment and gave me a haughty look instead. "That arrogant swine hasn't done your manners any favors. No matter. Your usefulness is nearly at an end."

Although her threat chilled me to my core, I couldn't help feeling the urge to roll my eyes at *her*, of all people, having the nerve to call someone else arrogant. "Yes, well, as long as AJ likes having me around, I guess I'll be fine," I replied with as much calm as I could muster. Hefting the garment bags to stress my point, I made to step around her. "I need to get these back upstairs."

Her hand shot out, claw-tipped fingers digging into my wrist. "What's this? Is that reprobate planning to attend the Solstice Festival tonight?" She grasped the receipt hanging off the bag with her other hand.

I moved back, jerking my arm from her grip and holding the bags out of reach. "So, what if he is? I don't think it's any of your business."

Her eyes narrowed, and I questioned my sanity. "You've developed quite the mouth," she growled as she took a threatening step toward me. "And what about you, *Nora?* Are you planning to drag your worthless carcass to the festival with him?"

I wanted to say yes and rub her nose in it, but the sneaking suspicion it might be the last thing I ever said held me back. Her fists clenched, and I fought a cringe. "No," I said at last, dropping my gaze. "I'm not going to the festival with him."

"Good. I knew you had more common sense than *that,* even if it hardly shows," she said derisively as she turned away. "Goodbye, Nora. I'm looking forward to the next time." I looked up to see her cast a particularly cruel smile over her shoulder.

Shuddering, I hurried into the next open elevator. No matter how the night turned out, it'd be one to remember.

25

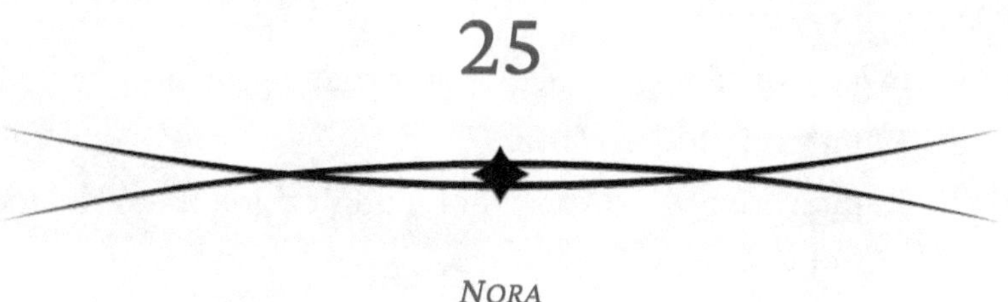

"READY?" AJ ASKED, closing his office door.

No. I nodded, wiping my already sweaty palms against my skirt.

"You're sure you don't want us to pick you up?" he asked once more.

"Are you sure you don't just want to arrive with two dates?" I replied, rolling my eyes. I'd thought long and hard about Izzy and AJ's offer to let me ride with them before ultimately refusing. If things went well with the vampires and badly with Cal, I wanted an easy exit without having to shame myself overly much.

If things went badly with the vampires... Well, it wouldn't much matter whose car we took at that point.

AJ smirked. "Maybe I do. Lina and Rachel could join us, too."

I laughed and pushed his shoulder. "Rachel would love that idea. I'm glad at least one of us will be safe tonight..." That sobered us both up in a hurry. I shook my head, trying to dislodge the encroaching anxiety, and took AJ's dry-cleaning off the coat rack I'd stowed it on. "Here, I assume you'll need this."

"Thank you. I probably wouldn't have gotten far without my tux. Did the delivery man give you a hard time?"

"He mostly just bad-mouthed you," I replied, distracted. "Did you say *tux*?"

He gave me an odd look. "Yes. Is that a problem?"

"But a tux is so—so *formal*."

"Right... It *is* a white-tie event. I don't think they'd let me in if I didn't wear one."

I gaped at him in mounting horror. Did it say white-tie on my invitation? There was no way I could've missed that!

"Are you alright?" AJ looked concerned now.

"Yeah. Just fine. I've gotta go." I may have wheezed a bit as I snatched up my bag and scurried for the elevator. AJ didn't follow. He was probably still trying to work through my weirdness. The doors closed, leaving me blissfully alone, and I collapsed against the wall.

The Solstice Festival was a *white-tie* event. That meant red carpets, tuxedos, and... "An evening gown," I whispered numbly.

I'd never owned an evening gown in my life. Even my prom dresses had been knee length, and they'd come from a rental place. I suddenly remembered the dresses at the shop Charna had taken us to. They'd all been floor-length, but I was so focused on getting information from the vamp, I'd basically zoned out of everything else.

What am I going to do?! This whole time I had planned to just wear one of the few cocktail dresses I owned and call it good.

I wanted to bang my head against the wall.

As soon as the elevator stopped, I shoved through the doors and practically sprinted to the parking lot, dialing Lina's number as I went.

"Hey, Nora. Are you heading home?"

"Just leaving work. Did you know the festival is *white-tie?!*"

"Uh, yeah, I did. Didn't you?"

"No!" I reached my car and thumped my forehead on the hot window. "I don't have a dress!"

"What?! Oh, no, what are you going to do? It starts in just a couple of hours!"

"I know! I don't know what to do!"

"I'd loan you one if I had it, but I had to borrow one myself. Maybe Izzy has something?" She didn't sound very confident. Understandable, considering Izzy was at least six inches taller than me.

"Maybe. I'll try calling her, anyway." Huffing out a breath, I dug in my bag for my car keys. "I'll get it figured out—don't worry. See you there."

"Good luck!"

A quick call to Izzy only confirmed my expectations—she didn't have anything even close to my size.

Unfortunately, the bad news didn't end there.

"My stepmom's dress was delivered yesterday. They told her nearly all the shops in town are sold out. Apparently, they invited a lot more people than usual this year."

I groaned. There was nothing for it—I had to make something from my own closet work. I raced home, narrowly avoiding a speed trap just outside the downtown area, and barreled into the house.

All four of my cocktail dresses were laid out on my bed within moments. Praying for creative inspiration, I stepped back to study them.

A minute later, I collapsed onto the bench at the end of the bed. It was no good. Only two of them were made from similar materials and they were nowhere close to being complimentary colors.

Besides the somewhat important fact that I couldn't sew to save my life.

I laid my head back on the bed, pillowed on a mound of fluffy orange lace, and blinked away tears. Once again, I couldn't seem to catch a break. Except this time, it was entirely my own fault.

The photograph on the nightstand caught my attention, launching me to my feet. My parents used to attend fancy parties together. *And Dad never cleaned out Mom's side of the closet!*

I bolted down the hallway and threw open their bedroom door. Ignoring the memories of the last time I'd seen Dad in this room, I rummaged through the closet and pulled out every garment bag I could find. Sifting through the contents, I uncovered three evening gowns. One was from a maternity line, but the other two looked like they might fit.

Returning to my room, I quickly tried them both on. One had shoulder pads and was molded for a body much more well-endowed than my own. The other was a lovely shade of soft pink and draped over my frame in a flattering way that reminded me of the dresses Greek muses wore in movies. It was too long, but I had a roll of hem tape still in my bathroom cabinet from my senior prom—my best friend had caught her heel in her dress and needed an emergency repair.

I pulled the dress back off and found the tape. Spreading the skirt out on the floor, I started folding up a few inches of cloth at a time, working my way around the hem. When I finished the front half, I carefully turned the dress over and let out a gasp.

There was a huge stain on the back. It looked like someone had spilled their drink down Mom's skirt when she was facing the other way. I stared for a few moments before gingerly touching the spot. The cloth was supple—someone had already tried to clean it.

I sat back on my heels, feeling crushed. I wasn't even thinking about Miroslav and thwarting evil paranormal plans—I'd just wanted to feel close to my mom. Wearing that dress had made me feel connected to her in a way I never had before.

Before I could sink too far into despair, the doorbell rang. Wiping my eyes, I threw on my bathrobe and padded down the hall, glancing at the clock as I passed. The others would be leaving for the festival soon. I needed to call them, so they'd know to adjust their plans.

A short, rotund man with patchy graying hair stood on the porch wearing a black polo and black slacks. "Are you—" he squinted at a small note card in his hand, his whole face pinching up, "Nora Jensen?"

"Yes," I replied, looking past him to the van he'd driven. There was a small logo on the door, but I couldn't make it out.

"Oh, good—those directions were garbage. I'll get your stuff." He trotted away and opened the back door of the van.

Stuff?

Confused, I shifted my weight from one foot to the other, noting the lengthening shadows. I was nearly out of time.

The door slamming reclaimed my attention. The man returned to the porch, carrying an opaque garment bag. He held it by the hanger, his arm nearly straight up in the air to keep it from dragging on the ground. "Here you go." He thrust a clipboard toward me. "Sign by your name."

"Uh... What is it?"

He gave me an unimpressed look. "Should I take it out and model it for ya? Just sign already! I've got four more deliveries to make!"

I took the clipboard and found my name near the bottom. Signing next to it, I traded the board for the garment bag.

"Thank you for your business," the man recited in a bored tone as he turned away, his eyes glued to the clipboard.

I watched him go in bewilderment. Shaking my head, I closed the door and took the bag to the living room. A logo on the front matched the shape of the one on the van's door— *Midnight Maiden Boutique*. It sounded like a vampire thing. Would there be a coat made of skin inside, courtesy of Loralai?

I shuddered.

Gathering my courage, I unzipped the bag and pushed it back to see the contents. A stunning dress in a beautiful royal blue glittered up at me. I gaped at it. How was this possible? A small card attached to the hanger caught my eye.

Nora, darling, you never decided on a dress the other day. I hope you'll consider this one. I'm sure it would catch the eye of a certain special someone... See you at the festival!
—Charna

Charna had bought me a dress? *Charna?!* I collapsed into the nearest chair. Here was irrefutable proof—I'd officially entered *The Twilight Zone.* I heard my ringtone faintly from the other room and hurried to answer the call, carrying the dress with me. It was Lina.

"I'm nearly ready to go. Have you had any luck finding a dress?"

"Well..." I stared down at the soft folds of glimmering blue. "Sort of. None of mine work, and my mom's has a stain on it. But a delivery guy just came by with a dress that's apparently from Charna. She sent a card with it."

"Charna? Seriously?"

"I know, right? The card says the dress might catch the attention of someone. What do you think she's playing at?"

"I have no idea... I'd hope she means Cal, but who knows when it comes to her? Do you have any other options at this point?"

"No," I sighed. "I don't. And I'd better get a move on if I'm going to get there on time. See you soon!"

I hung up and hurried to put on the dress. It fit like a glove. A wide neckline left my shoulders and a considerable swath of my chest on display. At least it wasn't plunging like the ones Charna seemed to favor. The waist cinched in before fanning out into the beautiful skirt, expertly placed gathers creating a waterfall of perfectly draped fabric down the length of it. It wasn't as voluminous as a ballgown, but also wasn't slinky. It suited me perfectly.

I started twisting my hair into a simple updo when Mom's pink gown caught my eye in the mirror. Smiling to myself, I took the dusky rose-colored ribbon that cinched in the waist and threaded it through my hair. I might not be able to wear her dress, but I could still take a piece of her with me.

Throwing on a touch of makeup, I stuffed some necessities in a black clutch, grabbed my heels and my invitation, and headed out. As I slid carefully into the driver's seat of my car, triple checking that I wasn't about to catch my skirts in the door, it suddenly occurred to me that this might be the last time I ever saw my home. If everything went wrong that night, it might be the last time my friends saw their homes, too...

We'll just have to make sure things don't go wrong, I told myself resolutely, doing my best to shake off the morose thoughts.

Half an hour later, I was in the middle of a long line of sleek, expensive vehicles waiting to round the white, circle drive of a massive house on the outskirts of the city. I had hoped to find the parking area and make my way into the party as unobtrusively as possible, ideally through a side entrance, but it turned out there was only one road in and out of the property. At least, that I was able to find. The grounds were expansive, so there was probably another road or two hidden somewhere.

With every tiny forward movement of the line, I felt my anxiety growing. The winged emblem of the Bentley in front of me wasn't helping. I could only imagine what the guy behind me was thinking as he stared at my dented bumper and crooked Toyota insignia.

My turn came at last, and all too soon. I prayed it would be obvious what I was supposed to do, since the Bentley turned out to just be dropping somebody off and continuing on.

A group of photographers lined the walk to the entrance. My hands grew slick on the steering wheel.

A young man in a black vest and bowtie ran up and opened my door, offering his hand to help me out. If I was a braver person, I would have planted a kiss on him in thanks. As it was, my knees felt wobbly from relief. He guided me around the car and set me on the path to the entrance with a friendly smile, then hustled back to jump in the driver's seat and pull away.

I realized belatedly he'd left a numbered ticket in my hand. I tucked it into my bag for safekeeping, taking advantage of the excuse to keep my head down and hurry past the paparazzi. A couple snapped photos, but they were clearly waiting for important people.

I caught up with the older couple who had arrived in the Bentley and had to slow to an awkward crawl as they dithered along, basking in the camera flashes. Once they ran out of people to take their photos, they finally picked up the pace. A thirty-something woman with a sleek, angled bob stood in the doorway holding a tablet and checking invitations.

"Dr. and Mrs. Winstone, we're so pleased you could attend again this year. Enjoy your evening." The spotlight-hungry couple nodded like they were bestowing a gift on the woman and strolled inside.

I stepped up and held out my invitation, clenching my bag with white knuckles. She took the thick cardstock and compared it to her list. "Ah, yes, Ms. Jensen. We're so pleased you could attend the festival. Enjoy your evening." She handed it back with a bland, practiced smile and promptly turned to the next person. Feeling a little taken aback that I was admitted with no questions asked, I fumbled with my clutch for a moment before managing to tuck the invitation back inside.

The doorway opened to a soaring entry hall with marble floors and murals painted on the ceiling. Garlands of flowers were hung along the walls and instrumental music spilled out of double doors at the far end. I trailed after the Winstones, gaping at everything.

The doctor and his wife disappeared through the open doors, and I hurried after them, realizing I was wasting too much time gawking at the decor. Stepping through, I found myself at the top of a grand staircase, looking over an impeccably dressed crowd. Strangely, most of them wore black masks.

Before I could do more than wonder at it, a voice blasted out of a nearby speaker, nearly sending me sprawling down the stairs in surprise. *"Presenting Dr. and Mrs. Harold and Martha Winstone."*

To my horror, the crowd turned as one to stare at me. The Winstones stood on a landing several feet below me, next to a guy with a microphone and two women stationed beside a small table. Apparently, I was supposed to wait at the door for my turn instead of standing right above them like a big, blue beacon. The spotlight trained on them rose slightly to fully include me.

At least I can't see the crowd with this light blinding me.

Gut clenching, I gathered up my skirt and focused on the stairs as I descended behind the Winstones. They had already continued to the second staircase. Microphone Guy smiled at me and held out a hand. I stared back. His smile dimmed a little, and he leaned toward me, covering the microphone. "Do you want me to announce you?" he whispered.

"You mean that's *optional?*"

He nodded.

"Oh, thank gosh!" I let out a gusty sigh.

The guy's lips quirked like he was trying not to laugh, and he gestured to the women next to him. Turning, I found they were manning a table covered in beautifully decorated masks. Despite being a uniform black, there were numerous shapes and patterns to choose from.

I had only begun to look when the nearer woman picked one up. "If I may?" she asked, holding it out for my perusal.

It was satin, but partially covered in a glimmering cloth similar to my dress's skirt. The material gathered over the right temple and fanned back over the mask's ties. I nodded and the woman deftly slid two hair combs over my ears and attached the ties to them. Whoever arranged this obviously didn't want to be blamed for wrecking women's elaborate hairdos with cheap elastic bands. The woman smiled kindly and directed me toward the lower staircase.

I kept my eyes down until I reached the bottom, determined not to fall on my face, no matter what else might happen that night. Feeling a thrill of success, I looked up with a small grin, which promptly fizzled out.

Everyone was still staring at me.

I looked around desperately for somewhere to retreat to, but the dim lighting and mask weren't doing my eyesight any favors.

A tuxedo-clad chest suddenly appeared in front of me. "Ms. Jensen, it appears you're once again in need of saving."

And, once again, I could have kissed AJ for his timing. I took his offered elbow with a grateful smile. Izzy gave me a determined nod from her place at his other side. They had both also donned masks—his a simple black velvet, and hers lace with tiny silver studs lining the cutouts, as though designed especially for her.

AJ steered us away from the base of the stairs, the crowd parting like water and whispers trailing in our wake. I held my head up and did my best to ignore them. Not for the first time since meeting her, I envied Izzy's seemingly impenetrable skin. AJ wasn't any help either—he swaggered along with a rakish grin plastered on his face, eating up the extra attention.

Despite his obvious enjoyment, the vamp, thankfully, took us to a quieter part of the room, partially hidden behind a support column. Now that I wasn't the center of attention,

I realized the huge room was even taller than the entryway and was flanked by twin rows of columns marching down the length of it. The architect probably interned in Greece.

Once we were somewhat secluded, Izzy turned and gathered us into a tight huddle. She handed me a tiny earbud from her purse and then stepped close and pantomimed fixing my hair. I recognized her cover and quickly stuffed the piece into my ear. It crackled for a moment before resolving itself into the sound of Rachel's voice.

"Can you hear me, Nora?"

Glancing at Izzy, and the tiny camera hidden in the silver pendant hanging around her neck, I gave a small nod.

"Perfect! Gosh, this is so cool! Lina should totally make spy movies or something!"

AJ smirked and glanced around the room. "If this plan actually works, I think any of you ladies could do anything you wanted."

"Tell that to my mother," Rachel sighed.

Izzy raised her eyebrows at me, and I tried to suppress a grin. "So, what now?" I asked.

The announcer cut off any potential responses. *"Presenting Demetri and Loralai Petrovic."*

Surprised to hear another person with that hated name, I peeked around the column to see the newcomers. Even from a distance, Loralai's twisted smirk was like a bucket of ice water down my spine. I jerked back, irrationally fearful of being seen. "Loralai is *married?!*" I hissed at AJ. "I thought you said her name was Evans!"

He grimaced as he tracked their progression down the stairs. "Her name as a human was Evans. That's why she was so angry when I called her by it—as a fellow vampire, she expected me to know better. Many of our kind choose to take on the surname of their sire when they're Turned."

"So that's the guy who made her a vampire?" Rachel asked. Izzy leaned past AJ to get a clear view with the camera.

"Correct."

"You don't sound very happy about it," I said, watching AJ's stormy expression.

"His presence makes this even more complicated. Loralai is unpredictable, but easily overpowered given her youth."

I didn't comment on the fact that AJ was the only one present who would consider her "easily overpowered."

"But Demetri has all the advantages of age," he gave us both a serious look, "and he's the main inspiration for Loralai's violent tendencies."

"Can you beat him if you have to?" Izzy, at least, wasn't afraid to voice our fears.

"Perhaps, if there were no humans to worry about. But not if Miroslav is also in the picture."

We all stared at each other, the same thought mirrored on our faces.

What have we gotten ourselves into?

26

CAL

SHE WAS HERE. And she looked incredible.

It didn't matter that I was standing on the far side of the room, or that she sidestepped the announcer—I would have recognized her anywhere. My slightly elevated position on a narrow landing near one of the garden entrances afforded me a perfect view of her shocked expression when the spotlight landed on her. It seemed the person manning it was more interested in the dazzling woman in the electric blue gown than whoever was actually being announced.

Mother noticed my attention. "Is that her?" she whispered, leaning away from the conversation she was having with Lind and some of the other board members.

I nodded absently, already stepping forward to meet Nora at the bottom of the stairs.

A hand on my arm stilled me. "Remember what I said, Caliban." Mother gave me a solemn look. "Be careful, dear."

I smiled reassuringly and pressed her fingers before pulling away. Turning back toward the entrance, I saw Nora had reached the floor and was looking around with a panicked expression. I hurried along the landing, trying to bypass as much of the crowd as I could.

Just as I stepped down, I saw a tall man approach her. Apprehension seized me, and I backed up to my higher vantage point. Nora turned to the stranger with a grateful expression that had me clenching my fists. I wanted her to look at *me* like that.

Her words from the Sunday before played through my mind for the millionth agonizing time, *"...I don't fit in...someone from your own world is better for you..."* The memory of the tears in her eyes as she finally admitted how uncomfortable she was with my notability was like a knife in my gut every time I recalled it. I couldn't believe how badly I'd misread everything.

As I watched the man lead her toward the far side of the room, I realized there was a dark-haired woman on his other arm. "AJ and Izzy," I breathed. I told myself it was a relief. The radiant smile was for them both, not just him. She didn't share that level of warmth with him every day at work.

Surely not.

The twist in my stomach tightened.

I took a deep breath and let it out slowly. We were all here for a reason, even if I would have been forced to come, regardless. I needed to stay focused on the bigger picture.

The announcer drew my attention once more. *"Presenting Demetri and Loralai Petrovic."*

Surprised, I watched Nora's nemesis sashay down the stairs in a skintight red dress, clinging possessively to the arm of a tall, forbidding-looking man. He looked uncomfortable in a suit, as if he'd prefer to rip it off and use it to strangle someone. I hoped he wasn't someone we would have to contend with.

Someone AJ *has to contend with,* I amended bitterly. I had accepted my role in the plans without complaint, self-aware enough to realize my prominence made me the most logical distracter amongst our group. But after what happened between Nora and me, I hated how useless I felt. I wanted to be able to protect her—to have her *want* my protection.

Fists clenching anew at the waves of envy and regret washing over me, I stepped into the crowd once more and began making my way across the room. I needed to coordinate with the rest of the group, so I might as well get it over with.

"Presenting Miss Alina Dumont, attending on behalf of the esteemed scientist, Dr. Markus Dumont."

A swell of conversation arose at the announcement, and I turned from my position directly across from the stairs. Lina, dressed in a rather daring two-piece yellow gown that seemed a little out of character for the reserved young woman, was receiving a mask from one of the attendants. Once affixed, she made her way down the second flight, gripping her bag with both hands but holding her head high.

I pushed through the remaining few attendees to meet her at the base of the stairs. She looked surprised but accepted my offered arm with a kind smile, prompting more whispers around us. I aimed us toward the others at the side of the room. Izzy and Nora watched our approach, and I found myself staring at the wall behind them rather than trying to hold Nora's gaze.

"Thank you, Cal," Lina whispered as we reached them. She squeezed my arm before letting go.

"Nice dress, Lina," said Izzy.

Lina grimaced and covered the bare strip of skin on her abdomen. "It's my sister's prom dress. Isn't it awful?"

Izzy chuckled. "It's not exactly your style."

Nora stared at me, color staining the bits of her cheeks I could see below her mask. I had no idea what to say.

"You're not wearing a mask," she blurted.

"No." I cleared my throat. "I thought any distractions I might need to provide would be more effective if people could see who I am."

Lina nodded supportively.

"Oh," Nora replied. Her voice was quiet. "Oh! This is AJ." She gestured to the side and stepped back, allowing me to move forward and see the man standing behind the column.

A pair of familiar red eyes came into view, despite being shadowed behind a plain black mask.

"*Alden?!*" I gaped at him in confusion.

My childhood friend smirked, and Nora looked back and forth between us. "Wait, *you're* Alden? Why didn't you tell me you two know each other?! Why did you tell me your name was *AJ?!*"

"To be fair, I said you could *call* me AJ. You assumed it was my name, and I didn't correct you," he drawled. "As far as not telling you I know Cal..." He shrugged and grinned at me. "I wanted to see his expression when he found out."

I couldn't decide if I wanted to laugh in relief or punch him. I settled for grabbing his arm and dragging him away from the girls. "How could you have gone all this time without telling me?" I growled once we were out of earshot.

"Quite easily," was his smug reply.

I rolled my eyes. "Fine. *Why* did you go all this time without telling me?"

"Why not? It wasn't hurting anything, and I really did want to see your face. It didn't disappoint, by the way." He gave me an exaggerated smirk.

I glared in return. "How did you meet her?"

"We rode the elevator together. Then later she came downstairs asking me about Miroslav. I'm sure she already told you all this."

She had, but I wanted to hear it from him. "Since when is your office in the same building as Jensen Publishing?"

"Since last year. Our new building still isn't done, so we started sharing space with another firm temporarily. You don't visit me at work, so I didn't bother to tell you."

Things Nora had told me about AJ suddenly clicked into place. Alden was one of my family's personal lawyers, but I'd assumed Nora meant the vampire belonged to one of the several firms V-Corp kept on retainer for corporate litigation matters.

AJ's last name was Hunt. Alden had told me once, a long time ago, that Hunt was his legal name but that he went by Lancaster among the vampires—and thus, V-Corp—because they respected his mother's bloodline over his father's. I was so used to hearing him referred to as "Mr. Lancaster," I'd forgotten all about it.

I narrowed my eyes at him, unable to completely dispel my suspicion now that it'd had time to fester. "What are your intentions toward Nora?"

He rolled his eyes and clapped me on the shoulder. "You can dispense with the drama. I wouldn't have spent all this time convincing you to go after her if I only wanted to scoop her up for myself. I'm not *that* obsessed with beating the competition."

The knot in my gut eased at last. I'd known Alden my whole life and trusted him completely. He'd let me tag along after him when I was just a youngster and, despite all odds, had become a true friend as I grew up. I suddenly felt much more confident in our plans now that I knew it was him we were relying on rather than a stranger.

"You're right," I replied. "I'm sorry."

"Don't be. You need to save your energy for winning her back. And I still want to hear how you screwed it up in the first place, by the way."

"Shouldn't I be saving my energy for fighting vampires?" I asked dryly.

"Naw, that's my job. You've got more important things to attend to." He slung an arm around my shoulders and pointed me back toward Nora. "I wouldn't mind a good word on my behalf to Isolde, though," he whispered just before we reached the girls. I looked at him skeptically and received a cheeky wink in return. He sidled up to Izzy and murmured in her ear, his body brushing against her in a way that would make most women blush. She looked like she wasn't aware he even existed.

I fought a smirk.

"Here, Cal." Izzy stepped away from Alden's flirtation attempts and discreetly handed me a small earpiece. "Everyone else already has theirs."

I maneuvered it into place and was rewarded with Rachel's bubbly voice. *"Hi Cal! Can you hear me okay?"*

"Hello, Rachel. I can hear you," I replied with a smile.

"Great! I'm so glad you're on our team, and I think it's suuuper romantic that you're trying to win Nora back. I have all kinds of great ideas for that, if you need them!"

Flushing, my eyes shot to Nora's, but she immediately looked away. I cleared my throat. "Erm, right. Thank you." I turned a glare toward Alden, who shrugged unapologetically.

"You knew we'd have earpieces," he said.

"Anyway," Lina interrupted. "I'm sure we've all realized that this masquerade business is going to make our plan a whole lot harder. I don't know about any of you, but I wasn't overly confident in my ability to recognize the people on our list even before they decided to wear disguises, so it's probably best if we start mingling right away and just do the best we can. Any last-minute pointers, AJ? Or Alden? What are we supposed to call you now?"

"Al," I supplied, smirking.

"Not Al," he said, returning my earlier glare. "Alden is fine, but I'm also used to AJ now that Nora has used it for so long." He grinned at her, and she scowled back. Sobering, he looked us each in the eye by turns. "Just be careful. If you see anything suspicious, or if you find a vampire, let me know immediately. Don't try anything heroic. I think we can do this if we work together, but you all need to remember that

your main role here is to be my eyes and ears. I can't do my part if I'm also trying to rescue one—or all—of you."

We each nodded our understanding.

"Good luck," he added quietly. "We're going to need it." He tucked Izzy's arm under his and steered them out of our little alcove.

Lina squeezed Nora's hand and gave me an encouraging smile before following the others out. As she passed, she slipped a small item into my hand. Glancing down, I saw it was a tie pin with a round embellishment on the end. As agreed upon beforehand, I would wear the other camera for Rachel. I pinned it on quickly and turned to Nora, holding my arm out. "Shall we?"

Her throat bobbed, and she stepped forward, not meeting my eyes. Wrapping tentative fingers around my arm, she quickly turned to face the crowd, clearly not wanting to interact with me. I tried to swallow the feeling of rejection and focus on the task at hand. As we moved out from behind the column, her skirts brushed against my leg with every step, further diverting my attention.

I'm not sure I can do this.

Thankfully, Rachel provided a timely distraction. *"Oh! There's one of our guys right over there by the drinks! Izzy, point me over there!"*

I glanced in the direction Rachel indicated, trying to look casual. Alden and Izzy were strolling toward one of the refreshment tables. The vampire reached out and clapped another man on the shoulder with a friendly smile, seemingly trying to politely move past him to one of the drink stands. The man did a double take before taking a large step back, dipping into what looked like an awkward bow. Alden nodded and turned away, pouring drinks for Izzy and himself.

"AJ says—I mean, Alden says the guy is human and not a priority. He got really weird when he saw Alden was a vampire, though, so Alden says let's keep an eye on him."

I tried to make a note of the man's appearance, silently cursing the vampires for choosing to have their big moment at an event where everyone looked nearly identical.

"Skinny weasel guy, got it," Nora murmured next to me. I grinned and squeezed her arm without thinking. A quick inhalation was all the response I received.

I took us back across the room to the landing, hoping to give us—and Rachel—a good overview of the crowd. I realized my mistake as soon as we stepped up and turned to face the room. People immediately began to notice us, elbowing each other and murmuring. Nora stiffened beside me. "I'm sorry," I whispered. "I thought it would give us a better view."

She didn't say anything for a long, agonizing moment. Then her fingers gently pressed my arm. "It was a good idea," she replied. "I see one of our people by the stairs, Rachel. That older lady with the weird hair."

I rotated, drawing Nora with me. "Purple dress," I added.

"Yes! Good spot, guys! Gray-haired lady, spangly purple dress, awful feather boa." There was a rustling sound. *"According to our notes, she is a vampire, but not one of the key players. Alden said she's sort of an assistant to one of the Circle members."*

"Caliban, dear, won't you introduce me to your friend?" Mother's voice made my stomach clench.

Turning, my smile was more of a baring of teeth. "Mother," I ground out.

"Uh-oh. Good luck!" Rachel whispered, even though my mother couldn't possibly hear her.

Mother smiled at me expectantly, the gleam in her eyes challenging.

"Of course," I said, gesturing to Nora. "This is Nora Jensen. Nora, this is my mother, Clara Vasile."

Nora smiled nervously and took my mother's offered hand. "It's very nice to meet you, Mrs. Vasile. Cal has told me a lot about you."

"Oh, please, call me Clara. And I'm sure he has." Mother gave me a rueful look.

I shrugged. "Nothing too terrible."

Nora's fingers crushed the fabric of her skirt. I longed to reach for her hand and offer whatever encouragement I could. Instead, I stuffed mine into my pockets, determined to respect her space.

Mother noticed, of course. She raised a questioning eyebrow at me before turning back to Nora. "Ms. Jensen, are you related to Adam Jensen, of Jensen Publishing?"

Nora flicked her eyes to me briefly. "Yes," she replied. "He was my father."

"Oh, I'm so sorry, dear. Adam was a wonderful man. I always admired how skillfully he ran his company."

"I, um, I wasn't aware you knew him."

Neither was I.

"Not well, I'm afraid. We only ever spoke at a few business meetings with the rest of the board. But the Jensen Publishing numbers painted an admirable picture of the man. The company maintained some of the lowest turnover rates and most efficient outputs of V-Corp's subsidiaries."

The glowing review seemed to encourage Nora. She gave my mother a genuine smile and nodded. "I'm glad to hear that. Dad always said a company's success depends on the happiness of its employees. He tried really hard to make sure everyone there enjoyed their work."

"It obviously paid off. I told the other board members several times that we needed to bottle whatever was happening at Jensen so we could share it with our other companies." Mother smiled and reached out to squeeze Nora's shoulder. "I'm very glad to meet you. Your father would be proud of the beautiful young lady you've become."

Nora blushed and Mother stepped back, her manner brisk once more. "Well, I'll leave you two to enjoy yourselves. Heaven knows no one wants a parent hovering around when you're trying to have a romantic evening." She waved and walked away, leaving me mortified.

I turned hesitantly to Nora. Her cheeks were bright red as she stared after Mother. She faced the crowd once more, refusing to look at me. Multiple people were still watching us, having obviously observed the whole exchange. Not for the first time, I cursed my family's fame.

The loudspeakers blared once more. *"Presenting Elder Lantz and Miss Charna Hersh."*

"Ooo! Everybody look! He's important!" Rachel chirped excitedly in my ear.

We turned to the stairs, along with most of the crowd. Vampires rarely attended human events, and important vampires never did. Charna wore what might be termed a shiny dishcloth, going by how much of her body it covered. Every step she took flashed skin all the way up to her hip. Elder Lantz was surprisingly short and bald-headed. He wore a similar robe to what Kael had worn when I met him. He wouldn't be easy to lose in the crowd.

"I don't remember her trying *that* on in the store," Nora murmured.

Before I could reply, a large group of people pushed through the entrance, causing a great deal of murmuring to break out. Even the soft music playing seemed to dim. I recognized Elder Kael at the front and saw several others wearing the same robes.

"Oh boy, guys." Rachel's voice crackled. *"I don't think we need to look around anymore. Everybody just got here."*

27

I WATCHED THE vampires descend the stairs with a feeling of dread. There were so many of them! How were we possibly going to prevent them from reviving Miroslav with a handful of humans and one much-younger vampire?

"Lina wants us all to meet back up. She said to head for the big potted tree in the back corner."

Cal stepped off the raised landing we were on, tugging me with him. The people nearest us moved out of the way, whispering to their neighbors. My hand clenched Cal's arm convulsively, and he tucked me closer to his side in response. We stopped at the drink table briefly before wandering toward the tree.

Izzy and *Alden* (*ugh!*) smiled and waved as we approached, as though we were just there to socialize. Lina arrived a moment later, pulling on her crop top in a fruitless endeavor to cover her stomach. "Remind me never to borrow one of Rosalie's outfits again," she grumbled.

"I think you look awesome, Lina!" Rachel reassured her.

Lina snorted. "Thank you, Rachel. Okay, everyone, what are we thinking here?" She looked at Alden.

"Things are complicated, but it's about what we expected," he replied. "The Elders have reached an age where they will avoid a fight, if at all possible, but if it comes to it, any of them would be more than a match for me. I think we need to continue operating under the assumption they're here for publicity, and not to start a bloodbath. Distraction and prevention are our goals and, frankly, really all we can hope to accomplish, anyway."

Lina nodded. "With that in mind, I think we might have the most luck if we can break their group up a bit and keep them occupied. I don't know what reviving Miroslav entails, but I assume there's a reason there are so many vampires in attendance."

"I agree," said Alden. "From what I was able to find out, they're likely going to try to perform a specific ritual that will require participation from all the Circle members. If we can keep them apart long enough, they'll lose their window of opportunity."

"Say all this works," Izzy spoke up for the first time. "What's to stop them from turning around and reviving him somewhere else tomorrow?"

"Nothing, unfortunately," replied Alden. "But we'll cross that bridge when we come to it."

Looking around at the grim expressions on my friend's faces, I gathered my courage. "I'll distract Charna," I volunteered. "Maybe I can get her to keep her dad out of the way."

"Perfect," said Lina. "Given Charna's reactions in the past, I imagine Cal will be able to help with that."

She was right, much as I wished I had a different partner in this endeavor. I suddenly pictured Cal escorting Lina around and realized I didn't wish that at all.

One problem at a time, Nora.

"My stepmother is over there." Izzy nodded toward where most of the vampires were grouped, a large buffer of empty space between them and the rest of the crowd.

"Excellent." Alden's eyes gleamed. "Let's go pay her a visit."

Izzy sighed, but took his arm once more.

"I don't have any connections to the vampires, so I'll try to talk to the humans on our list and figure out what they're planning," Lina said. "Rachel, please keep us all updated. And point out anything suspicious."

"Aye aye, Captain!"

We went our separate ways, Cal and I heading toward the glimmering golden beacon in the center of the room. We pushed through the crowd, primarily consisting of men, and I plastered a huge smile on my face. "Charna! I'm so happy to see you!"

She turned and gasped, clutching her hands dramatically to her chest. I'm sure I wasn't the only one to notice how the gesture made her cleavage swell excessively. "Nora, darling! You look exquisite! I knew the gown I picked would suit you perfectly!" She rushed over to embrace me.

I patted her back and did my best to maintain a pleasant expression. When she pulled away, I cleared my throat and leaned into Cal's side, praying he would play along. "Charna, this is Cal. I've told him all about you and how good of friends we've become."

Cal bowed over her hand. "Charna, it's an honor to meet you at last. I'm so grateful to you for the kindness and support you've shown to Nora."

Charna's eyes glittered in delight. She cast me a knowing look. "Oh, Mr. Vasile, the honor is all mine. Nora is my dearest friend. There isn't a thing I wouldn't do for her."

It was the opening I was waiting for. "You're too kind, Charna! Although, I must admit I've been very interested in meeting your father ever since you told me about him. Would you mind introducing us?"

Her smile twisted with glee. "Not at all! I know he'll be thrilled to meet you. Let me call him." She looked around for a moment before apparently spotting him—I was too short to see past the ring of people around us, who were eating up our performance like the latest blockbuster. Touching the shoulder of a young man nearby, Charna moved toward him until her chest pressed against his. "Excuse me, darling," she breathed and tipped her head to peer past him.

I expected her to do something awful, like screech across the room at her father, and braced myself for it. Instead, she did nothing more than stare intently over the shoulder of the guy, who tried very hard not to be obvious about the fact he was sniffing her hair.

A long, awkward moment passed before she turned back to us with a bright smile, ignoring the crestfallen expression of her admirer. "He'll be here in a moment," she said.

Sure enough, a commotion at the back of the crowd drew our attention. People parted ways and Elder Lantz stepped into view. I couldn't help gaping at him.

"What the heck just happened?!" yelped Rachel.

I wouldn't mind knowing that myself.

"Papa, this is my dear friend, Nora Jensen, and her lover, Caliban Vasile." Charna gestured to us with a wicked glint in her eye.

I couldn't get my voice to work. The word *lover* seemed to ring in my ears, drowning out everything else.

"Mr. Vasile, Ms. Jensen, it's an honor." Charna's dad tucked his hands into his sleeves and bowed to us both like some kind of monk.

"Elder Lantz, the honor is ours." Cal's voice sounded strained.

Lantz gave him a pleased smile as Charna draped herself across her much-shorter father's shoulders, the slit in her dress straining dangerously against her hip. I imagined a stiff breeze would be the highlight of every man's evening.

"So, Elder Lantz, Charna's told me a bit about the work that you do—it sounds very interesting. Would you tell me more about it?" I asked, praying he shared his daughter's penchant for bragging.

My hopes looked to be rewarded as the vampire's chest swelled and his expression turned smug. "Of course, Ms. Jensen! Perhaps you'd care to walk with me, and I can tell you all about it?" He held out his hand.

I glanced at Cal, who gave me a tiny nod. "That sounds delightful." I took the vampire's hand, which was shockingly cold, and followed him through the crowd. A look over my shoulder revealed Charna, now plastered to Cal's side, following close behind. When we left our audience, Lantz transferred my hand to his arm, to my immense relief. I discreetly wiggled my fingers, trying to work the feeling back into them.

We slowly circled the room as Lantz talked my ear off about how great it was to be a vampire (the greatest) and all the important stuff the Circle of Elders was in charge of (apparently everything). He glossed over the bits about Miroslav, but I was able to read between the lines of phrases like "We receive enlightenment" and "Our path is laid before us" as he talked about their pseudo-religion.

The music suddenly changed, and the crowd started pushing out to the edges of the room. *"Ladies and gentlemen, please clear the floor. The dancing is about to begin,"* said the announcer.

"How delightful. Would you care to dance, Ms. Jensen?" I tried to wipe the shock off my face as I stared at the vampire.

"Oh Papa, don't be silly." Charna stepped to his side. "Nora and Cal want to dance together, of course."

"Ah, you're right—young love!" He beamed at us before taking Charna's hand and leading her onto the dance floor.

I felt Cal's presence beside me. "We don't have to," he murmured.

"I'm not sure we have a choice," I sighed, meeting Charna's fierce gaze across the space.

"Don't worry, Nora and Cal, you're doing an awesome job of distracting Charna's dad! It looks like the vampires have tried to gather once or twice already, but he missed both chances.

"Izzy and Alden are doing great at annoying some of the others. Izzy plays a spoiled socialite way better than I would've ever expected, and Alden is keeping this Kael guy busy with pestering him about joining the Circle."

Cal took my hand and led us through the bystanders. "Thanks, Rachel. How is Lina doing?" he murmured.

"So-so. She's talked to several people, and is doing some fantastic acting, but none of the humans have any real idea what's going to happen tonight beyond it being important."

We reached the center of the dance floor, and Cal turned to face me, raising our joined hands and wrapping his other around my waist. The heat from his fingers seared through my dress, and I let out a gasp. "Is this the best use of our time?" I hissed, though it'd been my idea in the first place.

Cal flicked his eyes toward Charna and Lantz as they spun past, the small man looking perfectly at ease with his towering partner. "As long as they're occupied, I'd say it is."

I gulped and froze when he moved toward me, nearly causing him to step on my toes. Instead, we wound up unbearably close together. The smell of soap and warm skin washed over me, only adding to my edginess. "I don't know how to dance like this," I whispered.

Cal smiled down at me. "Just relax and let me lead," he whispered back. He slowly stepped forward again, and I moved to mirror him. A few more out-of-time steps later, I began to get the hang of it.

"Ready to join the others?" he asked, tipping his head toward the line of whirling dancers circling us.

I shook my head adamantly, but his smile just grew, crinkling adorably around his eyes. He guided me through the steps, moving us toward the outer ring. "Be brave," he whispered and spun us into the midst of the others.

I squeaked and fumbled the first few steps, but got my bearings back quickly. Before long, I was returning Cal's grin as we whirled around the perimeter of the dance floor.

The song was over all too soon, leaving me gasping in delight. "That was so much fun!" I exclaimed.

He beamed at me. "Care for another?"

Several songs later—all of which Charna and her father also danced—we stumbled back into the crowd, panting and elated. Cal brought drinks, and we stood together, giggling like kids, as we watched Elder Lantz sashay around his daughter to a thumping Latin beat.

"Do we have to label him a bad guy? He's got some sweet moves!"

Rachel wasn't wrong. The vampire looked like he'd enjoy nothing more than dancing the night away, much to the dismay of the line of men that kept waiting for an opportunity to steal Charna from him.

"Maybe we can convince him to give up evil and open a dance club," I snickered.

"Hey, I'd go to it," Cal said.

"Me, too," I replied, smiling up at him. He met my gaze and a spark lit in his eyes. He stepped closer, and the sound and crowd around us seemed to fade. His gaze dipped to my lips. I felt my cheeks flush, but I didn't turn away.

Maybe I don't have to tell him anything—maybe I can just show him.

Rising on tiptoe, I tipped my face upward. His response was immediate and stole my breath away. Snaking an arm around my waist, he pulled me flush against his chest and pressed his lips over my own, kissing me with the fervency of a man restored to life.

I finally broke off the embrace with a gasp. "Wow!"

"I missed you," he murmured, leaning his forehead against mine.

Closing my eyes, I basked in his warmth. "I'm sorry for hurting you."

He leaned back, and I opened my eyes. "I understand why you did it," he said, his gaze simmering. "But will you please try to trust me? I'll never want anyone else but you."

"I trust you," I whispered. "I'm not going anywhere."

His hand tightened at my waist as he dipped toward me with a hungry expression.

"Guys, I'm so sorry, but Charna and her dad are leaving!"

I pulled away in time to see Charna's caramel, glitter-dusted shoulders disappearing into the crowd on the far side of the room.

"Come on." Cal pulled me after him, cutting straight through the middle of the dancers, and plunging into the crush of bodies on the other side. I fell behind as we struggled to get through, but Cal kept a firm hold on my hand.

Someone suddenly latched onto my wrist, jerking me away from Cal, who was quickly swallowed up by the crowd. "I guess you lack that common sense, after all," a voice growled in my ear.

I blinked and stared dazedly around the balcony overlooking the garden. When did I go outside? Why was I out here?

"Nora! Are you there?!" Rachel's voice rang frantically in my ear.

Cal rejected you. You couldn't stand to be in there a moment longer.

The thought brought an abrupt stab of pain. "I'm going home," I sniffled. Tears welling in my eyes, I pulled the earpiece out and fumbled in my purse for my valet ticket. The notion of going back through the party to reach the entrance made me sick to my stomach.

Clenching the ticket, I crept through the door and peered around. No one nearby paid me any attention. I picked up my skirts and hustled toward the staircase, keeping as close to the wall as possible. The columns screened my flight, and I was nearly to the front of the room when strong hands gripped my shoulders and whirled me around.

"Nora! What are you doing?" I'd never seen Alden look so upset.

I struggled against him. "Let me go—I have to leave! I can't stay here!"

"Look at me."

"No, let go of me!" I scratched at his hands, desperate to get away.

He turned and propelled me toward a nearby doorway, clapping a hand over my mouth as my protests escalated. Dragging me through, he kicked the door shut behind us and pushed me against the wall. With his knees braced on either side of my thighs, he held my face in both hands, forcing me to meet his gaze.

A single glimpse of blood-red and I clenched my eyes shut, still fighting against his hold.

"Open your eyes, Nora," he growled.

"No! I won't let you control me!"

"I'm not going to compel you; now open your eyes!" He ripped off my mask, pulling half my hairstyle out with it.

I opened my eyes and glared at him. "I wish I'd never met you," I snarled. "Izzy is better off dead than with someone like you!"

His expression turned mournful. "Forgive me," he whispered. Tangling his fingers in my hair, he pulled my head to the side and swooped down. A sharp pain bloomed in my neck, and I cried out, pounding his chest with my fists. He pressed his body into me, crushing me against the wall and trapping my hands between us. I sobbed weakly. My knees buckled and my vision went black.

———

"Nora? Can you hear me?" The voice sounded like it came from underwater.

I peeled my eyes open and looked up at Lina's blurry face hovering above me. "Lina?" I croaked. "What happened?"

"Um. It's a bit complicated." She glanced to the side.

I followed her gaze and saw Alden sitting in a nearby chair, head hanging, and arms draped over his knees.

"Alden? Did you—did you *bite* me?" I raised a hand and found a wad of tissue at my neck.

Lina gently pushed my fingers away. "It's okay; you'll be okay." She glared at Alden. "Won't she?"

The vampire raised his head. "She'll be fine. What do you remember, Nora?"

"I remember...I was trying to leave. Cal upset me." But no, that didn't seem right. "Wait, I don't remember what he did. He—we were following Charna. Someone grabbed me." I gasped, blank spots in my memory slowly filling in. "It was Loralai! She told me to leave. She told me Cal didn't want me here." I stopped, puzzled. "Why did I believe her?"

Alden sighed. "Because she was compelling you. Judging by your reaction to me trying to help you, she's been doing it for a long time."

"She brain-bent me? But—but I thought that wears off quickly?"

"There are different levels of compulsion. The longer a vampire compels a human, the longer each new compulsion will take to wear off—and the more serious the effects."

Lina dashed a hand across her eyes and smoothed my hair, seemingly needing something to do. "Will it cause permanent damage?" she asked, her voice wobbly.

"It can. Hopefully, we caught it in time."

I touched my neck again. "Is that why you bit me?"

He gave me an apologetic look. "Yes. I'm sorry it had to come to that. The only way to break a deep level of compulsion is for another vampire to feed on the human."

"How does that break it?" I asked.

"The injection of my saliva into your blood creates an instant bond between us and dissolves any pre-existing bonds or compulsions." My eyes widened, and he held up his hands. "It's not enough to Turn you, don't worry. And it will fade. For now, you'll just feel a stronger-than-normal attachment to me. Not that it could be much stronger." He winked and I couldn't help chuckling.

"Thank you, Alden." More memories surfaced, and I winced. "I'm sorry I was so awful to you. I didn't mean any of those things I said."

"Don't worry about it. It's a side effect of bonding with a vampire. Now, if she comes around, you'll feel an instinct to fight against her for my sake."

I digested that for a moment.

"Is that why vampires have defined groups of followers?" Lina asked as she helped me sit up.

"Exactly why. Our influence doesn't mix well with that of others."

Lina opened her mouth to reply, but a faint ringing sound cut her off. She winced and touched her ear, reminding me I'd taken my earpiece out. Before I could look around for my purse, Lina's expression turned to horror, and she whirled toward Alden. He was already gone; the door swinging behind him.

"What's happening?" I asked as Lina jumped up and pulled me to my feet.

"I'm not sure. Rachel says Cal's in trouble."

Still feeling faint, I leaned on Lina as we hurried from the room. The crowd had shifted, the bulk of it pressing back against the edges of the room. We elbowed our way through and found the Circle of Elders, chanting in a strange language and standing in the middle of what had been the dance floor, their arms outstretched as they formed a ring surrounding two figures. The other vampires stood guard around them.

A struggle to the left caught my attention. Alden was grappling with Demetri Petrovic and another vampire. I took a step toward them, unsure what I planned to do, when a voice rang out.

"Nora, dear! You're just in time! Come be a part of the celebration." Charna moved into view and beckoned to me.

The humans in the room zeroed in on me, those nearest taking a collective step back. I felt like I was marching to my doom. Lina stayed close by my side. The other vampires' expressions ranged from smirks to snarls. The Circle ignored everything, maintaining their eerie chanting.

When we reached Charna, she tucked me under her arm, ignoring Lina, and pulled me toward the Circle. The vampires gave way until we had a clear view over the arms of the chanting Elders. "Welcome to your future, Nora. Isn't it glorious?" Charna whispered.

Kael stood in the middle of the ring, one long-fingered hand upraised and the other wrapped around Cal's neck as he kneeled before the vampire. I lunged forward, but Charna held me in an iron grip. I was dimly aware of the sound of Lina struggling behind me. Cal seemed to be paralyzed as he stared up at the Elder vampire, not moving a muscle.

As I watched in horror, dark lines appeared beneath Kael's fingers and began to climb Cal's neck. I realized they were his veins as they crept across his face, spreading over his ears and twisting around his lips. When they reached his eyes, the irises began to distort, the color swirling and spreading until his eyes turned completely black.

I screamed. I didn't stop screaming until Charna finally released me, and I collapsed, my eyes still riveted on Cal. On the horror they were creating.

28

LIGHT SEARED INTO my eyelids as heat scorched through my veins. I clenched my fists, feeling the strength in my arms. For the first time in over five hundred years, I had complete control of my body. I opened my eyes to see Kael standing over me. The pathetic worm grinned at me, his lips peeling back in a ghoulish expression. He stepped away, and I felt a sharp pinch in my neck. Something metallic caught the light as he tucked his hands into his sleeves. "My Lord Miroslav, we are honored you have returned to us," he said, bowing over his arms.

I continued to take stock of my body, out of practice with processing physical sensations. I realized I was kneeling and moved to stand. Kael rushed forward to assist me, but stopped when a low growl rumbled through my chest. I wobbled for only a moment, my enhanced strength and senses allowing me to quickly regain my former agility. Looking around, I recognized several members of the Circle as they surrounded us with similar looks of adoration plastered across their faces. Others were unknown to me. Beyond them stood a smattering of young vampires, as well as a handful of humans. A larger crowd of humans ringed the outer edges of the room we were in.

"Where are we?" I rumbled. My voice sounded unfamiliar, but then, it always did after a Ritual.

"The yearly Solstice Festival, my Lord."

Ah, yes. They had told me they planned to revive me in the middle of a human event. Looking around, I blinked at the harsh lighting. This was unlike any festival I had seen before.

"Cal?" A timid voice reached my ears.

Facing the speaker, I saw a puddle of blue fabric on the ground. The puddle shrank as a small, golden-haired woman rose out of it. She took a step toward me.

"Cal, is that you?"

This had happened with previous Rituals. Grieving loved ones believed I was their beloved brought back to life. "No," I said. Her features crumpled, and I turned away. I'd taken a mere step when a strange tugging sensation began in my chest. I stopped to analyze the feeling. It was like nothing I'd felt before.

No... I *had* felt it. Many lifetimes ago.

The sound of the woman's sobs intensified the feeling. Iva's face suddenly came to mind, tears running down her cheeks as she clutched her stomach. She'd wept for weeks for the loss of our unborn child, and I had been powerless to do anything but grieve with her.

The pull increased.

I faced the woman once more, placing a hand under her chin to raise her gaze to mine. She flinched but didn't pull away. "What's your name, child?"

"Nora," she whispered. Suddenly lunging forward, she pressed her hands to my chest. "You know me, Cal! I know you're still in there! You have to be!"

One of the young vampires dashed forward and yanked her away by her hair. "Get your hands off him, human filth!" he snarled.

In the blink of an eye, the vampire was lying at my feet, his neck twisted at an unnatural angle. Someone shrieked and a stampede of bodies started flooding toward the staircase at the end of the room. I ignored them and offered a hand to the woman. Nora. She gaped at me, fear in her eyes. "I won't hurt you," I promised, not knowing why.

Her fingers trembled as she took my hand, and I felt a shock of electricity at her touch. I pulled her gently to her feet and had the sudden urge to embrace her. I growled and clenched my hand into a fist. What had those incompetent Elders done to me? She shrank back at my expression, and I immediately smoothed my features, hoping to soothe her.

"My Lord, there is much to be done now that you are revived. Perhaps we should return to the manor?"

"I will do as I please, Kael," I said with a warning look at the sniveling rat.

"Of course, my Lord, of course." He bowed several times, looking like a ghastly imitation of a wooden toy I'd once seen in a traveling merchant's wares.

Turning my attention back to the fair-haired human, I pondered what I was to do. For centuries, I'd been plotting my revenge, planning every step in the downfall of the known world. Those plans hadn't involved forming an involuntary bond with the first human I laid eyes on.

Movement over the woman's shoulder caught my eye. Another human female, this one russet-haired, and clad in a scandalous yellow gown, stood nearby. She wrung her hands and looked as though she wanted to approach.

"Do you know this person?" I murmured to Nora. She followed my gaze.

"That's Lina," she said, turning back to me with a devastated expression. "Don't you recognize anyone?"

Another loved one of the deceased, then. I wondered if I would feel compelled to protect this one as well. "I do not," I responded to her question. "But if she is your companion, I will tolerate her presence."

Nora motioned to the other woman, Lina, who approached hesitantly. "Are you Miroslav?" she asked as she stepped to Nora's side. Nora shot her a sharp look.

"I am," I replied. "Nora informs me you are her companion, Lina."

"I am," she parroted.

I looked her over with a disapproving air. "Nora should keep more respectable company."

Nora gasped, and Lina wrapped her arms around her middle, covering the swath of bare skin on display. "It's not my dress," she grumbled.

Movement blurred across the room, drawing my attention to the arrival of a male vampire. He was older than many of the others present, but still just a child, by my estimation. He inserted himself between Nora and me, placing a possessive hand on the woman's arm. "Are you alright?" he murmured, keeping his eyes on me.

Nora nodded and placed her other hand over his. Interesting. Now that he was here, I recognized his scent all over the woman. His mate, perhaps?

For some reason, the thought made me angry.

"Who are you?" I ground out, feeling my canines elongate.

The russet-haired woman pulled at her companion's arm, trying to distance the two of them from us. Intelligent human. Nora held her ground, lifting her chin resolutely. Brave, but foolish.

"Alden Lancaster," the male said with a casual air. "Your host has known me his entire life."

I felt a stir of familiarity. Strange. "Who this body knew in its previous life is of no concern to me."

"If that were true, you wouldn't be so interested in these women. You woke up to a room full of mortals, many of them with much richer blood to tempt you, and yet you set your eyes on these."

He made a fair point—one which I refused to concede. My eyes narrowed on the hand still wrapped around Nora's arm. "What are they to you, whelp? Your sustenance? Your bedmates?"

Nora blanched and ripped her arm out of the male's grip. "Not even!" She glared at me and the other vampire by turns. "What is with you people? We have more important things to worry about right now than your little ego trips!"

The male looked contrite, and I felt a swell of pride for some untold reason. The vampires behind me stirred, angered by the human's lack of respect. I cared little for their opinions. I waved a careless hand. "You may go," I said. "I will call for you if I have need."

"But my Lord—"

The sniveling voice cut off at my growl.

Footsteps sounded behind us, and Nora's expression became panicked. She darted forward and clutched my arm. Brazen, this one. "No, Cal! They might hurt people if you just turn them loose!"

The plight of mortals had ceased to interest me countless years ago, but as I lost myself in the pair of blue eyes gazing up at me, I felt compelled to protect them once more.

"Kael," I called, not taking my eyes off Nora.

His rancid scent drew closer. "How may I serve you, my Lord Miroslav?"

"If any humans are harmed this night, you will answer for it."

I heard his mouth flapping like a fish thrown to shore. "Yes, my Lord," he said at last before hurrying away, no doubt on his way to stop whatever violent revelries he had already sanctioned.

Nora smiled, and I felt my heart give a strange jolt. When had my heart last beat? Frowning, I took stock of my body once more. My skin felt warm. My skin hadn't been warm since my Turning. I touched my throat. A strong pulse throbbed against my fingers. I staggered away from Nora, shocked. How could this be?

She frowned and stepped after me, her arms held out as though she were trying to comfort a wild creature. "What's wrong?"

"What happened to me? This body still lives."

She nodded excitedly. "Yes! I knew it! He's still alive!"

No, it was impossible. The Ritual required a recently deceased body. For many lifetimes, the primary role of the Circle had been to locate and prepare appropriate candidates for my possession. As the Original Vampire, I quickly learned my physical traits were vastly different from that of my offspring. My body withered and eventually ceased to function, much like that of any mortal, but my soul lived on. The Elders discovered the secret of transferring my life-force to a new vessel, reviving my physical self once more.

But a body could not be in possession of two souls. A living host was unthinkable.

Until now, maybe.

I blinked. That thought had not been my own. I turned away from the others and focused inward. Thoughts...feelings...*memories* began to surface that belonged to someone else. Images of Nora. And the male vampire, Alden, and Lina. Others I didn't recognize. So many of Nora.

Then...

I gasped, and my eyes flew open. *Iva.* My precious, darling Iva. How did she live in the thoughts of this mortal? Focusing once more, I searched for her, desperate to see her face. The memories came slowly at first, but then more quickly. Soon, they were rushing by in a colorful blur.

Holding hands with Iva, receiving her kiss on my cheek, her warm embrace. Sometimes she was scolding. Others, crying. She wore strange clothing.

The memories began to change. I found myself looking up at her. Her manner became more lighthearted. She held me in her arms and nuzzled my cheek. She tickled me and made animal sounds as she chased me around a brightly colored bed chamber. She sang to me and bathed me. She tucked me against her chest and whispered endearments.

A final memory played before me. It was dark, and I felt frightened. There were muffled noises and unseen things pressing against me. A sudden light blinded me, and I cried out. The air chilled me, rough hands grasped me.

Then she was there. I laid against her skin and basked in her comfort. She stroked my head and wept. "My sweet baby," she whispered.

Mother.

I opened my eyes and felt a tear roll down my cheek.

Thank you. A feeling of gratitude washed over me with the foreign thought.

"My son," I murmured, awestruck. "I have waited so long for you."

29

I STARED AT Cal's back, waiting for him to turn around.

Not Cal—Miroslav, I reminded myself. *But maybe...*

I wrung my hands and hoped against hope that the momentary *something* I'd glimpsed in his eyes was more than just my desperation causing me to see things.

His shoulders suddenly straightened, and he spun around, fixing me with an unreadable look. "Where is Iva?"

I shot a confused glance at Alden and Lina. "Who?" My voice wavered nervously. He might look like Cal, but the body lying a short distance away spoke to a drastically different truth.

His mouth twisted like he tasted something bitter. "This one's mother," he said, gesturing to himself.

"I can take you to her." Alden stepped up beside me. He leaned over to whisper something in my ear and Miroslav was suddenly there, inserting himself bodily between us with a glare at Alden, who backed away with his hands raised. "This way," he called, turning and sauntering off toward the end of the room opposite the staircase.

Miroslav clasped my hand and followed, tugging me after him almost as if he didn't realize what he was doing. Lina trailed behind, to my relief. The room was empty by that point, and I worried about Izzy. Lina must have understood my intent as I peered around every column we passed. "Izzy's safe," she whispered, tapping her ear with a significant look.

A load I hadn't realized I'd been carrying lifted from my shoulders. Izzy wasn't in danger, and Rachel was still looking out for everyone. I wished I hadn't dropped my purse so I could hear Rachel's updates, but satisfied myself with knowing we were all alive and well.

For the time being, at least.

Alden led us through a nondescript exit and down a maze of hallways until we stood before an imposing door. Steel plated, and featuring a crank instead of a knob, it looked like it belonged in a bank vault. Laying his ear against the door, Alden rapped his knuckles in an intricate rhythm on the surface. A faint tap sounded from inside. Alden sent another series of knocks. Something clanked, and the wheel began to turn. When it stopped, Alden pulled the door open, straining a bit. I couldn't imagine how much it weighed.

A crowd of people awaited us inside, Izzy among them. She stood near a severe-looking woman with silver-streaked hair. Her stepmother, I assumed. Our friend nodded at us but didn't approach.

"Caliban! Thank goodness!" Clara Vasile pushed through the group but pulled up short when she got a good look at her son, clapping a hand over her mouth in shock.

I couldn't blame her. Cal's eyes were still black, and his veins stood out in stark relief against his skin. Everything, down to the way he held himself, screamed *Other*.

"What have you done to my son?" she whimpered.

Miroslav dropped my hand and advanced on the trembling woman. The others shrank back, shoving one another to get away from the monster in their midst. A few beefy-looking men stepped forward, pulling handguns from their coats.

Cal's mother held her ground, even reaching out a shaking hand to touch her son's face when he was close enough. "Caliban," she whispered.

"No," Miroslav's voice was harsh, making Clara flinch. "But I believe he is still here," he added in a softer tone.

Clara stared at him in wonder, hope blooming in her eyes. He reached out and touched her cheek. She laid her own hand over his, turning her face into his palm.

He released a whisper-soft sigh. "You are not her," he murmured. "Though you wear her face."

I wondered at the sorrow in his tone. This Iva person was obviously very important to him. I ached to comfort him, but knew he wouldn't want that. He wasn't Cal, no matter how much I longed for him to be.

"Iva was Miroslav's wife before he became the Original Vampire." Alden inserted himself into the moment. He gave Clara an apologetic look. "She was the mother of the Vasile family line."

Clara gaped, and Miroslav shook his head. "Impossible. My Iva was—*murdered*." He choked on the word, his voice rough. "She never bore any children."

"That is true," replied Alden, bowing his head respectfully. "But the child she carried at the time of her death was saved. She grew up and had children of her own. I've been watching over those children for the past eight generations."

A myriad of emotions crossed Miroslav's face, from grief to hope to wonder.

Watching his reaction caused a lump to form in my throat. To lose your wife in such a horrific way, and when she was pregnant, no less... I reached for his hand without thinking and squeezed it tightly, pouring all the comfort and encouragement I could into the gesture. He pressed my fingers in return, surprising me.

Lina sidled up to me, clasping my other hand. "Who knew Alden was Cal's guardian angel?" she whispered.

I shook my head, at a loss for words. There were so many things I was still trying to wrap my mind around.

The room emptied as people scurried around us, giving Miroslav a wide berth. Soon it was just us, Clara, and a handful of people I assumed must be Cal's board members. My eyes nearly popped out of my head when I spotted Creepy Guy from the coffee house lurking nearby. He raised a cheeky eyebrow at me. Cal was lucky Miroslav was running the show right then, or else I would've had serious words for him.

The thought threatened to drag me down once more. I squared my shoulders and took a deep breath. Cal was alive. That was enough for now. We could figure the rest out later.

Izzy appeared in the doorway. I released Miroslav's hand and followed Lina over to her. "Are you okay?" I asked.

Izzy nodded. "My stepmom's lackeys dragged us off to the panic room as soon as the Circle guys started their ritual." She grimaced. "I'm sorry I wasn't there to help. They wouldn't let me go."

"Don't be sorry," said Lina. "We're just glad you were safe." She glanced toward Miroslav, who was speaking quietly with Clara and Alden. "I think it might have turned out as well as it could have. Nora convinced him to keep the vampires on a tight leash, and it looks like he's somehow connected with Cal's mom. Maybe it'll all be okay."

I clenched my fingers and hoped she was right. I wasn't sure how long I could keep up this optimism if Cal didn't resurface soon.

Lina bumped my shoulder. "We'll figure it out," she said when I met her eyes. "Look how much we accomplished together with just a few days and an apocalypse looming over our heads. I'm sure we'll find a way to bring Cal back."

"We failed pretty spectacularly at preventing Miroslav from coming back," Izzy pointed out helpfully.

Lina glared at her, but I just chuckled at her familiar bluntness. "Yes, but what might have happened if we hadn't been here? Miroslav was ready to send the vamps off on a killing spree until we stopped him."

"Until *you* stopped him," Lina corrected.

I blushed. "I suppose I did."

"And now Nora is free of Loralai's compulsion," added Alden, joining our group. He pulled his earpiece out and handed it to me. I took it with a questioning look. "I can still hear her," he said, pointing to Izzy's ear.

Vampires and their dang senses, I grumbled good-naturedly as I wiggled the bud into my ear.

"Rachel? Still there?"

"Oh my gosh, Nora! You nearly gave me a heart attack earlier! And then Alden didn't help things; I thought he was attacking you for real and totally flipped out!"

Izzy and Lina both nodded.

"I'm sorry. Alden says Loralai had me under compulsion for a long time. I had no idea." I frowned, suddenly remembering my trip to the lawyer's office. And who I ran into on the sidewalk outside their office just before the bike crashed into me. "That dirty—*ugh!* She *is* the one who got me into that accident!"

Another memory coalesced, and I gasped. "Jensen Publishing...it's *mine*," I whispered, hardly able to believe it.

My friends all stared at me, waiting for an explanation. I laughed and hugged Alden impulsively. "Thank you, thank you, thank you! You can bite me anytime you want!" He chuckled and patted my back until an angry snarl split us apart.

Miroslav stalked over, glaring daggers at Alden as he pressed himself against my side. I was too giddy to care. I danced a tiny jig in my heels, grabbing Miroslav's hand and spinning myself under his arm before leaping away to embrace Izzy and Lina both at once. My friends laughed, even Izzy, and Clara smiled somewhat bemusedly as she moved to stand beside Miroslav.

"Good news, I take it?" she asked.

"The best news!" I crowed. "I'll be seeing you in those business meetings soon, Mrs. Vasile!"

This time she laughed, too. "I insist you call me Clara, especially if we're going to be working together."

I suddenly sobered up. "Wait, didn't Cal take over as CEO?"

Clara cast a sad look toward her son. "It wasn't finalized. Under the circumstances, I'm afraid I'll be holding onto the role a bit longer. At least, until we find some answers."

I nodded. Of course, she would need to continue running V-Corp. As far as I knew, Miroslav had neither the knowledge nor interest to attempt it, and I doubted anyone outside the Circle of Elders and their cronies wanted him to try.

Eventually, all of us remaining in the panic room made our way back to the entrance. A small army of waitstaff were clearing away refreshments and taking down decorations in the ballroom as though nothing unusual had happened. The body had disappeared. Considering it was a vampire, I wasn't sure if his corpse was wheeled out, or if he just got up and went home.

The group peeled off in twos or threes until, at last, it was just our small, makeshift family. And Miroslav. He'd refused to go home with Clara, saying he needed to return to the vampires and make sure they weren't causing a ruckus. Of course, he said it much more eloquently.

We wandered out toward the overflow parking lot. Everyone else had called for a ride from the entrance, and several shiny cars rolled past as we walked down the edge of the road. Miroslav startled the first time but ignored the rest—I guessed it was the first automobile he'd seen. I pulled my heels off before we'd gone very far and was padding along the warm pavement in my bare feet.

"It's hard to believe it's over," said Lina, breaking the silence.

"I know," I replied. "It definitely didn't turn out the way I expected. *Either* of the ways I expected." I eyed Miroslav as he walked beside me, but he remained silent.

"I'd better be able to dress up and have the paparazzi fawn over me next time!"

We all chuckled. "Definitely, Rachel," I said.

"Where is this Rachel?" Miroslav's voice grated across my ears, so at odds with Cal's familiar tone. "Is she a spirit?"

I gave him a small grin. "Not quite. I'll introduce you to her soon."

We reached the mostly empty lot and Lina peeled off immediately, pointing. "I was late. My car's right over there." She hugged us all, skipping Miroslav with a wary eye. "I'm so glad we made it through, even if we didn't, um, accomplish our goals." She glanced at the forbidding vampire before turning toward her car. "Goodnight, everyone. Drive safe!"

We continued on, although Miroslav paused to watch Lina drive away, a furrow between his brows. I'd have to introduce him to cars, too.

I sighed. Miroslav was interesting, but I wanted Cal back. More than anything, I wished we could sit out on my deck together, looking at the stars and discussing everything that had happened that night.

Alden and Izzy stopped at a sleek Lexus. I whistled and Alden smirked. "Nothing in the guardianship rules says I can't have an enjoyable vehicle." He stuck his nose in the air, and I huffed a laugh, prompting a low growl from Miroslav.

Izzy rolled her eyes and opened the passenger door, plopping into her seat. Alden, halfway around the car, glared at her. "You're supposed to let me open it for you!" he griped. I snorted and strolled away, waving to Izzy. She waved back and shut the door, cutting off Alden's tirade about gentlemanly behavior.

My dented Toyota was at the very end of the row. I wasn't the first one there, so they must have been trying to hide it. Oh well. The stars were out, and the crickets and frogs were singing. It was a beautiful—albeit bittersweet— night.

"Thank you for walking me," I said. Miroslav gave me a puzzled look, and I remembered it was him I was talking to, not Cal. "Never mind. Do you need a ride somewhere?"

He eyed my car like some kind of festering sore. "No. I can travel faster on my own."

Likely true. "Alright. When will I see you again?" I tried to keep my hopes reasonable.

"Soon, I imagine. This mortal does not like to be parted from you for long." He sounded annoyed by the fact.

I grinned and unlocked my car. "Thank you, Miroslav. And please take care of him."

He nodded and vanished into the darkness.

Shaking my head, I slid into the car, settling into the driver's seat with a giant puff of blue fabric. After a minute or two of stuffing the skirt under my thighs and out of the way, I swung the door shut. It caught on something just before it latched. Frowning, I pulled harder, but it didn't budge.

"What on earth?" I muttered, trying to see what it was stuck on. The door suddenly jerked out of my grip, ripping clean off the car.

Before I could do more than gape, I was flying through the air. I hit with a sickening thud and lay wheezing, unable to draw a breath.

"Hello, Nora." Loralai appeared above me, a psychotic grin plastered across her face. "How I've missed you."

My eyes widened just before a fist smashed into my cheek. Stars danced in my vision, and I struggled to determine which Loralai I was seeing was the real one. I managed to roll over, hacking into the dirt as I belly crawled toward my car. A stiletto speared me into the ground, the heel grinding against my spine.

"*Ah-ah-ah*," she sang. "We've only just begun."

I peeled my face up. Another figure swam in my vision. The image resolved if I squinted just right. Demetri Petrovic leaned against my car, looking bored.

"Please," I whispered. "Help me."

He pulled out a cellphone and swiped the screen. Upbeat electronic music began playing as he tapped away.

I groaned and tried to pull myself forward, my nails digging into the dirt and grass. My face suddenly smashed into the ground and pain bloomed in my nose. She pushed harder. The pain became all-consuming.

Then my lungs started screaming for air. I couldn't breathe. I flailed, trying to catch hold of her hand on the back of my head. Sediment scoured my mouth, and my chest convulsed.

Her hand pulled away, ripping out a chunk of my hair. I gasped, dragging in a huge lungful of air until I choked on it. I gagged and pushed myself onto my hands and knees. Demetri was no longer by my car. Staggering to my feet, I made it one measly step before a hot, piercing pain knifed through my torso. I shrieked and fell back to my knees, looking down in shock at the bloody metal rod sticking out of me.

Loralai strolled into view, casually tapping another length of rebar against her palm. "Oh, Nora, it didn't have to come to this. You could have supported my takeover of the publishing house. You could have stayed out of the way when Caliban took over V-Corp." She stepped closer. "You could have minded your own business when Miroslav awoke." She reached out and twisted the metal fragment in my ribs. I screamed as fire scorched through my body. Smiling, she pulled away and licked the blood off her fingers with obvious relish.

Demetri appeared beside her in a gust of wind. "We need to leave."

She glared at him. "I'm not finished here."

"It doesn't matter—we don't have time."

"Then *you* leave," she snarled.

He just looked at her a moment before shrugging and vanishing once more. She stared after him, a nasty expression on her face. "Coward," she muttered. Turning to me, her lips stretched back into a sadistic smile.

I panted, feeling hot and cold at the same time. And tired. So very tired. I couldn't even muster the energy to keep looking at her face. My eyes dropped to her feet as she approached. Her stilettos sank into the soft dirt with every step, making her gait somewhat wobbly.

That must be annoying, I thought irrelevantly.

As she bent to meet my gaze, lights flashed across her face. She jerked back, shielding her eyes. A solid form smashed into her a moment later, carrying them both out of sight. She shrieked and snarled, but the sound cut off with a gurgle after only a few seconds.

My vision dimmed, and I felt myself falling backward.

"No, no, no!" Arms caught and cradled me gently against a soft lap.

I blinked bleary eyes up at Izzy. "Thanks, Izzy," I sighed. "You're much more comfortable than the dirt."

She laughed and sobbed at the same time. "I'll be sure and put it on my resume." She stroked my hair, and I closed my eyes, relaxing under her touch.

"That's nice," I whispered.

"No, Nora. You can't go to sleep." Alden jostled my stomach, wrapping a cloth around the rebar and making me gasp in pain.

"Don't do that," I hissed, turning my head toward Izzy's comfort.

"I'm sorry, but I have to. An ambulance is on its way, but you need to stay awake."

"I don't want to stay awake," I murmured. "It hurts too much."

Drops of liquid pattered against my cheek. Surprised, I opened my eyes. Izzy dripped another tear onto my face. "Please, stay with us," she pleaded.

Shocked to see so much emotion from her, I nodded weakly.

She smiled and scrubbed a hand over her eyes. "Good," she sniffed. "I couldn't bear to listen to another Ambassador Ravia story without you."

I croaked a laugh, but it sounded more like a liquidy burble and shot daggers of pain through my middle. I groaned. "Stop making me laugh."

"I'm sorry." She started stroking my hair again, and I relaxed once more. Sometime later, I realized she was humming. I hadn't noticed when she started.

"They'll never make it in time," Alden murmured. "I can't hear the sirens."

Izzy continued her soft humming. She stroked my hair, rocking me gently, and wiped away tears that slid down my cheeks.

I looked up at her once more. "I don't want to die," I whispered.

"Shh. You're not going to die. I'll take care of you, and you'll be just fine," she said firmly.

Alden sat close beside her. I did my best to smile at him. "Take care of her, okay?"

His lips pressed together, but he nodded.

I nodded gratefully in return, my eyes sliding shut. As I drifted off, I heard them whispering.

"Can't you do anything for her?"

"Nothing she would want..."

———

Molten fire pouring through my veins woke me. My eyes flew open as I screamed in agony. I tried to thrash, but something held me down. I bucked against it, screaming until my throat turned raw. The pain slowly faded, and my cries tapered off to whimpering sobs. The weight on my chest lifted and strong arms gathered me into a warm embrace.

I grasped at the chest, weeping bitterly. Hands rubbed my back and soothing words whispered into my ear. I heard other voices nearby but couldn't bring myself to make sense of them. My tears eventually slowed, and I tilted my head to see the face of my comforter.

Cal's warm brown eyes looked back at me. "Hey, beautiful," he whispered with a smile.

"Cal?" I whimpered. "How are you here?"

"I guess my soul thought it needed to be in charge for a while. It probably had something to do with seeing the woman I love in pain."

Love. I attempted a weak smile. "Really?"

He nodded and pressed a kiss to my forehead. "I would do anything for you, Nora," he murmured. "I love you."

"I love you, too, Cal," I whispered, my eyes sliding shut. When I opened them, I nearly gasped at the light in his eyes. He grinned and gave me a nearly imperceptible squeeze. It hurt, but in a dull, bruised way. "Why am I not dead?"

"You could stand to sound a little bit happier about that fact," he chastised, and my lips twisted. "Miroslav saved you. His blood healed you somehow."

No wonder my veins were burning. "How did you get his blood in me?" I asked, frowning.

"He bit his wrist—*my* wrist?" Cal rubbed his arm with a confused furrow to his brow before seemingly shaking the thought away and turning his attention back to me with a sheepish expression. "He pried your mouth open and made you swallow it. I'm sorry."

Now that he said it, I realized there was a metallic taste in my mouth. I grimaced at the thought. "So, it healed me? It didn't—I mean, I'm not..."

His smile was gentle. "You're not a vampire. I don't understand how it worked, but I could see Miroslav's thoughts about how his blood is able to heal wounds and diseases as he did it."

Despite my gratitude to the vampire, I couldn't suppress a shudder as I recalled the wracking pain his blood had caused. "I'll try not to put myself in any more life-or-death situations if that's going to be the solution." I pushed away from his chest, my arms trembling, as I attempted to stand.

"I hope you don't, regardless. I can't handle the stress." He helped me to my feet, but when my legs threatened to buckle, he wrapped his left arm around my waist and let me brace against his right, holding me upright against his side.

Lina, Izzy, and Alden hovered nearby. Lina and Izzy rushed over as soon as Cal had me stabilized. "Oh, Nora!" Lina threw her arms around me in the softest hug she'd ever given me, catching Cal in her embrace as well. "Thank goodness that worked! I was so worried the whole way here!" Tear tracks smudged her makeup.

"I'm sorry I worried you," I said, patting her back weakly. She hiccupped a laugh. "How did you all know to come back?" I asked when she pulled away.

"Rachel told us something was happening to you," Izzy said.

I forgot all about the earpiece. I touched my ear, but it was gone—it must have fallen out while Loralai was eviscerating me. "Please tell her thank you," I said, feeling an overwhelming rush of gratitude for my irrepressible friend.

Lina smiled. "She heard you. And said to tell you 'you're welcome,' and she loves you."

"More like, she yelled it," griped Izzy. She was quiet for a moment, then rolled her eyes. "Yes, Rachel, I told you I'll listen to your stories. I only said that to convince Nora to stay alive." She wandered away, still arguing with Rachel. Lina gave me a knowing look and followed Izzy as Cal's arm tightened around me.

"Wait, how did *you* know to come back? You didn't have an earpiece," I asked, looking up at Cal.

He grimaced. "Miroslav smelled your blood."

"Oh. What happened to Loralai?" I whispered.

Alden stepped forward. "She's gone. She won't bother you again."

"Is she...dead?"

He hesitated, then nodded.

My stomach clenched, but I forced myself to take a deep breath. "You did what you had to. I assume it was you that I saw?"

He grinned. "If you saw me, then I must be getting slow in my old age." His expression softened. "I'm glad you hung on, Nora. I told you before, you're important."

"But *why* am I important?" I asked.

Alden glanced at Cal with a smirk. "I'll let you figure that out on your own." Stuffing his hands in his pockets, he strolled away after Lina and Izzy, whistling a jaunty tune. With a start, I realized he wasn't wearing a shirt under his dress coat. Glancing around, I saw a bloody, ruined mess that was once white lying on the ground near our feet and smiled fondly.

Turning in Cal's arms, I tucked my head under his chin and wrapped my arms around his waist. He held me securely against his chest and pressed his lips to my hair.

"What now?" I whispered.

"*Now*, I finally get to hold you for as long as I want."

I smiled against his neck. "I like the sound of that."

30

TWO MONTHS LATER

"MS. JENSEN, WOULD you mind signing for this production order, please?"

I took the clipboard and looked over the order: another shipment of textbooks for the vampires. I had already reviewed the book and had my resident subject matter expert put her stamp of approval on it as well. Signing at the bottom, I handed it back to our new intern. "I told you before, Lisa, you can just call me Nora."

"Oh! Um, sorry...Nora." She gave me a nervous half-smile and hustled down the hallway.

I sighed. Despite it being a private event, pictures and witness accounts from the Solstice Festival had given me an unexpected measure of notoriety. I had once told Cal I wasn't comfortable with his fame, but now people stopped me in the street for my own sake.

Apparently, bringing the Original Vampire to heel was a noteworthy accomplishment. At least, that's the way the media painted it. Some of us knew better.

I smiled, thinking of that night. Despite all the horrible things that happened, I still managed to find my happily ever after.

Or happily ever before?

Once I recovered from my injuries, I returned to my father's lawyers and confirmed the truth of my hazy memories—Jensen Publishing really was mine. Mr. Barnes seemed a little worried about my sanity; it wasn't the first time he'd explained the will to me, after all. Apparently, Loralai had been using her compulsion on me practically since the day my father died to keep me from claiming my inheritance.

My friends insisted I get the full gamut of tests by a doctor, MRIs and the like, but I knew they wouldn't find anything out of the ordinary. They hadn't with Dad, either, after all. The only thing that calmed my fears was the fact I wasn't getting sick or suddenly suffering from migraines. Those symptoms had been the beginning of the end for my dad.

I walked back to my office, gritting my teeth. Alden explained to me in detail how vampiric compulsion works— the twisted bond it creates between the predator and prey— as well as the slow but steady damage it does to a human mind. Once it reaches a certain level of harm, there's no reversing it. I had been so sure Loralai was the cause of Dad's illness, but could never prove it. Knowing I was right all along but there wasn't anything I could have done to stop it didn't help my grief.

Reaching my door, I stopped and took a deep breath. There was nothing I could do but move forward, honoring my dad's memory to the best of my ability. It was a steep learning curve, especially since Loralai had kept me bogged down in menial work, but I was slowly settling into my place as the new head of Jensen Publishing. I had a major advantage in the form of the employees. They were all so grateful and supportive. Hardly a dry eye could be found the day I stepped off the elevator with Cal and announced the change of leadership.

Hello, beautiful.

Speaking of Cal... I smiled and turned around. He stood in the aisle between cubicles, his lips quirked to the side.

What are you doing here?

I'm here to pick you up for our lunch date. His warm voice caressed my mind, and my smile grew.

There had been some definite perks to Loralai's murder attempt. When Miroslav pumped his blood through my body to heal me, it had the side effect of creating the equivalent of a sire bond between us—complete with the unexpected (but very welcome!) gift of communicating mind-to-mind. To my understanding, the ability was rare, only manifesting between two individuals who shared a deep and unbreakable attachment before the Turning. Because Cal's blood was mixed with Miroslav's, it magnified the bond and resulted in our mental connection.

It also explained Charna's bizarre behavior with her father at the festival.

I glanced at the clock as I strolled toward Cal. *It's only nine am.*

He mirrored my steps, meeting me halfway. Wrapping his arms around me, he planted a kiss on my forehead. "I couldn't wait until noon."

"I have a lot to get done this morning," I protested.

"It can wait."

"No one else leaves this early for lunch. I need to set a good example."

"No one else is the boss of the company. And no one else is having lunch with the boss's boss."

I swatted his chest, and he chuckled, the sound rumbling through me.

"Alright, fine." I sighed. "Where are you taking me today?"

"It's a surprise. Get your stuff and meet me by the elevators."

Twenty minutes later, we drove slowly under the arched entrance of the Heritage Home Memorial Gardens.

"Um, Cal? I think you might need to take Rachel up on the offer of those romance pointers," I said, looking out the window at the passing gravestones.

He squeezed my hand but didn't reply.

As we turned down a familiar avenue, I suddenly remembered what day it was. Tears welled in my eyes as I turned to Cal. He gave me a soft smile and pulled into a small parking area. Helping me out of the car, he tucked my arm around his and directed us across the manicured grass, his other hand covering mine. We skirted a moss-covered mausoleum, and a large gravestone came into view. Alden, Izzy, and Lina stood beside it.

I'm not sure if I laughed or sobbed, but the feelings of love and gratitude that washed over me were strong enough to buckle my knees. Cal held me upright until we reached our friends and I fell into Lina's arms, tears running freely down my cheeks. "Thank you so much," I whispered.

She rubbed my back, and I felt her smile against my hair. "You're so welcome."

Reaching out, I dragged Izzy into our embrace. Alden joined a moment later, wrapping his arms around the three of us and eliciting a huff of complaint from Izzy. Finally pulling away, I leaned into Cal's side, his hand sliding comfortably around my waist. Alden grinned at Izzy, who ignored him, and I couldn't help chuckling.

"I'm so glad you're all here. I don't deserve such amazing friends." I wiped the tears from my cheeks.

"You're stuck with us, whether you like it or not. Deserving has nothing to do with it." Izzy smiled despite her gruff tone.

Lina opened her mouth, then shut it abruptly. A few moments later, she tried again. "Rachel says Izzy's right, and also that you deserve nothing but amazing things. And that we are *all* amazing, except Alden." Her lips pressed together in mirth.

"Hey!" Alden folded his arms and glared at the pendant hanging around her neck.

I snorted a laugh, and Cal pressed a kiss to my temple. "We'll give you a minute," he whispered.

As the others slipped away, I kneeled in the grass beside the grave. "Hi, Dad. I'm sorry it's been a while since I was here last. You wouldn't believe some of the crazy stuff that's happened. Well," I smiled, "maybe you would. You always were the first one to get fired up about something new and different.

"I'm running Jensen Publishing now. It didn't happen right away like you wanted, but I got there eventually. Loralai is gone. I was right about her. I wish you would have listened..." I sniffed and wiped my eyes.

"The girls are all still around. They're here with me today, actually. Rachel is still just as energetic as ever," I chuckled. "I know how much you enjoyed talking to her. Lina's still the most kind-hearted one of us. And Izzy has an admirer. He's a good guy, but she's not cutting him any slack. I hope she'll give him a chance one day—I think he would be good for her.

"I met someone, too. You would really like him. He's smart and kind, and he makes me feel so happy. He's kind of a vampire now, as weird as that sounds, but we're making it work. You met his mom before—Clara Vasile. She said a lot of nice things about you. She's been really good to me, too. I was afraid I'd feel out of place with Cal, but no one has ever made me feel like I don't belong. I struggled a lot with that at the beginning, but you and Mom helped me. You both taught me to shake off the bad things and focus on the good, and I'm doing my best to remember that.

"Thank you, Dad. Thank you for everything you did for me, and for how much you loved me. I couldn't have gotten through any of this without all the lessons and advice you gave me. I miss you so much..." Tears welled once more. "Give Mom a kiss for me, okay? I love you both."

Standing, I brushed off my knees and swiped the moisture from my cheeks. I followed the direction my friends had gone and found them setting out Styrofoam containers in a small pavilion.

"I did promise you lunch," Cal said at my questioning look.

I wrapped my arms around him and buried my face in his chest. "Thank you," I whispered.

He squeezed me gently and kissed the top of my head. *I love you.*

I smiled. *I love you, too.*

"Quit canoodling and come eat," Alden griped, tossing a plastic cup at us.

"Fine, fine!" I laughed, retrieving the cup and sitting down at the picnic table.

"How is work going?" asked Lina.

"It's good! I finally feel like I'm moving forward with the company instead of just playing catch-up."

"How is it having Charna work for you?" asked Izzy.

"Surprisingly, it's not bad. It was a really hard decision to let her stay, but it seems to be paying off. She's been my subject matter expert for a month now and hasn't tried to sneak a single thing past me in all the textbooks and propaganda we print for the vampires. I think she just likes the attention. She still tells everyone what great friends we are." I rolled my eyes and crunched on a potato chip. "How's the library, Lina? And your uncle?"

"Uncle Mark is...about the same. Some days are better than others." I gave her a sympathetic look, and she smiled back. "But the library is good. We're getting ready for a special paranormal collection to come through the exhibit room. Supposedly, there's a werewolf that acts as caretaker for the set and travels with it everywhere. The staff is really excited to meet him."

"Wow, that *is* exciting!" I had never even seen a werewolf that I was aware of. "I'll have to come see the exhibit."

"Definitely! You should all come."

"What do you say, Izzy?" asked Alden. "Care to visit the library?"

Izzy swatted his hand as he tried to eat off her plate. "I visit the library often. I'm sure I'll see the exhibit."

Alden looked disappointed, but perked up almost immediately. "What about you, Cal? Ready to meet your *arch-nemesis?*" He waved his hands in a dramatic gesture.

Cal chuckled. "I highly doubt the Original Vampire *has* an arch-nemesis. But I wouldn't mind seeing the exhibit and maybe meeting a werewolf." He squeezed my waist. "Will you go with me and mourn my death if my nemesis defeats me?"

I held the back of my hand to my forehead. "Oh, my dearest! I couldn't possibly bear to see you defeated!"

Alden snorted into his drink, and Lina and Izzy both smirked.

I grinned and bumped Cal with my shoulder. "Besides, Miroslav wouldn't let that happen."

"True. He definitely has an easier time taking control than I do."

My grin softened, and I squeezed Cal's hand. I knew he was more frustrated with Miroslav's presence than he let on, especially since the vampire seemed capable of hijacking his body at any given moment, but Cal struggled immensely to regain control. Alden seemed certain there was a way to separate the two—ideally without Miroslav gaining a fully autonomous body. For now, Cal's presence provided a necessary deterrent to the vampire's destructive instincts while the rest of us continued to search for a solution.

Cal pressed my fingers in return and leaned in for a kiss.

"Not at the table," scolded Izzy.

"You wouldn't say that if you were at the receiving end, my sweet," said Alden, waggling his eyebrows at her.

Her answering look would have turned a lesser man to dust.

Chuckling, I settled for tucking my head against Cal's shoulder and smiling around the table at my friends. As we shared our meal and laughter and fond memories, I basked in the love of my family and realized I couldn't ask for anything better.

Epilogue

THE ANCIENT CREATURE prowled the darkened hallways, his footsteps echoing off the craggy stones. A nameless minion scurried at his heels, but he barely noticed—the slaves were little more than insects in his estimation.

The mortals had surprised him, much to his displeasure. Rather than fleeing in terror like lambs before the slaughter, they had rallied around his abomination and convinced themselves they could help it. That it *deserved* their help.

His lips curled in a sneer.

No matter. There was nothing he relished more than bending the vermin of this world to his indomitable will. The more they resisted, the more delicious their ultimate submission.

A cold wind lashed his skin. Turning a corner, the hallway ended in a gaping hole. He stepped to the edge and surveyed his domain. Pungent sulfur filled his nostrils from the molten pools far below. The wind raged, whipping his face with stinging chunks of ice. The creature shadowing him cowered against the wall.

Pathetic.

Throwing back his shoulders, he roared his challenge into the gale as his features elongated, his fingers curving into wicked claws, the wildfire at his core building into a raging inferno.

The minion whimpered and scurried away, narrowly avoiding a fatal strike from his iron-spiked tail. He launched himself into the abyss, his powerful wings bursting free from the confines of the narrow passage.

"Let them resist me," he thundered as the wind screamed past his ears. "I will grind them into the dust until they beg for my mercy and forgiveness. And then," his lips peeled back from his razor-sharp fangs, "I will feast on their corpses."

The story continues with Lina's adventure in:
The Lycanthrope's Exile

Available now!

Thank You!

Thank you so much for reading *The Vampire's Masquerade*. If you enjoyed meeting Nora and her friends and learning more about the world of paranormals, I'd so appreciate if you would leave this book a rating or review.

Reader reviews and recommendations are the best way for independent authors to reach new audiences.

Please visit www.nelliepeters.com/pls1review or scan the code below to leave a review, get the next book, and join my newsletter—the best way to stay up to date on my writing progress and new releases (plus, you'll receive a FREE *Paranormal Literary Society* prequel novella!).

Also by Nellie Peters

Visit nelliepeters.com to learn more about my books!

WORLD OF PARANORMALS:
A Promise of Eternity
(contemporary dark fantasy)
A House of Torment
A Vow of Mercy

Paranormal Literary Society
(contemporary fantasy; fairy tale inspired)
The Vampire's Masquerade
The Lycanthrope's Exile
The Apparition's Rebirth
The Shapeshifter's Deception

Companion Novellas:
Werewolves and Weddings
Murders and Madness

ROMANTASY:
Kingdoms of Darkness and Deliverance
(high fantasy; fairy tale retellings)
Repaying the Wrongs

Acknowledgments

First and foremost, thank you to God for giving me the gift and desire to write. You always provide—even when what we need is a lifetime supply of elaborate imaginary adventures.

Thank you to my husband, Daniel, for your never-ending support and encouragement. And for educating me on the amount of thinking men do while kissing (answer: none).

To my early readers: Rheannan, Jess, Janalee, and Casey, you guys are the best! I can't tell you how much I appreciate you taking the time away from your busy lives to help me. I love you all!

To Elaine Lanmon, thank you so much for making the effort years ago to teach a random college student how to create book covers. I treasure the time I got to spend with you and am beyond grateful for your friendship and inspiration.

To the rest of my family, thank you for your love and support. It's been a long road to this point, and I wouldn't have made it without you.

Finally, to my mom. You first taught me to love reading and to nurture the imagination all those wonderful books instilled in me. You were the first to tell me I could be an author, and the first to listen to and encourage my own creative writing attempts. I hope you know how much I appreciate everything you did for me. I love you so much.

About the Author

Nellie Peters lives with her own Prince Charming and their four littles on the wild, windswept plains of Wyoming (don't worry, it sounds a lot more romantic than it is). When she's not writing, she's cleaning up sticky messes, helping endlessly renovate their house, reading an embarrassing number of books, and dreaming up exciting adventures that may or may not wind up on paper.

Visit nelliepeters.com to learn more about the author and her books.

www.ingramcontent.com/pod-product-compliance
Lightning Source LLC
Chambersburg PA
CBHW021019310726
48969CB00006B/1456